Spirits of the Mothers

Europe 15,000 years ago

Cristi Fernández Narvaiza
and
Martin Bless

Uitgeverij Aristos *bv*

Original title *Geesten van de moeders*
Uitgeverij Aristos bv, May 2009

English version

Publishing House Aristos bv
First edition: October 2009

Design: Studio of Publishing House Aristos

ISBN 9789089730282
NUR 300, 683

www.publishing-house.org
postmaster@publishing-house.org

Spirits of the Mothers
Europe 15,000 years ago

English version by
Cristi Fernández, Martin Bless and Jan-Manuel Bless

To Maruja, Cardin, Olivia and Edward

The significance and motivation of the figuration of [prehistoric] women evidently belongs to the domain of hypothesis.

Henri Delporte,
L'image de la femme dans l'art préhistorique, 1993

Contents

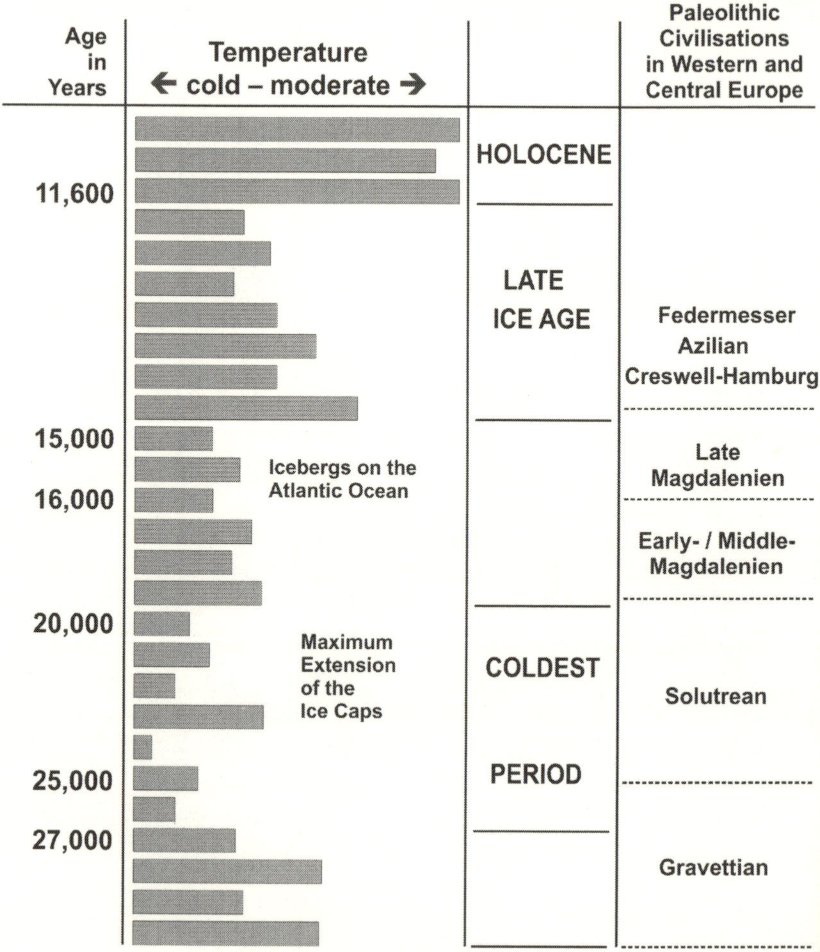

Schema of generalised temperature changes and late Paleolithic cultures at the end of the last Ice Age

Introduction

Climate change only became a hot issue when our father (-in-law) had already reached a great age. This did not keep him from saving clippings on the subject and discussing these with us. And so, one day we wondered how prehistoric people had managed to survive the tremendous changes at the end of the Ice Age. This stimulated us to broaden our fairly limited knowledge. Only much later did we realise that this question had been the beginning of a long and unpredictable adventure that would end with writing a book.

It took us years to understand that our distant Paleolithic ancestors were not the primitive savages so often portrayed in caricatures, on the contrary! They formed a complex society with its own standards and traditions, which – unfortunately for us – have not been documented, but passed from generation to generation through orally transmitted tales and myths. Awe-inspiring drawings, paintings, engravings, sculptures and other objects prove the existence

of skillful artists amongst them. Even Picasso admired their art. We became anxious to know more about their life, to understand their feelings and read their thoughts. Bit by bit we became enthralled by highly stylised depictions and figurines of women without a head, which have been discovered throughout Southwest and Central Europe. They play an important role in our story.
Of course, we were deeply impressed by the extreme conditions of life in the Ice Age and especially by the catastrophic changes of 15,000 years ago, when our ancestors had to cope with an unprecedented temperature increase, rapidly melting glaciers and a dramatic rise of the sea levels. The last mammoths and rhinoceros disappeared from Central Europe due to irreversible changes in the environment. Herds of horses, reindeer and bison were decimated or disappeared, and the same happened to some of the widely scattered nomadic groups.
The Magdalenian civilisation, the last culture of the Paleolithic or Old Stone Age, was at that time already four thousand years old and extended from Spain into Poland. It did not survive this climate change either. They were succeeded by many other cultures with new tools and arms, often restricted to much smaller regions; proof that mankind was flexible enough to adapt to new conditions.

Our lineage goes back to the same prehistoric hunters who 50,000 years ago marched into Europe and stayed here to this very day. According to the DNA-based theory of Bryan Sykes, almost all native Europeans descend through the maternal line from one of the 'seven daughters of Eve,' seven ancestral 'clan mothers' who 50,000 to 10,000 years ago lived in the Near East and Southern Europe (Bryan gave these European clan mothers the names Ursula, Xenia, Helena, Velda, Tara, Katrine and Jasmine).
After the Ice Age their blood mixed with that of farmers and herdsmen from Asia, but part of our genes trace back to the late Paleolithic hunters who survived all these climate changes.

Two of Eve's daughters, Helena and Velda, were descendants of a small group of nomads that migrated during the coldest period of the last Ice Age from the Middle East to Southern France. At the time Europe was populated by the clan of Ursula who had been born in Greece 45,000 years ago. Nobody noticed their arrival in this then sparsely populated region. According to Sykes, Helena was born 20,000 years ago near present-day Perpignan, on the foothills of the French Pyrenees. Almost fifty percent of native Europeans belong to her clan. Velda's mother lived three thousand years later in the surroundings of present-day Santander, in Northern Spain.

Just before the onset of the Magdalenian civilisation Helena was born. Her offspring may have played an important role in the development of this culture. Who knows? The same holds for Velda's children. They may have painted the bison on the ceiling of Altamira, that famous cave near Santander. Anyhow, Ursula's, Velda's and Helena's descendants moved 16,000 years ago from Northern Spain and Southwestern France into Central Europe, completely uninhabited in those days, spreading the Magdalenian civilisation into Czechia and Poland.
The children's children of Helena, Velda and all other daughters of Eve survived the end of that culture and also the end of the Ice Age. Shepherds and farmers from Asia did not enter an empty Europe 7,000 years ago, on the contrary. They came across flourishing communities of hunters, fishers and gatherers who were not starving to death.

Of course, we were curious enough to check Bryan's theory and took advantage of the possibility to have our own DNA analyzed by him. Everybody can do this, by the way, and enlarge his or her family tree with ten or twenty thousand years. The results surprised us nonetheless. Martin happens to descend through the maternal line from Helena and Cristi from Velda, with the special annotation that Cristi's cradle, as well as those of her mother, and grandmother and great-grandmother, stood in the native region of Velda, where also our eldest daughter Kitina was born.

Now you understand why we look at the ashes of a Magdalenian campfire from quite a different angle since we know that it may have warmed a direct ancestor. The thought that distant relatives have handled all those stones and bones and created the beautiful cave paintings and other artistic products, gives us a feeling of pride. We can only guess what they said or thought, theorise about their religious beliefs and wonder whether they expressed these in those images. Of course, all sorts of ideas and hypotheses have been suggested, but everyone is free to form their own view, and so we did.

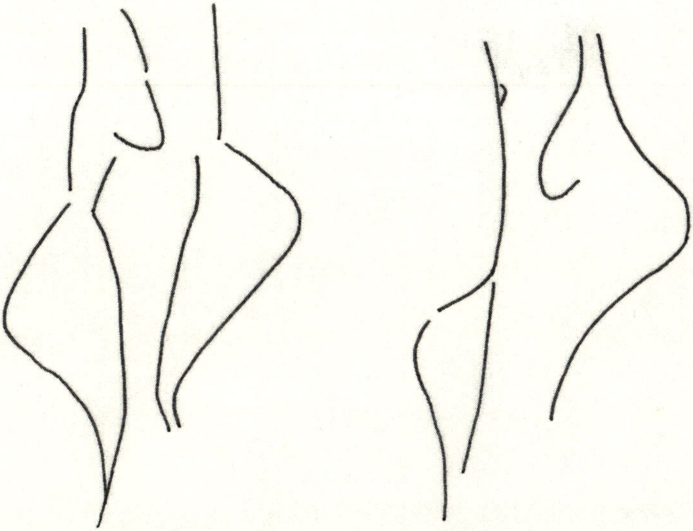

Engravings of stylised women of Lalinde-Gönnersdorf type
(*Spirits of the mothers*)

Left: couple from Gönnersdorf
(Neuwied; after Bosinski a.o., 2001).
Right: couple from Magdeleine
(Penne-Bruniquel; after Ladier a.o., 2005).

The distance between these localities is 1,000 km.

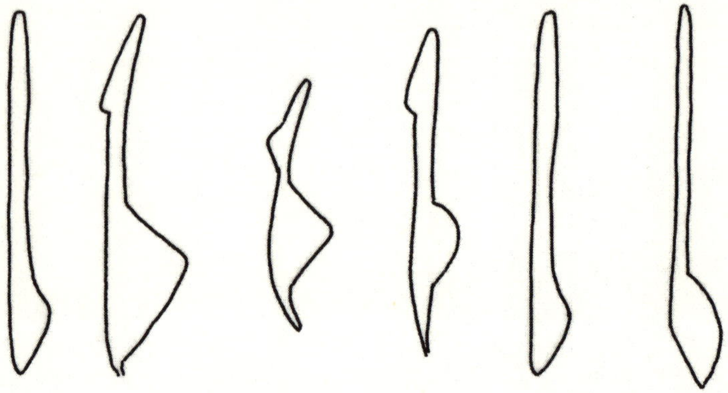

Ivory figurines of stylised women of Gönnersdorf type
(*Spirits of the Mothers*)

From left to right
two specimens from Gönnersdorf
(Neuwied; after Bosinski & Fischer, 1974),
one from Oelknitz
(Jena; after Bosinski, 1982),
two specimens from Nebra
(Nebra; after Bosinski, 1982)
and one from Garsitz
(Königsee; after Bosinski, 1982).

Distance between Gönnersdorf and other sites is 300 km.

15,000 years ago

The Womb of the Earth

As usual, all camp residents had gathered in the largest hut. They sat closely packed together around the smoldering fire. A few grease lamps completed the sparse light. Leya was seated between her mother and Krasser, her partner. Absorbed in thought he doodled on a piece of slate. His flint graver drew a round face with large eyes.
Many winters ago she had met Krasser for the first time: a tall, strong youngster with an infectious laugh, returning after several summers from a long journey with his family to the Western Water*. She had been enchanted by his enthusiastic description of an immense lake, in which the sun disappeared at night and whose water tasted like tears. Everybody was amazed how easily he drew with a few quick lines the mysterious animals he had observed there, seals and turtles. No-one was able to match him at reproducing the details in those drawings. Krasser they had called him, a name that suited him perfectly. Many girls had courted him, but fortunately, it did not take long before he noticed her.
One of the places of honor, which were reserved for the elder, was occupied by her grandmother, Great Narrator.

She passed on all the stories to younger generations and she had taught Leya the art of telling a good story. Everyone knew the tales since childhood, but they could not get enough of them. The stories were a welcome antidote to the daily monotony, whereas the meal afterwards, with lots of hot tea, helped increase their solidarity.

Ursa and Durfal were seated behind her and Krasser. Before Leya met Krasser, her cousin Durfal and Ursa had already become a couple. Ursa's family lived south of the territory of Leya's group. Although both her children had died shortly after being born, Durfal had stuck with Ursa. She for her part had no interest in another man. Together the four friends had wandered eight summers and winters through unknown regions living the most fantastic adventures.

Her brother carefully lifted hot stones from the fire and introduced these to the boiling water within the cooking pits lined with hides. A delicious aroma of herbs ascended and filled the room. Having been absent for so long it felt great to enjoy that marvelous drink once more! Leya noticed in surprise that her brother had become an adult member of the tribe with his own family.

Her uncles and aunts awaited with great anticipation the story of the journey to the distant unknown South. Nobody had ever traveled that far. What had the friends seen there? Had they really met relatives?

In the half dark of the hut she observed Krasser's family. Together they had covered the last stage of their journey. She also recognised two young men from the East. They were looking for a young, strong girl to share their life. She had learnt that they had left their families three summers ago and were curious to learn from her adventures.

Yet again Leya realised full well that she would never have completed the journey without Krasser, Durfal and Ursa. They had supported her unconditionally when she unfolded her plan to go to the South. Deeply touched she looked at her travel companions, her friends. Somebody passed a horn with warm herb tea that she gratefully emptied in one swallow. Then she straightened her back and cleared her throat. The buzz died down and everybody fell silent.

"It feels so good to be back! Eight summers have passed since our departure, but our thoughts were always with you. In the darkness of the night your faces appeared in our dreams, and sometimes we recognised your voices in the sounds of the wind. As you all know from the tales of visitors who came to see us many winters ago, the road to the South is long and dangerous, but it was a most rewarding adventure. At that time our visitors brought a splendid necklace of snails, for Great Narrator, the mother of my mother, a special gift that she still wears as a token of her dignity."

All eyes focused on Great Narrator and admired once more the ornament around her neck.

"We, Krasser, Durfal, Ursa and I collected similar snails in the South, near the shore of an immense lake with undrinkable water and without an opposite side. We have brought these snails as evidence that we speak the truth."

She signaled to Ursa who carefully opened a purse of rabbit fur filled with small pink snails. Respectful looks were directed at the four friends. These exceptional objects proved that Leya was telling the truth! The pouch was passed from hand to hand; everybody had to handle one of the snails. They even tried to sniff the exotic perfume of that distant Southern Water*. What a luxury! Once her audience had quieted down, Leya resumed her account.

"An inner restlessness drove us to set out on a journey to the region, where our families once lived. We hoped to meet people who, just like us, passed the stories about the past to next generations. They might be interested in ours, since we are descendants of men and women who long, long ago left the tribe to start a new life here in the North. We wondered over and over again why our ancestors had decided to abandon the territory of their parents and never returned. Was famine the cause, or disease, or a family feud? Did people in the South have the answers? As you all know, our elders doubted at first. What was the point of such questions? Would it be good to know the answers? We would certainly learn from this, we argued. After long deliberations you finally agreed and so we started our journey at the onset of spring. And now, eight winters later, we are sitting again with you around the fire."

"The South is different from the world we know. We have seen mountains of rock, ice and snow, completely inaccessible to even a goat* and equally inhospitable as the region around the great ice lake in the distant North. It is devoid of any tree, bush or herb. However, wide, lush valleys in between teem with all kinds of animals, just as here in our own territory, and fast-flowing brooks and rivers are full of fish. People there speak our language although with a strange accent, and they all are descendents of our ancestors. They too cherish the spirits who guide our souls to the womb of the earth. They carve their images in stones, ivory or bones that are kept in their huts or carried in a pouch, in the same way that we and all our relatives have done since the beginning of time. In addition they scratch and paint these figures in the darkness of the womb of the earth, the residence of the spirits."
Shouts of surprise interrupted her story. The womb of the earth, no living human had ever seen it! That place in the inner-earth was accessible only to the souls of the dead and to the spirits of animals and mothers. That's what they had always learnt. Her mother doubted if she had correctly understood her daughter's words. She gave Krasser, Ursa and Durfal a questioning look, but they nodded in affirmation. Leya had told the truth. They too had ventured inside the womb of the earth, met spirits and walked out alive as anybody could see.

"What does the womb of the earth look like?"
"Is it as soft and warm and filled with lifeblood as the womb of our mothers?"

"Where is the entry?"
"Can we find it as well?"
"What does that entry look like?"
"How do you get into it?"
"Tell us!"
"Explain yourself, Leya!"
"Did your soul leave your body before entering the womb of the earth?"
Animatedly they all called out at once, until Leya raised her hands to calm them down. They finally fell silent, impatiently awaiting the rest of her story.

"The interior of the earth differs completely from the womb of our mothers. It is cold and chilly because each winter snow and ice cover her belly and bosom. Even the summer sun can't warm its interior."
Her audience nodded thoughtfully. For them this was a good description. Things were not so easy for the earth. Winters were hard. Leaving your hut in winter to hunt meant returning stiff and numb because of the cold, despite warm fur clothes. It took a long time before fire, warm herb tea and many rubbing hands managed to dispel that cold from your body.

"The cold does not seem to affect the spirits. The size of womb of the earth is immense. There is plenty of room for all spirits. She can accommodate all souls of the dead, our own souls and those of our children and children's children. No-one should worry that his or her soul can't fit in.
The womb of the earth consists of countless large and small cavities. Some are wide enough to accommodate all the huts of this camp. But it also happens that you have to squeeze your body through a narrow passage, like a child leaving the womb of his mother. Some walls are rough and hard as a rock. Even Krasser had difficulty with marking lines in spite of his sharp graver. In other places however walls are smooth and soft like mud so that you can easily draw images of the spirits with your fingers."

"A thick coat of thin whitish hairs, hard as stone, covers the ceiling of some cavities in order to protect the womb against the cold from outside. The environment is moist however and water drips continuously from these stone hairs to the floor. We have seen places with white and grey, freakish rocks resembling tree trunks, petrified souls of the dead or spirits of unknown animals turned to stone. To put it shortly, these places are unfit for living humans like us. Complete darkness reigns these places, as in a cloudy night without moon or stars. People only enter the cavities imploring the help of the spirits or guiding the souls of the dead through signs on the walls. Not only living humans, but also the souls of the dead might easily get lost in the many twisting passages of the womb of the earth."

"Why are these cavities not filled with lifeblood, just as the womb of our mothers?" Great Narrator repeated the question she had put forward before. She was visibly impressed by the story.

"As you well know, water is the lifeblood of the earth. Originally water filled all the cavities when the Maker brought humans and animals to life on the first day. When they left the womb of the earth, all the water poured away as well, just as happens at the birth of a child or an animal's young. This explains why today most cavities are dry and empty. We can't rule out that new unknown life is forming in cavities still filled with water. Red staining on the floor in some places may be remnants of the blood from her interior. The color was as red as the powder we use in preparing the hides.

The womb of the earth has many openings similar to the caves and caverns that protect us from rain and snow. Some are wide enough to let us all walk in side by side, but others are narrow, even narrower than a fox hole, so that we can hardly enter. People in the South believe that the Maker designated each hole for a different creature. Large ones were used by big animals, such as bison, mammoth, rhinoceros or bear. Bears feel so comfortable in the innerearth that they return every winter for sleeping and giving birth to their young. Small ones were intended for small animals, such as hare, rabbit, fox, birds, lizards, frogs, salamanders and snakes."

One of the men from the East raised his hand. "Did you see the opening used by the first men and women?"

She shook her head. "No-one could tell us. Of course, we asked. People neither know which animal emerged from which cavity. It happened so long ago that the tales have been forgotten completely. However, I would like to add a few words about a woman we met during our stay at the shore of Western Water. Her family lived far away, somewhere south of the lake, behind high snow-covered mountains. There she claimed to have seen the opening used by the first men and women; but no-one believed her."

This time an exclamation from a young woman with a baby at her breast interrupted her. "Bah! Dirty child! You have been pooing again on your mother's lap!"

"It's your own stupid fault," joked one of the men. "You should have wrapped him in a fur."

"I did! But he fouled it immediately just like two other ones. Who might have expected that he would shit again so quickly?"

Everybody exploded with laughter. Highly offended about such lack of understanding she found her way to a corner of the hut to clean her baby. One of the women passed her a handful of dried moss and a clean rabbit fur.

Since the tension had been broken some of them rapidly left to relieve themselves. A niece put pieces of meat on the glowing charcoal and one of her uncles added new fat to the lamps. Suddenly everybody felt thirsty.

Despite the hum of voices in the huts around her Leya slept well. Her audience however was unable to catch much sleep after the sight of the wonderful snails and the revelations about the womb of the earth. They had spend most of the night talking together, initially whispering, but as voices raised and talks degenerated into real discussions even the children woke with a start.

Why did they live so far from that immense Southern Water, the high mountains, and not to forget the magic openings to the womb of the earth? Why had their ancestors left a region, where everything existed that they suddenly desired? They felt discriminated and cheated by those distant relatives who were allowed to live there. Why had that distant family given up what was rightfully theirs? They concluded that their predecessors had thrown away a privilege without getting something in return, without taking into consideration the interest of their children's children. It went without saying that the last word had yet to be said.

Next morning most people woke up ill-humored, not only because of the lack of sleep, but mainly because of the idea that they would have been much better off if these stupid ancestors had stayed in the South. Day-to-day work came to nothing. When dusk fell and everybody gathered again in one of the huts, they continued to grumble. It took quite a few horns of warm herb tea to calm their feelings. They all wondered what Leya might tell.

Of course, Leya, Krasser, Durfal and Ursa got wind of this sudden dissatisfaction. They really had to laugh at it. How could men and women who had always been pleased with the life they lived suddenly lose their head after a story about the womb of the earth or a handful of tiny snails?

"Imagine," said Durfal, "that some people in the South would like to come here to see mammoth and rhinoceros. Maybe you should explain this tonight."

"But the South is teeming with fish," argued Ursa. "Seals abound on the shores along the Southern and Western Waters. Remember also those curious birds. Their wings were too small for flying, so we could easily catch them, and they tasted quite nice."

"Don't forget the incredible things we have seen." It was Krasser who came into the discussion. "Just think of that mountain belching smoke and fire, and huge clouds of dust which covered everything in the area."

"I recall stones flying through the sky," said Durfal, "as if the spirits were trying to chase us away from there. Terrified and not daring to get closer we kept watching from a distance, fearing that it might be the spirit of a monstrous animal. At night glowing rivers of fire descended the mountain while the earth beneath our feet was trembling and shaking, just as we did. I shall never forget the filthy smell and thundering noise as during a heavy storm."
Even now, after so much time, they were still impressed by that frightening experience.
"Under normal circumstances spirits keep very quiet and invisible," pondered Leya. "The same holds for the souls of the dead. All that noise, smoke, dust and stones may have been released by the inner-earth. She may have had a bad fit of coughing because of some unknown illness, just as sometimes happens to us. The problem is that nobody could tell us what caused this. One thing is sure: everybody was scared. Animals and humans had fled the neighbourhood for fear of the fire and stones. No wonder that some people would like to come to the North. I agree with you. We should talk this over tonight and make our family understand that our ancestors did the right thing coming here."

A soft cough broke the silence. Leya understood that they were anxious to know her view. She looked around and started with a question.
"Can someone give one good cause for being angry at our ancestors? Thanks to them we are living in this region with plenty of water and game. Neither we nor our children are starving and nobody has ever seen the limits of our hunting grounds.
Those beautiful snails and our account of the interior of the earth have upset you, with good reason, because all this is new for us. But don't overestimate their importance. Rather ask yourself why we did not stay in the South, because that was a real option. People in the South are just as hospitable as we, and several young and attractive women hoped to be

coupled to Durfal or Krasser. Ursa and I have also met handsome, strong men willing to share their life with us. We nevertheless decided to return to our hunting grounds around Big River. We were born here in the North and here we will die some day if that is the will of the Maker, because also from here the spirits accompany the souls of the dead on their way to the inner-earth. That is beyond all doubt as our mothers have taught us in the same way as they learnt it from their mothers."

There was a murmur of approval around her. She looked around and saw them nodding in affirmation. Leya had convinced them completely.

"Here we honor the spirits of mammoth and rhinoceros, something unknown in the South, because mammoth and rhinoceros don't live there. I will tell you about this another time."

The heads nodding at the rhythm of her words suddenly froze. Her audience tried to imagine people not honoring the spirits of mammoth or rhinoceros. How would their souls ever find the womb of the earth? It was bound to fail! Had Leya really said there were no mammoth or rhinoceros in the South? A profound silence reigned in the hut. Some of them tried to visualise a steppe without those beautiful creatures. Why could such a place be all right for grazing horses and bison? They had a vivid recollection of the enormous amount of snow killing so much game last winter. Would it be conceivable that all those animals could disappear some day? How could their tribe survive this? Everybody tried to digest her words. No-one spoke. Even the children kept quiet as if they understood the gravity of this moment. They were all stunned into speechlessness. They had expected and hoped that Leya's description of the South would make that region even more attractive. Instead she had thrown them into confusion.

The sputtering noise of one of the lamps returned them to reality. One of the men replaced the wick with a fresh juniper twig and added bone marrow to the grease. Aimlessly staring, they awaited some comment from their neighbours, but nobody dared to put his thoughts into words. Leya was also making up her mind. Should she continue her story or would it be better to drop the theme, at least tonight? Durfal and Ursa patted her encouragingly on the back. The two men from the East who had come looking for a wife envied the scene. They would so love to change places with Krasser or Durfal. Leya's frail figure held a great attraction to men. The long journey had lined her smiling face whilst her eyes radiated willpower and wisdom. They too desired Ursa, a skillful fisher and always good-humored. Leya read their looks, but did not let them distract her thoughts.

Suddenly she got a bright idea. She bent to the right, where a young woman next to her mother was breastfeeding her baby. She picked a tuft of moss from her lap that the girl had prepared for drying the child if necessary and held it in the light of a lamp.
"Look at this little piece of moss! The leaflets are so small that they are barely visible. If I peel off one of these and put it on the palm of my hand you see nothing. Moss is only recognizable when all the leaflets are stuck together." She handed the moss over again to the woman. "That is just the way it is with stories. Don't attach too much importance to a single word or an isolated remark. These are like leaflets of moss. Wait until you have learnt all the details. Then you will have time enough to think and ask questions."
Her audience heaved a sigh of relief. For the moment they did not need to worry. It had been only words and casual remarks. They would wait until they had learnt all the details. It was so good to have Leya again in their midst.

The dogs around the camp suddenly howled. Wolves were possibly roaming across the hills. Dogs were tolerated in the neighbourhood since they tended to keep predators like wolves, bears, wolverines and even lions at a save distance. Some of the hunters pricked up their ears. A wolf answered

far away, and then another and another. Loudly barking the pack ran in their direction making clear that this was their territory. The dogs lived on the offal that had to be shared with foxes, martens, gulls, crows and ravens. During periods of food shortage they might be absent for days, hunting together on the steppe. Dogs were not tolerated within the camp because time after time they tried to steal a portion of meat. Even babies were not sacred to them. With sticks and stones one had to scare them away.
The howling reminded Leya of a tale in which a dog played a leading part. It might be a good idea to relate the story. With a gesture of her hands she demanded attention. They reacted immediately because all eyes were focused on her that night.
"The baying dogs reminded me of a story on an incident that happened long ago during the Time of Great Change*. That is the time when many families like ours left their native soil to try their luck elsewhere."
She turned to her grandmother. "Great Narrator, would you please tell us once more the story of the dog?"
They laughed. It was a positive sign. For the moment, all the gloomy thoughts had been banned from their heads. Her mother softly pinched Leya's hand approvingly. They all looked excitedly at Great Narrator who immediately accepted to comply with the request.

"Most of you already know the tale, but for some it may be new. I shall tell you about something that happened ages ago, long before my grandmother had been born. All our ancestors were still settled in the South. They became so numerous that famine reigned from time to time. That's why several families decided to follow the northward migrating herds. Somewhere along Big River they hoped to find game sufficient to live on so that they never would suffer famine again. One of those groups was led by an older man who had been in the North before. He knew all the tracks they had to follow. In spite of his age he was still a leader who commanded respect. His many scars and tro-

phies proved that he had even won a combat with a bear. Just as happens in our days the group was followed by a pack of dogs. That was good. The way they barked warned them against the presence of predators. One of these dogs was a bitch with two pups who frequently begged in vain for food because there was no much to eat on that journey. One day the man killed a horse, enough food for the whole group. People were happy, put up tents, made fire and prepared the meat. They kept singing and dancing until late in the night. The dogs for their part tried to catch part of the takings, but only got a few bones. It was very late when everybody went to sleep. Only the man kept watching the fire. Suddenly he saw the bitch appearing from the shadows of the night. She was not barking or growling. Cautiously she crept nearer and nearer, paused for a moment, moved closer again and finally laid down in front of him, her eyes focused on him begging for a small piece of meat. The man looked surprised. He never had experienced something like this. Impulsively he grabbed his bag, got a piece of meat and gave it the dog. She sniffed at the meat, grabbed it with her teeth and disappeared wagging her tail into the darkness to share it with the pups.
Next evening exactly the same happened. This time the bitch licked his hands and she put her head on his lap. The man had to laugh to himself. Inside he praised the dog because of her smart way of begging. He touched her head and neck and she let him without protest. Then he gave her a piece of meat from his bag. Again the dog disappeared with the meat for the pups. The following night the man awaited the arrival of the bitch with the meat already in his hand. He was happy to see her because she meant company. He had no wife to sleep with and no-one showed him so much gratitude as this dog. From that moment onwards a sort of friendship existed between the man and the dog. During the day she kept away with the rest of the pack, but at night she came and sat next to him. He stroke and patted her, telling her of his loneliness. The bitch on her part licked his hands, looked at him and put her head on his lap.

The other members of the group observed this curious relationship. They secretly laughed about it, but made no comments to the man. He alone knew the way in the North and he was one of the most experienced hunters. Spring passed by and so did summer. Autumn arrived. The bitch no longer cared for her pups. They had found their own place in the pack. But every night she went to the man, licked his hands and put her head on his lap, whilst he rewarded her with a piece of meat, stroking her and speaking to her."

"One day the group wandered along the Big River. It was cold and there was snow. Suddenly part of the bank collapsed. A young woman walking there by chance on it fell in the water. Her screams caught the attention of the rest. They dashed to rescue her, but the water was deep and ice-cold and the current very strong. Petrified with fear, everybody watched. Only the man reacted. Looking at them with contempt he threw down his cloths and jumped into the water to save her although she had never slept with him and did not have any special feelings for him.
They noticed immediately that he would not succeed to get her out of the water. He got tired because of the strong current and the ice-cold water robbed him of his strength. Together they drifted away from the bank. At first the dog had watched the scene loudly barking, but now she started howling in despair. Suddenly the bitch jumped in the water and made a frantic effort to reach him. The man extended his hand and grabbed her fur. The rest watched breathlessly. Would the animal be able to bring the man and the woman ashore? For a short moment they thought she would make it, but then they were drawn into a whirlpool and disappeared."
In the hut nobody dared to speak a word. In their imagination they too witnessed the tragedy.
"It took two days to find the bodies of the man and the woman. The dead man's hand continued to hold on to the fur of the bitch in the hope that she might save him.

The pouch on the woman's neck contained a beautiful figure of the spirit of a hind that would accompany her soul to the inner-earth. The purse of the man had vanished and they feared that his soul would wander forever without finding a resting-place. The elder of the women however pointed at the dog. 'Her spirit will have guided his soul, because some kind of friendship tied her to the man, even though she was a despicable beast. In the womb of the earth they will be happy together, she licking his hands and he stroking her head.'

They then dug a burial pit and laid down the bodies, first the body of the woman with the image of the spirit of a hind by her head and then the body of the man who had tried to rescue her although she did not sleep with him and did not have any special feelings for him. Finally they laid down the body of the bitch with the head on the chest of the man. They dusted the bodies with red ochre, filled up the pit and covered the grave with stones, white ones for the man and the woman and dark ones for the dog. If the stream has not removed these stones during high water, they may still be there."

Great Narrator fell silent; letting her audience quietly come to their senses. Then she asked: 'Is there some warm tea? I have got a dry throat after all that talking!"

They all at once started lively conversations. Someone hummed softly, the rest followed the tune. One of the women sang a song, inventing the words; a song about a man and a dog, about friendship and affection. In the end it had been a very good night.

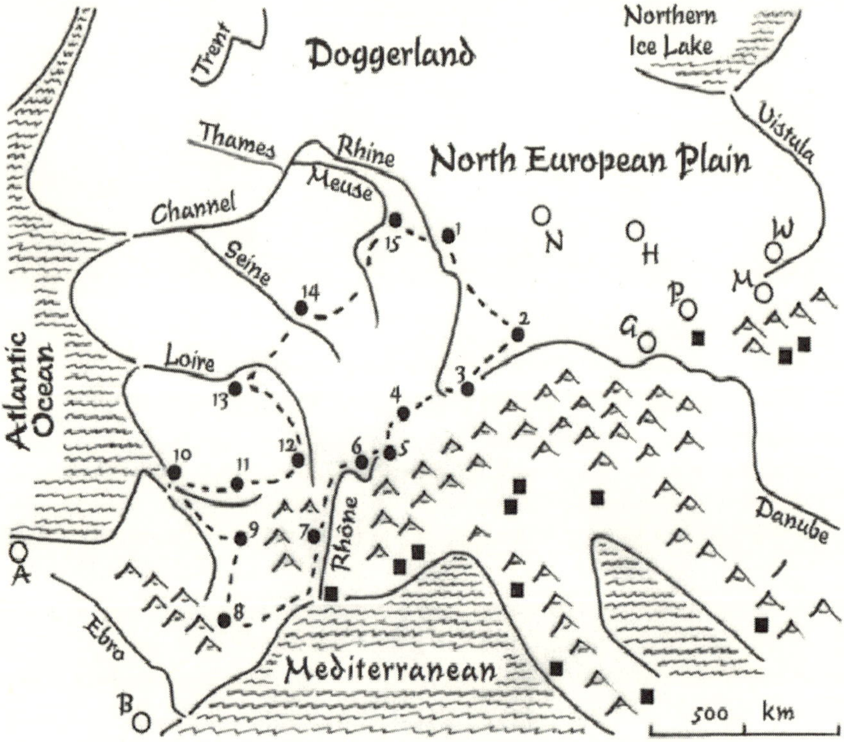

EUROPE DURING LATE MAGDALENIAN TIME, 15,000 YEARS AGO, WHEN SEA LEVELS WERE ONE HUNDRED METERS LOWER THAN TODAY. LEYA'S VOYAGE IS INDICATED BY A DOTTED LINE

1 – Gönnersdorf (Rhine), winter camp of Leya.
2 – Hohlenstein (Nördlinger Ries) and Hohlenstein (Lonetal), family of Ursa.
3 – Petersfels (Brudertal), reindeer hunt.
4 – Champréveyres (Lake Neuchâtel).
5 – Veyrier (Lake Geneva).
6 – Pierre-Châtel (Rhône).
7 – Planchard (Ardèche).
8 – La Vache (Ariège).
9 – Magdeleine (Aveyron), ancestral mothers.
10 – Gironde, seal hunting.
11 – Saint-Cirq (Vézère), First Tribe.
12 – Enval (Allier), volcanoes around Clermont-Ferrand.
13 – Roc-aux-Sorciers (Angles-sur-Anglin).
14 – Étiolles (Seine), Northerners.
15 – Eyserheide (South-Limburg), Krasser's family.

A – Altamira, El Linar.
B – Blaus, Matutano (Valencia), Southerners.
G – Grubgraben (Donau), meeting between Magdalenian people and Eastern Tribes, flutes.
H – Hostim (Bohemia), Stille's family.
M – Maszycka (Cracovia), Middle Magdalenian massacre).
N – Nebra, Oelknitz, Garsitz (Saxony-Thuringia), eastern neighbours of Leya.
P – Pekarna (Brno), winter camp of Prater.
W – Wylczyce (Cracovia), summer camp of Prater.

■ – Eastern Tribes (Late Epigravettian).

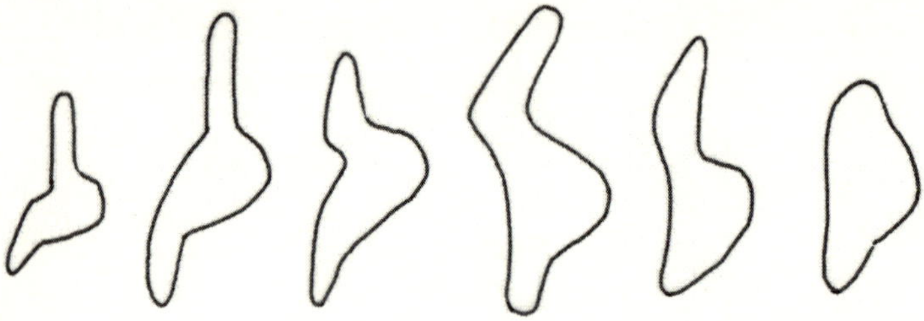

FIGURINES OF STYLISED WOMEN OF GÖNNERSDORF TYPE
(*SPIRITS OF THE MOTHERS*)

FROM LEFT TO RIGHT:
CHARM OF JET
(FOSSILISED WOOD)
FROM MONRUZ
(NEUCHÂTEL; AFTER BULLINER, 2006),
TWO CHARMS OF JET FROM PETERSFELS
(BRUDERTAL; AFTER BOSINSKI, 1982),
IVORY FIGURINE FROM PEKARNA
(MOKRA-BRNO; AFTER DELPORTE, 1993),
FLINT FIGURINE FROM WYLCZYCE
(KRAKOVIA; AFTER FIEDORCZUK A.O., 2007),
SANDSTONE FIGURINE FROM DOBRANICHEVKA
(130 KM SOUTHEAST OF KIEV; AFTER DELPORTE, 1993;
AREA OF EASTERN TRIBES).

DISTANCE BETWEEN MONRUZ AND PETERSFELS IS 175 KM,
BETWEEN PETERSFELS AND PEKARNA 750 KM,
BETWEEN PEKARNA AND WYLCZYCE 300 KM AND BETWEEN
WYLCZYCE AND DOBRANICHEVKA 900 KM.

Mass Migrations and Unbridgeable Boundaries

According to the most pessimistic prognosis of the IPCC, the Intergovernmental Panel for Climatic Change created by the United Nations in 1988, the global average temperature (compared to that in 1990) might increase by seven degrees during the twenty-first century. This is based on the assumption that the more coal, oil and gas we burn, the more carbon dioxide is introduced into the atmosphere. It will not only melt ice around the poles but also on Greenland, the Alps, Andes and Himalaya. Subsequently, sea levels will rise and complete coastal areas will be flooded. No-one really knows how fast and to what extend. This is not so surprising since our generation is the first that realises a climate change is happening. Modern climate studies will help us understand the how and why.

During the Little Ice Age*, between 1430 and 1850, people were unaware of the slight decrease of average temperature since they had no instruments to measure this. At the very most they were surprised by the fact that rivers froze several winters in succession or that consecutive harvests failed. That follows from ancient chronicles because even during the Little Ice Age these were not annual phenomena. Besides, they had never heard of statistics. Only afterwards do we conclude that artists have painted more winter landscapes during that period than in other epochs. Modern equipment measures temperature changes of a tenth degree or sea level rise of one millimeter per year. So we know that temperature has increased since the start of industrial revolution. We no longer depend on unverifiable pronouncements that 'earlier winters were so much colder and summers less warm,' because our human memory is highly unreliable in this aspect. One or two severe winters during our youth may be remembered as a yearly phenomenon.

Imagine however a mean temperature increase of say five degrees within a few decades; would we notice this without adequate measuring equipment? Something similar happened 15,000 years ago at the start of the Late Ice Age. Did our ancestors realise that climate change? They should at least have noticed the consequences. The abrupt temperature rise at the beginning of the Late Ice Age caused rapidly shrinking ice sheets and glaciers. Rivers could not absorb the huge amounts of melt water and frequently burst their banks. Repeated flooding must have completely isolated some human groups from the rest.

In less than five hundred years sea levels rose twenty meters and especially in flat lowlands the sea may have engulfed complete settlements during storm and spring tide. Years later the skeletons of these former dwellings were still visible above the water. Caves along the shore, in which people had been painting during their youth, may have become inaccessible within decades due to the rising water. In amazement they found the steppe being overgrown by trees and bushes, reducing the space for large herds, their principal food supply.

Their daily life changed drastically. They spend all their time adapting to new conditions and food supplies, relegating art and religion. This explains why the start of the Late Ice Age heralded the end of the Magdalenian civilisation.

Long before that moment even the smallest climatic changes had left their stamp on the evolution and expansion of the Magdalenian. 16,000 years ago, for example, the eastern border of the North American ice sheet suddenly started to crumble away. No-one really understands why, since temperatures at the time were much lower than today and so were carbon dioxide concentrations in the atmosphere. Sidney Hemming imagines an 'armada of icebergs' that drifted through the Labrador Strait across the North Atlantic to the Gulf of Biscay and Southwestern Portugal. Sea water cooled down because of this immense amount of ice. Temperatures dropped in Southwestern Europe, where the climate became drier, with far-reaching consequences.

Partly due to long-lasting drought in the western part of the Mediterranean, mammoth, rhinoceros and musk ox, the icons of the Ice Age, disappeared from Southern France. Since the major part of the North European Plain*, from the Netherlands into Poland, remained an inhospitable polar desert, many animals migrated to the slightly more greenish steppes of Central Europe, a hilly region extending from the Ardennes in the west to the Carpathian Mountains in the east. Reindeer, horse, bison and saiga (an antelope species) were among the first to go.

Drought most likely caused repeated periods of famine in Southern Europe and many families may have decided to seek their salvation elsewhere. Some of these followed the herds to the North, to the surroundings of present-day Paris, where they hunted mainly reindeer and horse at watering and crossing places for game along the Seine, Marne and tributaries. They ended up in the Meuse valley in the French and Belgian Ardennes. The many cliffs, caves and overhanging rocks reminded them of the valleys of Dordogne, Vézère and Lot, their original homeland.

Other groups landed in the valleys of Allier, Loire and Saône, from where they went eastward to the French, Swiss and German Jura, or to the northeast along the Mosel, to the hills of Rhineland, Saxony, Thuringia, Bohemia, Moravia

and Southern Poland, all areas, which before had been stricken by drought, permafrost* and icy sand and dust storms.
Finally we should not forget the groups migrating to the Pyrenean mountain valleys as soon as glaciers began to retreat.

Imagine all those people, young and old, even mothers with babies on their trek from Southern France and Northern Spain, walking in bands of ten to forty individuals bearing or dragging all their belongings. How many completed these journeys or succumbed due to illness or accidents? Within at most a few generations they spread across Central Europe.
This ancient migration somehow resembles the nineteenth century colonisation of Australia and the Wild West of North America, the main difference being the fact that in those days Central Europe was uninhabited. Migration from Southwestern Europe to the north and northeast was not at the expense of an autochthonous population that had to be chased away from its territory. It was virgin territory for both animals and humans.

Alps and Carpathians acted as natural buffer between this region and that of the tribes in Southeastern and Eastern Europe, Italy, Greece and the Balkans up to Russia, Caucasus and even Siberia. There was no competition to contend with from that side. The less well defined boundary on the North European Plain in Poland coincided with the water rich Vistula discharging at the time into a gigantic ice lake of melt water from the Scandinavian ice sheet. This Northern Ice Lake occupied the place of the current Baltic Sea.
Crossing these natural borders met with heavy-handed punishment. Stefan Kozlowski and Eva Sachse-Kozlowska describe the fate of a Magdalenian family in the Polish Maszycka Cave. Two thousand years before that mass migration, one of the first attempts to make a living elsewhere ended in mass-murder.

Some of the tools excavated at this site were made from stones from the Ukrainian territory of Eastern Tribes. No-one can tell us any more if they collected these stones there themselves or if they obtained them as a gift or in exchange.
But it is clear that the Eastern Hunters have not appreciated their presence in that border region.
Perhaps somebody escaped the massacre and informed his fellow tribesmen in France with all the horrible details. Since then Magdalenian people avoided the territory of the Eastern Tribes and vice versa as if it were under taboo. This might explain why the characteristic Late Magdalenian harpoons have been excavated only once within the territory of the Eastern cultures.
It may sound cynical but in the end that expedition seems to have yielded something positive. The Maszycka group almost certainly got in touch with people of the Mezine-Meziritch culture* in the environs of Kiev in Ukraine, characterised by extremely stylised feminine figures. Gerhard Bosinski, the leader of the Gönnersdorf excavation near Neuwied, suggested that these served as a model for the stylised feminine figures, which subsequently became the icons of the Late Magdalenian in Spain, France, Switzerland, Germany, Poland and Czechia.

In Southeastern France, since the coldest period of the Ice Age, the Rhône was the boundary between the Western People in the Ardèche and the Eastern Tribes in the Vaucluse and Provence. They could have crossed the river for a visit, but for some reason they never did. Late Magdalenian hunters only colonised the Vaucluse after the disappearance of the Eastern Tribe and the last mammoth from that area. Did people leave on their own initiative because of famine or was the group exterminated by accidents, famine and illness? Whichever reason, the Eastern Tribe never returned to that region.
One or two thousand years later Late Magdalenian hunters entered a no man's land. They did not have to argue with

anyone to make their claim. At the same time, slightly farther south, members of the Eastern Tribes bivouacked in the eastern Rhône delta near Istres. Perhaps both parties met, but the sparse contacts did not produce an exchange of knowledge and skills.

Most likely though, rumours persisted on both sides about the other ones*, rude people, inferior thieves and murderers, better kept at distance. It is also conceivable that Magdalenian people avoided the Rhône delta for being too swampy, whereas the Eastern Tribes did not like the deep valleys in the Vaucluse. Be that as it may, some boundaries can't be bridged.

This contrasts sharply with the excellent contacts between the tribes inhabiting Europe 30,000 years ago. The then existing Gravettian culture extended from Portugal to the Don Basin in Southern Russia. This explains the widespread distribution of figures and reliefs of women often characterised by very big breasts, belly and buttocks, as for example in the 'Venus of Willendorf,' which have been discovered in many sites in Russia, Czechia, Slovakia, Germany, Austria, Italy and France.

These contacts were interrupted by the start of the coldest period of the Ice Age. The increasing cold made Northwest and Central Europe inhospitable and people abandoned England, Wales, Northern France, Belgium, the Netherlands, Germany, Czechia and Poland. The rapidly extending ice sheet on the Alps and Carpathians and rivers like Vistula, Danube and Rhône separated the Eastern and Southeastern Tribes in Russia, Ukraine, Crimea, Hungary, Austria, Slovenia, Greece and Italy from those in the west, in Southern France, Spain and Portugal. That boundary separated people for ten thousand years.

First there were physical obstacles: mountains, cold, snow, ice and water. Later psychological barriers developed of distrust and mutual fear of people who had mentally drifted apart, did not know each other anymore and were literally and figuratively incapable of speaking or understanding each other's language.

Imagine a period of ten thousand years! That is twice the time that separates us from the Egyptians who built the pyramid of Cheops or five times the period elapsed since the birth of Christ. At the start of the Late Ice Age ten thousand years had passed since the moment that the bond between peoples in East and West Europe had been disrupted due to the decreasing temperature. The extreme cold at the peak of the Ice Age, 22,000 years ago, made even some parts of Southern Europe inhospitable. Crossing that boundary six thousand years later brought about the massacre of the Maszycka family. How could the Alps, Carpathians, Rhône, Danube and Vistula separate humans with the same ancestors for so many years? Can we envisage something similar in a far future?

Gravettian bivouacs, 27,000 – 30,000 years ago, before the coldest period of the Ice Age

Climate was mild enough for people to explore the hills and valleys of Northwest and Central Europe (including England and Wales). They avoided the North European Plain and Doggerland (the North Sea region that had become a dry land area) because of the lack of adequate weapons to hunt on the open steppe.

Many bivouacs were occupied from just a few days to several months.

SOLUTREAN BIVOUACS, 22,000 – 25,000 YEARS AGO, DURING THE COLDEST PERIOD OF THE ICE AGE

HARSH CLIMATIC CONDITIONS (FOR EXAMPLE, THE SCANDINAVIAN ICECAP EXTENDED TO HAMBURG AND THE BRITISH ICECAP TO SOUTH WALES, WHEREAS THE FRONT OF THE RHÔNE GLACIER REACHED THE PRESENT-DAY CITY OF LYON) FORCED PEOPLE TO STAY IN SOUTHERN EUROPE. GREAT BRITAIN AND CENTRAL EUROPE HAD BEEN COMPLETELY ABANDONED. THE RHÔNE RIVER BECAME A MAJOR BOUNDARY BETWEEN SOLUTREAN HUNTERS IN THE WEST AND THE EASTERN TRIBES.

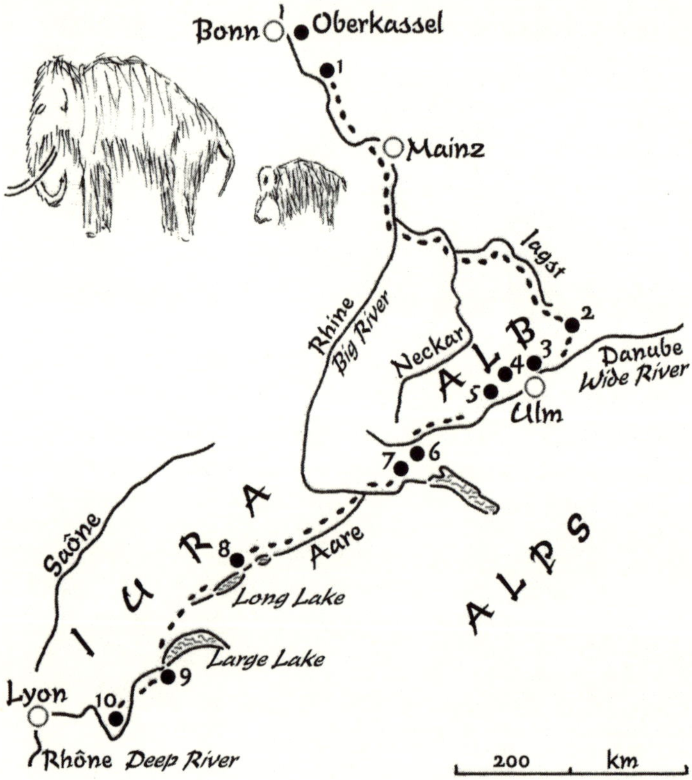

LEYA'S JOURNEY, FIRST TWO SUMMERS, FROM HER FAMILY'S WINTER CAMP AT BIG RIVER TO THE CAVE BY DEEP RIVER

1 – Gönnersdorf (winter camp of Leya).
2 – Hohlenstein, Nördlinger Ries
(abandoned campsite).
3 – Hohlenstein, Lonetal (Ursa's brother).
4 – Blaubeurener Tal
(summer camp in Blue Valley).
5 – Felsställe, Mühlen.
6 – Petersfels, Gnirshöhle, Brudertal
(Brothers' Valley, reindeer hunt).
7 – Kesslerloch, Schweizersbild, Schaffhausen, Rhinefall
(winter camp of Durfal's great-aunt).
8 – Champréveyres, Monruz, Lake Neuchâtel
(spring camp by Long Lake).
9 – Veyrier, Geneva
(summer camp by Great Lake).
10 – Pierre-Châtel, Virignin
(winter camp by Deep River).

15,000 years ago

Journey to Brothers' Valley

The past days and nights had been bitter cold. The last two moons they could cross the frozen Big River from one bank to the other without any difficulty. A severe snowstorm from the northwest forced them however to shelter in tents and huts. Trapping foxes and hares because of their sought after winter coats had been suspended. The forced inaction easily produced irritations and everybody longed for the moment that the wind would die down. Fortunately, Krasser distracted the minds. Young and old stared open-mouthed at effortlessly drawn lines carved in dark shale, lines transformed as by magic into animals living on steppes and hills.

"What is this?" he asked.
"A rhinoceros," shouted the children simultaneously, even before he had finished the drawing.
"And this?" Only a cluster of short, diagonal lines, followed by a slightly curved one, was visible.
"A horse, the mane and back of a horse," called out one of the girls with excitement.
"Very good," he praised.

"This one will be more difficult," he warned. The stone burin drew a single vertical line. He saw them doubting. A curved line followed.
"The spirit of a mother!" The same girl enthusiastically screamed it out.
"Excellent!" Krasser congratulated her with a laugh.
A little boy protested: "I miss the head, the arms and legs. Where are the boobs? How can this be a mother?"
"Spirits don't need it in the womb of the earth, you fool!" was the girl's sharp answer. "Even without eyes or ears the spirits of the mothers find their way in the darkness. They are never hungry so they don't need a mouth. They have no arms or legs since they weigh less than a spider's thread borne by the wind." Everybody nodded in agreement. That was what they had learnt since childhood. The boy hung his head in shame.
"Don't worry," Krasser comforted him, stroking his head. "We all have had to learn this and even today Leya and I don't know everything. Next winter you will be as smart as the rest if you listen carefully. By the way, would you like to help me making this drawing disappear?"
The boy beamed with pride. It was quite an honor helping Krasser making a drawing disappear! He bent over the drawing and spat on it. Wiping the stone with a piece of moss he made the white lines vanish.
"Which of you would like to draw his favourite animal," asked Krasser. Of course, they all liked to do so. He passed around shale slabs and flint burins. They set to work in a good mood.

Someone suddenly remarked that he had missed Leya's tales.
"We have been very busy," apologised Krasser. "This is the time of snaring ptarmigans, and trapping foxes and hares as long as these have a snow-white coat. We have to tan skins, make clothes and belts. We had to construct a new hut for ourselves, and also the maintenance of the other huts and tents takes up our time especially since it is snow-

ing so much. We have to replenish wood stocks and renew tools and arms."

"But tonight the moon is completely round. The winter's fifth moon begins. That should be enough reason for coming together and listen to the tales of Leya."

Krasser laughed: "You are quite right! Hunting is impossible now. We will ask Leya to tell us a story tonight, as long as you take care of the fire and provide enough meat and herbs for everyone."

They did not need to be told twice. The children ran away to collect wood, whereas the adults got dried and smoked meat and herbs from the store holes, which had been cut out in the frozen soil.

At nightfall all families gathered again around the fire in the hut that Leya and her friends had finished only a few days before.

Large shale slabs with on top a layer of dried grass and horse hides prevented the rise of humidity and cold from the frozen subsoil. The ochre used for the removal of fat had left reddish stains on the hides. A lamp illuminated the image of a mammoth cow and her calf resting against the central pole.

The children had filled the pits with snow. With a pair of sturdy willow branches they fetched hot stones from the fire and dropped these into the pits. After melting the snow they brought the water to the boil in the same way. Then they added small pieces of meat and herbs to make soup.

Men and women proudly showed off their new clothes, bags of white fox and hare fur, bracelets and necklaces with beads of black jet*, and deer and fox teeth. Someone had decorated his fur cap with feathers of a snowy owl. They ate roasted meat, hazelnuts and dried mushrooms, whereas bone marrow and cooked meat had been put apart as always for the elders. Despite the flapping hides on the hut they forgot the storm while they ate and talked. When everybody had had enough they fell silent. Now it was Leya's turn.

"Do you recall why we went to the South? Some of you imagined that we only did it to collect snails and other treasures, but a long and dangerous voyage like this does not serve that purpose. Those snails and other objects only provide proof that we really have been in the South. Everybody has received a few of these as a reminder of our save return."
Her audience automatically checked if the snails were still firmly attached to their clothes. They fully realised that the four friends had given them a precious present. The groups they met from time to time did not have such valuable snails. It would certainly increase their prestige.

"We hoped to discover the reasons why our ancestors had left the South, and find out whether it would be wise to stay here in the North, far from the origin of our tribe, or to go back to that region."
The elders remembered very well that the friends had used the same arguments when they asked permission for the journey to the South. At that time they could not predict the enormous amount of snow that last winter had caused serious problems to humans and animals. Countless animals had died or were so weakened that they became an easy prey to carnivores. Especially females with young did not survive. Next spring even fewer animals would be migrating to the northern plains if it snowed that much again. The group would have to cover greater distances to hunt enough game. Whatever Leya had to tell them, it would be good to know her opinion. Looking back, their decision to let them go on this expedition had not been so stupid!
"Now you understand why we returned not only with those snails but foremost with many memories of everything we saw and learnt. We will gather many nights around the fire and spin out the stories of our adventures. We have been away so many winters and summers that some of you perhaps imagined that we had died on the way. We for our part were afraid not to find you here after such a long time. You will never comprehend our intense joy when we discovered

the huts and tents by Big River and laid eyes on the smoke of your fires.
Eight springs have passed since our departure. At first we followed Big River upstream to the big bend south of the hills. Some of you have been in that region. Beautiful white snails and fish live there underground. Only after death do their remains emerge from the mud. We collected these as a gift for the people we hoped to meet during our journey. That region also forms the northern boundary of the territory of our southern neighbours, the family of Ursa. We found no signs that they had stayed there during the past winter in spite of the presence of abundant game, enough for a big group of people during many winters and springs. Horse, reindeer, rhinoceros and mammoth migrate every autumn from the northern plains to that region, where they pass the winter, since Big Valley is wide enough for all these beasts. Her family was not there, however.
At the beginning of the second moon of the spring we shifted our search to one of the tributaries, which flow from the east. Ursa recognised the place and remembered her family taking that route on occasions. A whole moon we followed the narrowing river upstream to the east, in the direction where every morning the sun rises above the horizon. We caught plenty of fish and also eggs since ducks, geese and swans were breeding everywhere along the river side.
As the days got warmer, we were pestered more and more by mosquitoes. In vain we tried to repel them. We were covered in terribly itching gnat bites. Especially in swamps did their ceaseless attention make us despair. Horse, reindeer and even bear with their thick coats were attacked by the wretched things. Many horses and reindeer migrate therefore to the high plains behind the mountains in the east as soon as summer begins. There the wind blasts mosquitoes away.
It was finally a real relief losing them. The plains teem with horse and reindeer, but we did not see any mammoth or rhinoceros."

"In one of the valleys we came across the remnants of an old bivouac that had seemingly been abandoned last fall. It might have been made by Ursa's relatives. We found smashed horse and bird bones and tracks of foxes, wolves and also of a bear that had clearly hibernated in one of the nearby caves. This offered new hope. On Ursa's advice we went to the southwest, where we discovered more and more signs of the recent presence of a small group of humans."

"Half a moon later in the early morning we observed smoke in the far distance. 'That's the place to be,' we said. At midday the smoke had disappeared, but above the same spot a flock of birds could be seen, a couple of ravens and some gulls, birds usually occurring in the neighbourhood of a carcass or bivouac.
We increased the pace and eventually looked down on a westward narrowing valley. From there a few horses galloped the gentle slope in our direction, a bleeding stallion with an assegai in his ribs followed by two mares and two foals. Four people ran after them with cries of despair seeing how the quarry escaped. Durfal and Krasser reacted at once. They motioned Ursa and me to drive the beasts back to the valley. We dropped our supplies, grasped our assegais and ran loudly screaming to the approaching horses. Visibly shaken by our unexpected appearance the animals were confused. The stallion reared up, turned neighing around on his hind legs and ran back into the valley, where one of the pursuers hit him fatally with a spear. The mares and foals swerved aside and headed for freedom.
We collected our stuff and walked down the hill to the people, a man and three women who had run to the stallion to drink the warm blood pouring from the wounds.
On our arrival they made room for us as a token of gratitude for our part in the hunt. We greedily drank the blood since we had only had some water that day. When everybody felt satisfied we looked at each other. They only hesitated for a moment and then Ursa and Durfal started

cheering as did the man. Between laughing and crying they hugged each other. Krasser grinned from ear to ear. 'We did it! We found Ursa's family!' She had recognised her older brother and also an aunt, her mother's sister. The other two women joined us and everyone embraced again. That's how we got to know the wife of Ursa's brother and also a widow of a nephew who had died hunting a few summers before. Ursa glanced questioningly around. 'Where is the rest of the family?' Her brother cut the questions. 'Later! We will talk after dinner. We have to work.' He pointed at the dead horse.
Together we dragged the body of the dead stallion to their camp down the valley. Three little children ran frightened away from the tent to hide behind the rocks. They had never met someone beyond their own family. Even their aunt Ursa had left the group before they were born. Only after realising there was nothing to fear, did they approach us slowly. We divided the entrails eating these immediately. The liver was for the kids. Then we skinned the beast and cut it to pieces. The gulls and ravens around the camp boldly flapped closer, but the children were smart enough to keep the birds at a distance with stones. Before nightfall we had scraped the fat from the hide, collected and cleaned the tendons, and sliced the meat into slivers to dry and smoke. The quarters were roasted above the fire. Brains, tongue and the rest of the meat from the skull and neck were put into bags to get boiled. We ate part of the marrow from the long bones and mixed the remainder with fat for the lamps. Being that busy little came of talking, but we felt happy together."

"When everyone was full conversation got going. We told how we left early spring on our journey to the South, taking the opportunity to visit them. Durfal described our great anxiety when we were unable to find them in Big Valley, in our eyes the best hunting place in spring time. Ursa's good memory had finally put us on the right track to trace them.

They for their part were extremely happy with our visit, her brother said. Without our help they would still be in trouble since their group was too small to successfully hunt horse or reindeer. That was the reason they had left Big Valley. Their present camp was situated at a strategic position, where the valley was narrowing, but they were not enough to drive game to this spot and kill it. After Ursa's departure her family had been overtaken by disaster. Her mother, her two uncles, her younger brother and all her nephews and nieces had died due to illness and accidents or disappeared during hunting. They were the only ones still alive, he sadly concluded.
Ursa initially refused to face reality. When she left five springs earlier to follow Durfal everybody had still been strong and healthy. Although it had been a sad farewell she did not imagine then that she had seen them for the last time. We were incapable of comforting her or drying her tears."

"It took quite some time before her brother could continue. He hoped that Ursa would find solace in the thought that the spirits of mothers and animals had guided their souls back to the womb of the earth. He carefully produced a small ivory idol from the pouch on his necklace showing his unbroken faith in the spirits of the mothers. Lately, he gloomily explained, they lived on occasionally snared birds and rabbits, on trout from the brooks and herbs collected in the vicinity of the camp. They wandered around compelled by the need to try their luck. Their worn-out clothing and footwear urgently needed replacement.
We, Durfal, Ursa, Krasser and I gave each other a knowing look. No words were needed, we nodded in assent. 'I think that it might be a good idea to stay here this summer,' said Durfal to Ursa's family putting into words our unspoken thoughts. 'We have seen today that hunting together is easier, not only for you but also for us. After summer however we will continue our way to the South. It is important that you try to join another group. Perhaps you know where to

find one.' They stared at us as if they were not sure of Durfal's saying. Then their faces beamed with joy. You should have seen it! They were so happy! Deeply moved they grasped and shook our hands expressing their gratitude. We on our part felt pleased helping them. Krasser showed his feelings by carving several spirits in a stone. We all knew that it was thanks to them that we had found them."

"The next day we prepared our gear to hunt and fish. Somewhere in the valley the children discovered reindeer antlers, which we used to cut new spear tips and harpoons. We made awls and needles of a long bone after the children had sucked the raw marrow, whereas Ursa's aunt spun the tendons. Next we made strong moccasins out of the horse hide. Durfal put the remaining long bones on the hot ash of the fire warming the marrow and I prepared a nice herb tea in the same way that we tended to do here. We were all in high spirits. Someone started singing about the horse hunt that turned out so well and about food in abundance. Durfal took care of the rhythm tapping two stones. For a moment the children looked on, in surprise at the merriment. They had never seen anything like this. Then they followed the cadenza clapping their hands. Loudly singing we repeated each phrase of the continuously lengthening song. At night we roasted part of the meat, having rubbed it with chives and other herbs. After a well-earned sleep we made an early start to the Southwest.
A few days later we reached a valley with steep slopes and many caves, which served as shelter. The brook was teeming with trout and burbot. We also discovered a well with ice-cold water, nearly as blue as the sky above. We therefore called that place Blue Valley*. We saw grazing horses and reindeer, and also a few deer and goats. Moreover, the valley narrowed at several places, where game could de easily ambushed. In short, an ideal hunting ground for the rest of the summer. We stayed there until the onset of fall when berries and currants were ripe for the picking. Most currants we dried for the winter on a sunny spot, while the

children tried to shoo away the birds. The remainder was put with some water inside intestines, which we hung in the sun. Within days we got a nice sour drink getting us in the right mood for a feast.
The day before leaving Blue Valley we honored the spirits, which had been so well-disposed towards us. No-one had gotten hurt and we had collected lots of food and hides. We all had new footwear and clothing, embellished with feathers and small pieces of bone. At nightfall we painted our faces with yellow and red ochre. We ate and drank, sang and danced deep into the night. Krasser carved the figure of the spirit of a horse in a stone that we covered with red ochre as a sign of our gratitude. We threw it into the well, where it went straight to the inner-earth. Next morning we woke up when the sun was already high. Lack of sleep produced a raging headache and we felt sick after the abundant food and drink. A dip in cold water however solved the problem."

"Days before, we had constructed stretchers of willow branches and leather straps. We fixed the hides and supplies on these, cast a final glance at the surroundings and walked the whole day eastwards, until the place where the Blue Valley ends at the Wide River*. From there we went upstream to the Southwest, in turns dragging the stretchers.
Just before the beginning of the second moon of fall we reached a place, where large herds of reindeer crossed Wide River going northwards to overwinter. We had never seen so many beasts together. They were slightly smaller than reindeer in this region, but big enough to replenish our food supplies. So we decided to look for a suitable spot to hunt them down.
The same day we discovered many smoke plumes slightly farther southward, a sign that other people were also interested in hunting the animals. We therefore lit a fire as well in order to draw their attention to our presence. At dawn we walked in the direction of the smoke.

Some hunters, preceded by loudly barking dogs, met us halfway. After a warm-hearted greeting they took us to their camp in one of the many valleys. There we discovered to our surprise, because no-one had ever told us before, that a sister of Durfal's grandmother was a member of that group. She really rejoiced about our visit.
In his youth her mate had reached the shores of the Northern Ice Lake, a horrible region, practically without any vegetation, where neither man or game have a chance to survive. He had been one of the very few that had dared to go so far to the north. He had told this story to the eldest among us when he visited our family many winters ago, long before I was born, and so he had met his wife.
Being one of the eldest he immediately invited us to stay with them. 'We are all family,' were his words. 'We are all brothers and sisters, members of the same tribe. You know what; let's give this valley a name to remember this joyful meeting. Let's call it the valley of brothers and sisters, or simply Brother's Valley!' It would have been an offense to refuse so much hospitality and we thus accepted his invitation. As a token of our gratitude we gave him and the rest of the eldest the fish teeth and snails we had collected in spring.
Our new friends had discovered Brother's Valley just a few days before our arrival. They were still busy installing the camp that comprised at least ten huts, as many as the fingers of our hands. The site was situated at the narrowest spot of the valley, by a small cave with a clear view on the surroundings that also served as residence for one of the families."

"Our group was large enough for a drive. Part of the men and women separated with torches as many beasts as possible from the herd and drove these into Brother's Valley. We had distributed the children along the valley flanks. Throwing stones, yelling and howling like wolves they prevented any game escaping to the hills. The animals ran straight to the campsite, where all fires had been extinguished. In terror they ran to the only visible escape route between the camp and the northern slope. The hunters waiting in ambush looked incredulously at the huge herd rumbling in their direction with the beaters behind. They had not expected so many beasts.

The hunters swung into action as soon as the herd reached the narrow passage. At that short distance each throw came home. The first reindeer fell roaring to the ground. There was no time to kill them. Hastily they grasped a second spear, then a third and a fourth. Our cries of triumph overwhelmed the death cries. The beasts trampled one another in mortal fear. Only a few managed to escape. The last ones turned round and tried to run back. They were killed off by the beaters.

We slaughtered the wounded reindeer with knifes and stones. Blood gushed in broad streams from the wounds forming large pools on the ground. Everybody, young and old, ran closer as usual to drink it on the spot. Impatiently we cut open the beasts for the liver. You should have seen us: faces, hands, clothing, everything was red stained by the blood. Everyone was dancing and laughing, unable to talk, the mouth full with bloody liver. It felt just like having drunk that grape juice in Blue Valley, as if we were floating and dreaming at the same time.

We only came to our senses when dogs and foxes neared to seize their share of the catch and ravens, gulls and eagles flew above our heads. The smell of blood and entrails might soon attract wolves and perhaps also a bear or a wolverine. We laid fires around the slaughter field in order to keep predators at a distance. Next we removed the entrails before these got tainted. Alas, it was far too much. We selected the best pieces to eat or cook these immediately. We separated stomach, intestines and bladder for washing and drying.

The remainder we threw outside the camp for dogs, foxes and birds. It took days to skin the bodies, cut meat into pieces and remove the tendons. Hides had to be cleaned, fat sampled, meat dried and smoked.

We heated the long bones and broke these for sucking the marrow. It is routine work if a few animals are involved, but not if you have to deal with so many. Our smarting hands were severely chapped, but it was really worthwhile. Each family got a number of hides, enough for clothing and footwear and reparation of tents. We had collected enough food for the winter and a surplus of bones and antlers for to make spear points, awls, harpoons and needles. Never before and never afterwards did we kill so much game in a single day. Neither did the people of that group ever experience something similar. I am sure that they will talk many winters to come about that incredible event, the reindeer drive in Brother's Valley."

"Wow!" One of the young hunters had imagined himself into her story. "Here we content ourselves with two or three horses! At this very moment, we depend on our last supplies. It must be marvelous to see such a large herd pass here tomorrow."

"Oh, yes! You forget it is still winter and reindeer hide somewhere far in the South," stopped someone this wishful thought. "They will not come back before spring. Be realistic! Within a few days, if it stops snowing, we may at least snare hares and ptarmigans, or perhaps kill a stray horse."

"Stop talking!" Another person intervened. "We want to hear the rest. Leya, ignore these triflers!"

'At the beginning of the winter's first moon we organised a celebration to thank the spirits. Fires burned in front of each tent and people cooked or roasted meat and made soup. Everyone had made himself up with black, yellow and red colors. Following their traditions men, women and children had small charms on their neck representing the spirits of the mothers. They carve these out of black wood found locally along the brooks in that region. Here we carry these figurines with us. The elder showed off our snails and shells, a sign that they appreciated our gifts. For their part they presented us assegais with yellowish brown flint blades of an exceptionally good quality. Mine may look now heavily damaged but the blades have survived almost eight winters. They assured us that this special flint only occurs at many days walk from Brother's Valley.

A few days later we broke camp. It was useless to stay any longer. Each day we had to walk a little farther collecting dry branches for the fire. Moreover, game had stopped coming to Brother's Valley."

Engravings of stylised women of Lalinde-Gönnersdorf type
(*Spirits of the Mothers*)

From left to right
one specimen from Andernach
(Andernach; after Bosinski a.o., 2001),
two from Gönnersdorf
(Neuwied; after Bosinski a.o., 2001),
two from Roc-la-Tour
(Monthermé; after C. & J.G. Rozoy, 2004)
and one from Fontalès
(Saint-Antonin-Noble-Val; after Duhard, 1993).

Distance between Gönnersdorf and Andernach is 5 km, between Gönnersdorf and Roc-la-Tour 300 km, between Gönnersdorf and Fontalès 1,100 km and between Roc-la-Tour and Fontalès 850 km.

Spirits and the Womb of the Earth

As we have seen before, the coldest period of the Ice Age made Central and Northern Europe uninhabitable and people were driven back to Southern France and the coastal regions in Spain and Portugal. According to Bryan Sykes they descended from Ursula, one of the 'seven daughters of Eve' who had been born 45,000 years ago on the foothills of Mount Parnassus in Northern Greece. Because they were completely cut off from the outside world, this community developed its own (Solutrean) culture. We should however take the concept 'completely cut off from the outside world' with a pinch of salt. As already stated in the introduction, during that coldest period a small band of nomads succeeded in migrating unnoticed from the Middle East to Southern France. They formed a very successful group whose descendants rapidly spread over Southern France and Northern Spain.

Among them were Helena, born 20,000 years ago, and Velda, born 17,000 years ago. We have talked about this already.

Thanks to those famous boreholes in the Greenland ice cap we know that 20,000 years ago temperature raised a little bit, just enough to make the conditions of life slightly more bearable for plants, animals and men. Rivers carried more meltwater and this resulted in a noticeable sea level rise. How could this minor temperature increase cause so much ice to melt, as mean annual temperatures in Europe beyond the Mediterranean and Atlantic coastal areas remained below freezing point? Despite these low temperatures, sea levels rose twenty meters within five thousand years. It implies the melting of an ice mass three times as large as that on Greenland today!
In an extremely dry climate however it may be very warm during the day as practically no clouds can temper the sun. Moreover, no significant precipitation compensated the loss of ice. Melt water carried to the sea does not come back in the form of snow. Therefore sea levels rise.
Particularly in Southwestern France a diverse fauna could be found. The many lifelike drawings, paintings and carvings of mammoth, rhinoceros, and bison suggest that they have been frequently observed by the artists. Horse and saiga possibly preferred dry steppes, whereas lush valleys and greenish coastal plains formed the domain of reindeer. Salmon, trout and eel teemed in brooks and rivers. A wide variety of seal species was found by the sea shore, whereas mountain goat and marmot lived on steep slopes and rocks. We should not forget the many birds and hares. All in all there was enough game for the prehistoric hunters.
The fact that more trees were growing in Southern than in Central Europe was equally important: mainly pines, willows and birches, but locally also oak, beech, lime, alder, elm and hazel. People needed enormous quantities of kindling and also long, straight stems and branches for tent poles and assegais.

It is highly likely that the descendants of Helena and Velda rapidly outnumbered those of Ursula. They invented new weapons and tools characteristic of a new culture: the Magdalenian*. They also proved to be very gifted artists. The Middle Magdalenian, 16,000 – 18,000 years ago, was a golden age of prehistoric art. The superb ceiling with bison in the cave of Altamira is one of the highlights. Because of the supreme quality of the bison paintings the specialists initially refused to believe that these had been made by 'primitive cave-men'. Similar multicolored paintings in the cave of Font-de-Gaume, near Les Eyzies in the French Dordogne, are indicative of close contacts with Northern Spain.

Many people automatically associate the Stone Age in Europe with cave paintings, not knowing that the artists at the time also produced beautiful engravings and reliefs. In Combarelles, at less than five kilometers from Font-de-Gaume, they engraved hundreds of images in the cave walls. We tend to regard this as some kind of competition between the makers: in Font-de-Gaume those who used red and black earth (iron and manganese oxide) for drawing and painting bison, mammoth, reindeer, lion, rhinoceros, bear and wolf on the walls, and in Combarelles people who made do with a piece of flint for engraving the same animals. Of course, it is doubtful if they ever have seen each others work, since the period of the making, the Middle Magdalenian, lasted two thousand years.
In spring 2008, an information center opened for the public in Angles-sur-Anglin, east of Poitiers. A replica of the eighteen meters long sculpted frieze of Roc-aux-Sorciers occupies the central stage. It is the largest one known from the Paleolithic. It has been made some 18,000 years ago, during the Middle Magdalenian, by means of simple flint tools. The Sorcerer's Rock, this is the textual meaning of Roc-aux-Sorciers, is located slightly north of Angles-sur-Anglin. It is an overhung rock shelter at a bend of the Anglin, a favourable location with regard to sun and wind. In winter Sorcerer's Rock protected the residents against the

cold wind from the north, whereas the sun warmed the spot from sunrise to sunset. The rock also formed an ideal observation post for hunters since the surroundings were practically treeless at the time. From there they had a good view on the animals grazing in the wide valley south of them. When walking from Anglin to Sorcerer's Rock, we imagined a small group, coming the same way, driving the game slowly into the direction of the rock, where the valley suddenly narrows. At that point they had nowhere to escape because of the deep, fast-flowing river on the left side. An ambush of a few hunters will have sufficed to kill them.

The residents ornamented the back-wall of the shelter with up to one meter large reliefs. Starting at the left is a scene with two bison, a cow following a bull. Next we see two horses, the mare on the left looks back at a snorting stallion, his forelegs wide apart and head lowered, that tries to attract her attention. Three human female bodies, showing thighs up to half the torso, dominate the third panel. They are cut off just below the breasts and have a prominent vulva, symbol of fertility and procreation. The last three panels form an entity, a herd of mountain goats with the watchful leader in the center. On his left two males fight for the favors of a female closely followed by two kids, whereas another male on his right approaches a female. Look also at the other engravings in the frieze: lions, a mammoth and various human faces. They may stem from an older period before the sculptures were made. Some reliefs have been readjusted afterwards. A sculpted bison, for example, gave way to a fourth female body that later on was partly replaced by a mountain goat. It implies a repeated change of mind of the makers. An overwhelming sound and light show accompanied our visit to the center. It really made us think.

What was the meaning of those images? All sorts of theories have been suggested. What strikes us most is the absence of any background. Paleolithic animals have never been portrayed within their natural surroundings.

Where are trees, sun or moon? Perhaps the artists were incapable of drawing the sun or a tree? Nonsense! Someone with so much feeling for detail when painting a bison would certainly have been able to reproduce a primitive landscape. Apparently they thought that this was completely unimportant. All attention was focused on specific animals or humans. The rest, including the background, did not matter at all.
We can only guess at the underlying motives for reproducing whenever and wherever similar scenes, on all possible substrates and materials, with all possible techniques. Some scientists believe that these figures were drawn by shamans. Others have forwarded the hypothesis of hunting rituals or art done for its own sake. Still others interpret many drawings as fertility, totemic or animistic symbols. It is impossible to find out what the artists really intended to depict. That would have made it so much easier for us. On the other hand, this gives us the liberty of advancing our own interpretations.

Why should Paleolithic artists have portrayed living beings? In our opinion many drawings may just as well represent souls or spirits of humans and animals. Imagine they believed that souls or spirits were living within a different reality, and then we have an account for the absence of a background.
We are convinced that Cro-Magnons had already formed an idea about life after death, about some kind of hereafter. Even though their mental capacity may have been slightly smaller than ours, they did not differ in this respect from us. They did not know electricity, did not live in apartment buildings and the wheel had not yet been invented, that is true. However, were our grandparents perhaps less intelligent than we because they did not have computers? Of course, mobile phones and internet offer more possibilities than fax, telex or Morse, which for their part replaced the ancient smoke signals. Is an internet user however smarter than someone producing or interpreting smoke signals?

These are merely different ways to communicate.
Our body of thought goes back to Greeks and Romans, to the Ten Commandments of the Old Testament. You may safely assume that the stories of Creation in the Bible book Genesis are based on oral traditions, on stories already told around the fire in the Ice Age. The mere fact that they buried the dead with so much care shows that they imagined a life after death. The contents of their thoughts remain open to speculation. Did they believe in a Supreme Being, in some kind of creation? We think they did. We assume that the essence of Genesis already took shape in the Ice Age. We have only to find out or imagine how they understood 'creation'. In Genesis, for example, we read that the earth already existed. According to the author 'the earth was welter and waste'. Therefore the Cro-Magnon story of creation may have been limited to the creation of humans and animals.
The question remains what they imagined to have happened. In this context it is worthwhile to look at the countless fertility symbols, phalluses and vulvas. They knew that fertility and procreation formed the basis of life, even if they had no conception of sperm and egg cells. They were well aware of the fact that a woman needed a man in order to get pregnant. Just suppose they believed in a Supreme Being who 'fertilised' (of course, they will have used a different wording) the earth and so begot the first humans and animals emerging through these holes from the womb of the earth.
Then it is conceivable too that they imagined that the spirits or souls of the dead returned to their 'origin' by using the same holes, thus finishing off the circle!
This is, of course, a product of our unbridled imagination. Let's however elaborate the idea. Perhaps, dear reader, you will accept to follow our argumentation. For example, did our Paleolithic ancestors really think that caverns and caves represented the womb of the earth? Look in this respect at publications by Carmen San Miguel who studied the cave of El Linar, near Santander in Northern Spain.

According to her, two narrowing passages in one of the galleries obviously resemble life-sized vulvas. Our ancestors improved this resemblance by carving lines in the wall. Imagine how they squeezed their way through these virtual vulvas, symbolically leaving the womb of the earth, celebrating some sort of ritual birth!
Moreover, not only animals have been depicted in El Linar, but also an almost one meter large silhouette of a stylised woman without a head. Why did they portray the spirits in so many caves? What was the hidden message? We assume that they have tried to visualise that the spirits lived in the inner-earth, somewhere near the image.

Some of these figures occupy a preferential place, for example the 18,000 years old, Middle Magdalenian 'god with horns' in the cave of Trois-Frêres in Southern France. This half-human, half-animal figure (with deer antlers, eagle head, bear claws, horsetail and human arms and legs) is distinguished by its central position in the cave, the relative height on the wall (above the other images) and by the fact that it has not only been engraved but also painted. The 'sorcerer' or 'shaman' of Saint-Cirq-du-Bugue, with an enormous phallus, also occupies a central position in the cave. A similarly half-human, half-animal sculpture, the 'lion-man,' has been made 30,000 years ago near Ulm in Germany.
Some scholars assume that these represent sorcerers, witches or shamans. However, the artists have portrayed the Supreme Being with both human and animal characteristics. The Middle Magdalenian images are characterised by a striking male (but not necessarily human) member. This fits the thought of a Supreme Being who made the earth fertile and so begot the first humans and animals. The name 'god with horns' was not so stupid after all!

Furthermore, in at least some cases, they tried to visualise that spirits were somehow able to continue their former life, that the interior of the earth was not an obscure underworld, nor a gloomy twilight. In Font-de-Gaume the guide asks the visitors to pay special attention to a painting of a couple of reindeer, a male courting a female. He lowers his head and licks her muzzle while she bends her forelegs, a sign of submission. Time and again we feel overwhelmed by the tenderness of this image. The scene might suggest that the womb of the earth was a beautiful place for the spirits of animals, where they copulated and lived together in peace.

We remember something similar from Rouffignac: a chance meeting of two mammoth herds. The leading females exchange greetings with their trunks. The artist did not intend to portray living animals but only their spirits, spirits which meet on a virtual steppe in the interior of the earth. In fact we usually observe peaceful scenes, rarely animals fighting one another. They have most likely wanted to emphasise that the souls of the dead would find a place in that idyllic world. This must have formed the base of their thoughts about the hereafter, because exactly the same scenes have been engraved in the walls of the cave of Pair-non-Pair, north of Bordeaux. There we have seen a deer with a hind, a male mountain goat with a female and two kids, a stallion with a mare and her colt, a bison bull with a cow, and a mammoth cow with her calf. Of course, the archaic style of the engravings differs from the later Magdalenian ones, since they were made 30,000 years ago, fifteen thousand years before the time we are dealing with. Try to imagine: fifteen thousand years! They reproduced the same scenes over and over in this period of time.

We instinctively compare the stereotypical presentation of some drawings and figurines with Christian icons and images of saints. Christians recognise saints by their clothing and attributes; Saint Sebastian for example by his body tied to a post and shot with arrows or Saint Peter by the keys of the heavenly gate. Something similar happened in prehistoric times. We frequently see half-finished animals, such as the manes and dorsal line of a horse, the stylised horns of mountain goat, a single line indicating trunk, head and back of a mammoth. Those people never asked: 'what's this? Why's this drawing unfinished?' No, they knew very well that those manes and slightly bend dorsal line represented the spirit of a horse. That was all they needed.

For us it may be difficult to interpret the meaning of those abstract forms. Many scholars suggest that it was taboo to portray humans. Are they right? Perhaps human spirits and souls were visualised through for them familiar signs and symbols, which were commonplace. André Leroi-Gourhan interpreted vulvas and phalluses, points and lines and dozens of other enigmatic signs in caves and on objects as female and male symbols. What more do we need? Points and vulvas may represent spirits of women and lines and phalluses spirits of men. No-one knew, of course, what the spirits of the dead really looked like. Points or lines in a cave may just as well have represented primitive obituary lists!

The obvious difference between the realistically portrayed spirits of animals and the stylised or symbolic representation of humans suggest different roles. It is possible that animals may have been regarded as guardian spirits of mankind. Leroi-Gourhan noticed that animal drawings were quite often associated with abstract symbols. Points and lines on or near a specific animal figure may represent people commending themselves to that specific spirit. This prehistoric imagery may thus be compared with a cross, signature or fingerprint on a modern contract.

These artists not only portrayed spirits in caves, but also on stones and pebbles, which they deliberately abandoned at the campsites instead of carrying these with the rest of their luggage. The act of drawing and engraving may have been sufficient to get into contact with spirits. Placing the stones with the figures facing down may have strengthened the contact as spirits resided in the interior of the earth. In this way the picture served as a kind of transmitter between the living and the world of spirits. Each time one needed a spirit he could repeat the act. That's why they have portrayed some spirits more than once.

15,000 years ago

The Other Ones

She felt dizzy when she woke up, dizzy and sick at the same time and wondered why. She carefully staggered outside, hoping that fresh air might do her well. Fortunately, the wind was dying down although it continued to snow a little. She took a deep breath and felt better off for the moment. She saw dark smoke rising from behind the tent of her neighbours.

Someone was making a fire, but the branches and leaves were wet, creating a nasty smell that reached her nose. The urge to vomit suddenly got the upper hand. She could only bend forward, her hands pressed against her waist. Groaning she puked the contents of her stomach on the snow. A woman tried to help, patting her on the back and holding her head.

"Leya, what's happening? Are you in pain? Can I help?"

She shook her head, while tears were rolling down her cheeks. She blew her nose between two fingers, gratefully accepted a bladder with cold water and drank to clean her mouth. Through her tears she looked at the woman.

"What have you eaten last night?" asked the woman in a worried voice.

"Nothing special, roasted meat and herb tea, just as everyone else."
"Perhaps the meat was bad."
She shook her head. "I would have noticed. My stomach is bothering me; that's the problem. It may be a winter disease. I shall ask my mother if she has still some ground willow bark or root."
She went to her mother's hut, where Great Narrator remained in bed since she was feeling unwell.

"What's up," asked her mother. "You don't look well."
"I just like to ask you for some ground willow bark or root, or something like that. I felt sick since I woke up. I even had to vomit."
Her mother placed her hand on Leya's forehead and face. "Nothing special," was her reaction.
Next she felt her belly, without result. She kept thinking for a moment, then suddenly raised her head and looked at her daughter.
"Did you loose blood during the past moon?"
"No, but that is not unusual."
Her mother looked at her once more, carefully feeling the breasts. "What made you vomit?"
"I felt sick. I sniffed the cold air, outside the hut, to get rid of that feeling when suddenly a bad smell of smoke and wet wood reached my nose."
"Leya, you don't need anything. You are pregnant!"
"That is impossible," faltered she confused. "Why should I be pregnant, after so much time? I am too old for it, just like Ursa."
"You think you are too old," laughed her mother. "Why do you think so? I have seen many women who were much older than you when they got pregnant for the first time. Don't worry about your age, my child. Remember all these years of wandering around, all the hardships you have suffered. You have been so busy with other things that your body was not ready to get pregnant. You have been here a full moon, you had time to rest and eat and it did you well."

She embraced her daughter, together dancing mad with excitement across the hut. "I am so happy! My daughter is getting a child! I have secretly hoped for this through so many summers and winters, and now the time has come."

Leya turned to Great Narrator who had had taken in the news. Her eyes radiated joy. Leya sat down and hugged her. "Did you get it? I am pregnant! I am awaiting a child!"
"I can hardly believe that I am living to see this," said her grandmother. "It makes me so happy! My granddaughter is getting a child! It will be a daughter, as pretty as you. That's for sure! The Maker has fulfilled my wishes. The spirits will guard you. Some day she will pass all the stories to her children and all her family."
Seeing the tears of joy in her eyes made Leya feel deeply moved. She softly rocked the old woman in her arms. "I am getting a child, Great Narrator, a child! If it will be a daughter I will teach her all the stories I once learnt from you."
Leya could not remember that she had ever felt so intensely happy. She silently wondered how Krasser might react. Would he be as happy as she? Could someone really feel so much happiness, was that possible? In the past they had often talked how wonderful it might be to get a child. He preferred a boy, he always argued. The group needed strong, brave boys, although he would also content himself with a girl, beautiful and smart as her mother. The subject had faded into the background during the past winters. She never got pregnant and feared that this pleasure would pass her by. She slowly returned to reality.
"I must tell Krasser," shouted Leya. "He has no idea!"
She ran away, leaving the two overjoyed women behind. Her man sat in front of the hut, working a reindeer antler. He gave her a questioning look.
"Krasser," exclaimed she excitedly. "Krasser! You will not believe it! I am pregnant! I am getting a child!"
The antler slipped from his hands. "This is not real," was his first thought. "I must be dreaming!" Giving Leya a searching look, he saw her radiant eyes and understood

that he had not misheard. He jumped to his feet, his strong hands grasping her middle. He tenderly kissed her lips, nose and eyes, holding her close to his chest. His hand slipped below her clothes touching her belly to make sure that the child was really there.

"No," whispered Leya, "be patient. You can't feel it, it is still too small."

The news got around very fast. People came from right and left to share her happiness. Everyone kissed her, caressed her cheek or patted her on the back. It had always been like that when a woman got pregnant, hardly surprising since survival of the group depended on the birth of more babies. During he forthcoming moons everyone would be offering help and take good care of her.

That night a cheerful company gathered around the fire. Leya was also present. They had forbidden her to tell a story, afraid that this might be too much for her. 'Come on,' had she argued, 'I am not sick, only pregnant!' In the end she relented in order to please them. 'If it makes you feel happy, I will keep silent, but just this night!'

One of the men from the East had offered to tell about his family. They called him Prater, their pet name for a talkative one, because he tended to do most of the talking during the meetings around the fire. He slept with one of Durfal's nieces. She adored him, although being many summers younger than he, and she hung on his every word when he was speaking. No-one knew if he would take her with him to the East, or stay here in case she got pregnant.

The place of Great Narrator stayed empty. She complained about cold hands and feet in spite of being covered with many hides. She had decided to remain in her bed. 'I am old, Leya,' had she said. 'It will not take long before the spirits of the mothers and mammoths will accompany my soul to the womb of the earth.'

'What about us,' had Leya asked, 'what will happen to us without you? My child will be born next winter. Don't you like to see it and take it in your arms?'

'Of course, I would like that, but by body is exhausted, don't you see? Don't worry, if the Maker wishes, my spirit will come back to protect you, even if I do not know how that is possible. You better go listening to Prater's stories. It would be good for our group if he decides to stay here.'

"Come on, Prater," called someone out, "tell us something about the other ones! Don't they live somewhere in the East, just like you?"
"Are they humans or animals?"
"Perhaps you have seen them yourself," suggested a third voice. "Maybe they frightened you."
Everybody roared with laughter. Prater was big and sturdy, stronger than most of the men in the camp, as they had experienced more than once. No, Prater was not so easily frightened. That was unthinkable. He too laughed at their comments.
"OK," said Prater, "I will tell you the truth, one condition, that you first give me something to drink."
He emptied the horn in one, whiped his mouth with the back of his hand and made himself comfortable. He was really in his element now.

"As you all know, my family lives far from here, at three summers walk in the direction of the rising sun. First you cross the extensive territory of your eastern neighbours, who so generously received me and my friend last winter. They sent us on to you. Just like you, they hunt horses, which roam the vast northern plains in summer and seek out the southern valleys in winter. They also kill reindeer, saiga, fox and hare. We did not see any of the few mammoths living in that region. Just as you, they don't like to kill these, because the spirit of the mammoth accompanies their souls after death. My family also honors the spirit of the mammoth, but their images have been made long ago, long before I was born, when the last mammoths still lived there. Nowadays you only find their bones and tusks lying on the steppe.

It was not until last summer that I, for the first time in my life, set eyes on a living mammoth on your hunting grounds. I shall never forget it. The enormous hairy body, even bigger than that of a rhinoceros, the long trunk for bringing grass and herbs to his mouth, the giant tusks of the bull, and, of course, those large piercing eyes. Even now I can hardly imagine that I have really seen him. No other animal has ever impressed me that much. In my native region people will not believe me when I tell them about this encounter or show them the reddish hairs that got stuck in the bushes. They will suppose that I drunk too much currant juice and invented it."
They burst out laughing, remembering how excited Prater had been after seeing the mammoths. He had kept staring open-mouthed, completely motionless. Only when the beasts had disappeared into the distance, did his jumping and dancing show his emotions.

'I have seen mammoths,' had he cried, 'living mammoths!' Time after time he had asked them if they had seen them as well, making sure that it had not been a dream.
'Now you understand,' had they explained to him, 'why we don't kill these beautiful animals. They are the strongest of all animals. Even in a storm or in the dead of the night will they find their way and never get lost. Their spirit always knows the way to the womb of the earth, which is why many of us entrust our soul to the spirit of the mammoth.'
'Is his spirit perhaps stronger that the spirit of a mother?' had Prater asked.
'Without any doubt, but the spirits of your mother and the mother of your mother love you as only a mother can do. They are caring and tender; calm your spirit, lulling it to sleep in the interior of the earth. We however need more than one spirit.'

"Yeah, just laugh," was Prater's reaction. "You are used to seeing mammoths from childhood. For you this is normal, but for me it was a unique experience I shall never forget."

Once more he emptied the horn and quietly waited until everyone had calmed down.

"The group of my friend Stille, the pet name you gave him because he is not so talkative, lives farther eastwards between the mountains, at the upper course of a mighty river that streams to the northwest. You have to cross their territory in order to reach the hunting grounds of my own people. To appreciate the beauty of that region, you should have lived there like I did. We overwinter in the Southwest, where many caves offer a shelter against rain and snow. Game includes reindeer, horse, goat, bison, hare, fox and many other animals, so we have enough food. In spring we cross the mountains to the northeastern steppes to hunt horse and rhinoceros. Yes, don't be shocked. We also honor the spirits of the rhinoceros, just like you, but they are so numerous that it can't be bad killing one of them in times of need. It is always cold there in the northeast; even in summer does the ground stay frozen as we notice each time when we are looking for stones. To that purpose we have to dig deep holes, big enough to make a man like me disappear almost completely, except for my head. It is hard work digging holes in the frozen soil, but it is the only way to obtain good quality flint for making tools and weapons. From similar holes we also collect red ochre for make-up and cleaning hides, but those are dug in a different region, much farther to the north."
"How did you find out where to dig these holes in order to get the right quality stones? Did the other ones tell you?"
"Of course not! We did not need anyone. Only our family knows the secret. We dug these holes even before my grandmother was born. We have learnt this from the eldest and they for their part had heard it from their grandmother. No-one knows when our ancestors started doing this. We only dig the holes in summer, when the topmost layer turns into soft mud during the day. With a piece of reindeer antler we dislodge the stones. We also remove the soft mud until reaching the hard frozen soil below.

This in turn changes into soft mud the next day when it gets warmed by the sun. We continue this work until fall when the soil stays frozen even during the day. Then we start snaring ptarmigans, and also fox and hares for their white winter coat. Only when we have collected enough furs do we return to the winter camp. Half the winter may already have passed before the last families set off."

"And the other ones, Prater, where live the other ones?"
"Why are you so keen to know this?" grinned Prater when he returned the question. "Is someone interested to meet them? Well, I shall tell you about them, but only because you keep insisting on the subject.
As a child I already heard talk about the other ones; at night around the fire, in the dark. 'Beware of the other ones,' tended to say my mother when I went playing with other children outside the camp. 'Stay in the neighbourhood, don't go too far!' I understood, that the other ones lived somewhere in the South, far away from our winter camp. Each time when the hunters returned empty-handed, they blamed the other ones for it. According to them they were thieves and robbers who used to kill or chase away our horses, or, even worse: murderers, people who would kill us without remorse. We learned breathlessly how they had abused our hospitality. Complete families had been cowardly caught in their sleep, women and daughters first being raped, then their bodies cut to pieces and eaten as if they were animals. Luckily, as a child I never met the other ones since they never came to visit us. In my imagination they were bad-tempered like a rhinoceros; they had wolf's teeth and bear's claws and the strength of an infuriated bison. They had to be invisible, like ghosts, always ready to rip us to pieces."
Gestures and faces underlined his words. His audience imagined the other ones as freaky monsters, half-human and half-animal. The children took a covert look at the adults, doubting whether or not these might be strong enough to protect them against the other ones. Prater got

all the attention he might have wished for.
"Five winters ago, when I still lived with my family, we welcomed a visitor I had never seen before. He appeared to be a nephew who had disappeared long ago during a hunting party. After several useless search operations they had accepted that he had died somewhere. They hoped that the spirit of a horse had taken his soul to the womb of the earth. No-one was capable of surviving alone on the steppe in winter. If he had not perished with the cold, he should have succumbed as a victim to wolves or, even worse, of the other ones.
After getting lost, he told us, he became convinced that his end was near. Fresh snow had wiped out all tracks and a dense fog made any orientation impossible. Day after day he screamed himself hoarse without getting any answer. He had no food, found no twig to chew on. He cried, begging the spirits of the mothers for help. Completely exhausted he finally collapsed and overcome by cold he fell asleep."

"He next woke up by a fire in a small tent. Strong hands rubbed his arms and legs, his back and his head in order to get him warmed up again. He heard voices and murmuring without understanding a word. Someone placed a horn with warm drink to his lips. 'This must be the womb of the earth,' was his first thought. But the smell and taste of herbs was unmistakable and he felt the warmth returning into his body. Before he could wonder about this, he went off in a deep refreshing sleep.
When he woke up again, he found himself firmly wrapped up on a stretcher that was being dragged through the snow. They stopped when they noticed that he was awake.
Unknown but not unfriendly faces bent over him, uttering unintelligible words. He gave them a look of non-comprehension. Suddenly he understood. These must be the other ones! He was terror-stricken. They had tied him up in such a way that he was unable to move, a clear indication that they plotted against him, taking him to their camp to kill

and devour him. He desperately tried to free himself, but one of the women of the group – he felt sure she was a woman and certainly not a monster – lifted her hand. With a kind smile she showed him an ivory figurine of the spirit of a mother indicating he had nothing to fear. 'Imagine,' so he told us, 'the spirit of a mother! The other ones know and venerate the spirits of the mothers, just like us! Who would have thought that?'"

His audience jumped to their feet. The spirits of the mothers, did the other ones honor the spirits of the mothers? Forget it! But Prater kept his mind on the story and continued.

"We were very surprised to hear this. We could not believe it and asked if perhaps he had dreamt it. But he repeated his statement with emphasis. 'Oh yes, a figurine of the spirit of a mother, I know very well what I am telling you.' The woman gave him a piece of meat and a skin with tepid water she had kept under her clothes to prevent it from freezing. She nodded satisfied when seeing him eat. After a short rest they continued walking to the East. In spite of all the excitement and the jolting stretcher he once more fell asleep.

Days passed. He lost count of the times he saw the sun rise and disappear. He did not recognise the landscape they crossed. They finally reached a wide valley with here and there some isolated spruces and birches. Huts and burning fires marked the campsite, just as any other he had visited before.

Yet, when he gave it a better look, he noticed the difference. The construction of the huts consisted of heavy mammoth bones and skulls with the tusks still fixed in place and a cover of hides and reindeer antlers. He never had seen such structures. Children started drumming on mammoth shoulder bones as soon as they saw the group nearing the camp. He inhaled an odor of roasted meat. Later on he discovered that they used mammoth bones instead of wood for the fire.

People came closer and released the belts of the stretcher. Someone got him on his feet and kindly patted him on the back indicating to follow him. With unsteady steps he went with the man to one of the huts, where men and women signaled him to sit down. They also spoke that curious language. As they noticed that he did not understand them, they used gestures to make clear that he was a welcome guest. The eldest of the women rose from her place and showed him a figurine of the spirit of a mother. It was the second time that one of the other ones did so. Moreover, this figurine was a very special one. It was as if the light of the lamp behind was shining through it with a reddish glow. He for his part pulled out the flint figurine of the spirit of his mother from his pouch and placed this in her hand. They all laughed with delight and nodded, as a sign of recognition. They offered him drinks and food and new clothing of fox fur.

He needed many days to understand that he was not a prisoner. A young woman clearly showed that she liked him, sewing beads of bird's bones onto his clothes and preparing his food. After he regained his strength, they took him hunting mammoth and reindeer. No-one seemed to consider him as a stranger. Thanks to the girl he began to understand their language and after some time he could speak it as if he had lived there all his life. Bit by bit he learnt that the other ones were no monsters or beasts, but humans just like him, venerating the spirits of the mothers and always carrying their image. In the end he realised that there was no difference between the other ones and the members of his own tribe. Their hospitality for example was in no way inferior to ours, and they immediately accepted him as one of the group.

Only after the death of his wife, before she could give birth to their first child, did he feel the need to return to his native region. At first his new family could not understand why. Of course, the other ones lived a harsh life, but there was enough game, including bison, musk ox, mammoth, rhinoceros, fox, bears and ptarmigan, to ensure the survival of the group. Imagine: there lived so many mammoths in that region that the other ones were able to hunt them, whereas my family had never even seen a single living one! When he tried to explain that he missed us, they were very surprised. In their opinion we were the other ones, people to be afraid of. Why should he, having adapted so well to them, return to his previous tribe? Reluctantly they helped him find his way back to us."

His audience had been listening in growing amazement. Prater nodded: "Well, I think that you have something to consider. People tended to talk about the other ones without knowing them. I have learnt that there are also humans living beyond the limits of our tribe's territory. They may speak differently or have other customs, but they are just like us: kind, loving and hospitable, and, what's more, they also venerate the spirits of the mothers."
"Prater, could you tell us how the story ended?"
"Sadly enough he could not convince us to put aside our prejudices about the other ones. Some even accused him of having become one of them. To think that a tribesman could stick up for those terrible beings, that was about the worst we could imagine! We could no longer trust him. At the onset of spring he left us and we have never seen him again. Nobody is willing to talk about it, but I hope and believe that he feels happy again with the other ones."

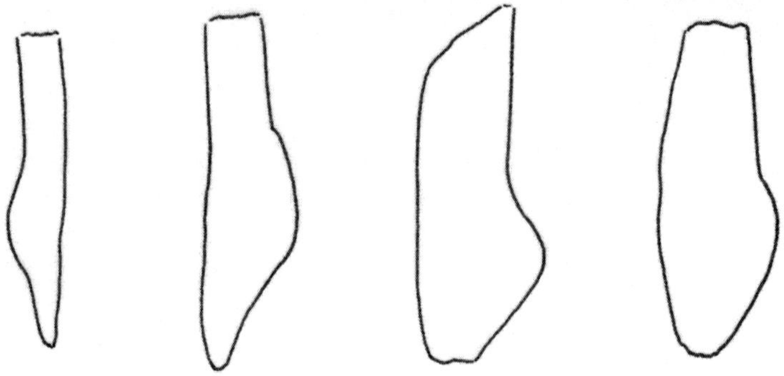

FIGURINES OF STYLISED WOMEN OF GÖNNERSDORF TYPE
(SPIRITS OF THE MOTHERS)

FROM LEFT TO RIGHT
IVORY FIGURINES FROM GÖNNERSDORF
(NEUWIED; AFTER BOSINSKI, 1982),
HOHLENSTEIN-LONETAL
(ULM; AFTER HAHN A.O., 1985),
WYLCZYCE
(KRAKOVIA; AFTER FIEDORCZUK A.O., 2007),
AND AMBER FIGURINE FROM DOBRANICHEVKA
(130 KM SOUTHEAST OF KIEV; AFTER DELPORTE, 1993;
AREA OF EASTERN TRIBES).

DISTANCE BETWEEN GÖNNERSDORF AND HOHLENSTEIN IS 300 KM, BETWEEN WYLCZYCE AND GÖNNERSDORF 900 KM, BETWEEN WYLCZYCE AND HOHLENSTEIN 900 KM, AND BETWEEN WYLCZYCE AND DOBRANICHEVKA 900 KM.

Spirits of the Mothers

It is always a pleasure to look at the mirror image of weeping willows in the water of the Vézère, by the bridge of Le Bugue. We automatically wonder if our ancestors 15,000 years ago enjoyed this view as much as we do, even if there were no weeping willows at the time and fewer trees and bushes. The present-day village square could have been a campsite, protected against the cold northern winds by the surrounding hills. In autumn people may have enjoyed fermented berry juice on the waterfront and, similar to us, watched the sun setting behind the hills and wisps of fog forming above the water.

Sometimes we watch a man wade through the water with a fishing rod. We daresay that similar scenes could be observed 15,000 years ago. Those fishermen did not possess such fine boots and casting tools but used harpoons made from reindeer antlers. In the shallow water fish could be easily spotted, especially large salmons.

After several days of heavy rain however, the water became too deep and the current too strong to keep a foothold, whilst the river transported so much mud that they could no longer see the bottom. They could neither fish in winter when ice covered the river, nor in summer when the uphill snowmelt resulted in higher water levels. This is confirmed by the results of Oliver Le Gall's investigations. Most of the fish was caught at the beginning of spring and at the end of fall.

Reindeer, horse and occasionally bison grazed on the far side of the river, whilst bushes and rock masses offered an ideal shelter to aurochs, goat, bear and ptarmigan. Just as nowadays, ducks swam in the water. This is suggested by bones and engravings of animals, which have been unearthed at Limeuil, only five kilometers from Le Bugue, near the place where the Vézère joins the Dordogne. The presence of harpoons proves that the campsite at Limeuil was not just frequented by hunters but also by fishermen. Only 16,000 years ago, at the onset of the Late Magdalenian, did people start to use these harpoons.

As we have seen in a former chapter, this coincided with the beginning of mass migration from Southern France to Central Europe, what resulted in a rapid expansion of the Magdalenian civilisation. The Late Magdalenian period, that lasted some fifteen hundred years, was not only marked by the introduction of harpoons in West and Central Europe, but also by a new symbol: figurines and engravings of stylised women without a head. They must have given a very special significance to these images, how would we otherwise explain their wide distribution?

Some twenty kilometers from Le Bugue, two Late Magdalenian sites, Lalinde and Gare-de-Couze, are known for their stylised human female silhouettes engraved in profile in pieces of chalk. Some of these can be admired in the prehistory museum at Les Eyzies. These depictions, and similar ones from Gönnersdorf in Germany, are as like as two peas in a pod, as if they had been made by one and the same artist. With good reason have some scholars defined these images therefore as 'stylised women of the Lalinde-Gönnersdorf type'.

Apart from engravings, figurines also occur, made from ivory, bone, reindeer antlers, amber, jet, shale, limestone and flint.

Time and again we are struck by the enormous geographical spread and the large number of sites, where these have been found. Each year new discoveries are made, as for example in the Margot Cave near Saulges in Western France. Today the images are known from practically the entire area of distribution of the Late Magdalenian: Spain, France, Switzerland, Germany, Poland, and Czechia.

Even when the Magdalenian civilisation was fading away and after it had disappeared, some groups continued to make these depictions, for example at Gouy and Orival, two latest Magdalenian or Azilian sites along the lower reaches of the Seine, and even much later in Niederbieber, a campsite of the Federmesser people in Rhenania. The Creswell hunters may have stuck to this tradition too, as suggested by images at Mégarnie in Belgium and the English Creswell Crags, however these are open to interpretation.

More than four hundred shale engravings of stylised women have been found in Gönnersdorf, all in profile, invariably without head or feet, with pronounced buttocks. The legs and torso are usually reduced to just one or two simple lines, whereas breasts are uncommon and arms even less so. Dale Guthrie compared their profile with one of those magnificent bronze bodies created by Rodin, without head or arms, in a seductive pose; the lower back intentionally curved, pronouncing her buttocks and the torso pushing forward.

Coupled depictions are common, standing face to face or belly to buttocks, as if they are dancing. Some lined up images may even be interpreted as chorus dancers. However, why have the artists chosen to depict a choral dance of headless and feetless women, usually even armless? What was the hidden message behind this? Perhaps they never intended to depict living women, but instead their spirits. They had no idea what a spirit looked like. We discussed this before. In their view a spirit was invisible, but they used their imagination and left out as many details as possible. Feet or hands were superfluous, just as eyes, mouth or nose. They even left off the head, possibly influenced by abstract figurines from Ukraine, which the massacred family of Maszycka may have observed as well. In fact, they probably would have preferred to omit every last detail, at the cost of losing every meaning. So they restricted themselves to a few lines, creating an extremely stylised figurine that everybody immediately recognised as the spirit of a woman; or the spirit of a mother, a much better name. The spirit of a mother protecting her children, her family. The special position given to the spirits of the mothers like guardian angles in their every day life, must have been conceived at the beginning of the Late Magdalenian.

Of course, this concept did not appear out of the blue. Aurignacian* hunters carved the first female statuette from a mammoth tusk some 35,000 – 40,000 years ago at Hohle Fels in the Suabian Alb, and ten thousand years later people continued manufacturing numerous female figurines. Engravings from this Gravettian* period, such as the images in the caverns of Cussac and Pech Merle, closely resemble later examples from La Vache, Aveyron Valley and Enval. The meaning of these images may have varied in time and from one region to the other, and the cult of those female spirits apparently weakened during the coldest period of the Ice Age; but, for some reason, it experienced a remarkable revival in the Late Magdalenian. In less than no time they embraced the spirits of the mothers almost everywhere. Today these depictions have been discovered at dozen's of sites in Europe.

These gave people encouragement in turbulent times. They faced famine, the disappearance of mammoth and rhinoceros from Southern France, and the forced departure of their relatives. Those hard times may have created the need to call on the protection of the spirits of the mothers. Apart from stylised female images, small figurines were made out of stone, bone, reindeer antlers or ivory, especially in Central Europe. These usually measured just a few centimeters, so that they could easily be taken along by our nomadic ancestors. Perhaps we may compare them with present-day mascots or images of Saint Christopher, which are frequently observed in cars in Southern Europe. They could have had a similar function, a figurine as an aid to experience and literally feel the presence of your guardian angle, just by touching it. Why not? Figurines from Petersfels and Monruz even had small holes so that they could be carried as charms on a necklace or bracelet.

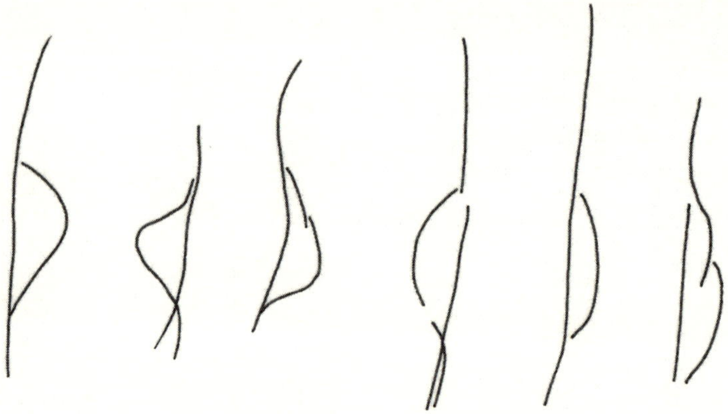

Engravings of stylised women of Lalinde-Gönnersdorf type
(spirits of the mothers)

From left to right
specimens from Lalinde
(Dordogne: after Duhard, 1993),
Gouy
(Rouen; after Martin, 2007),
Orival
(Rouen; after Martin, 2001),
Gönnersdorf
(Neuwied; after Bosinski a.o., 2001),
Teufelsbrücke
(Saalfeld; after Bosinski a.o., 2001)
and Petersfels
(Brudertal; after Bosinski, 1982).

Distance between Lalinde and Gouy is 600km, between Gouy and Orival 10 km, between Orival and Gönnersdorf 550 km, between Gönnersdorf and Teufelsbrücke 300 km, between Teufelsbrücke and Petersfels 450 km, and between Petersfels and Lalinde 800 km.

15,000 years ago

Journey to Deep River

Half asleep Leya snuggled up to Krasser, longing for the warmth of his body. His response came immediately. "I am expecting a child," she knew, "I am not sick, just pregnant. I don't have to worry." Holding on to these thoughts she stayed in bed, enjoying the moment. She rose rather late, and then visited Great Narrator who was still deep in sleep. "Let her rest," suggested her mother. "It is too cold for her to go outside."
Walking through the camp she listened to the comments on Prater's story the night before.
"Imagine," said someone, "that something like this would have happened here. Would we behave like Prater's family and mistrust the other ones? Would we suspect a relative of plotting with them against us?"
"Of course not," remarked a second voice. "That is impossible here. We live too far from them. You don't have to fear, not as long as the other ones don't come here."
"They have never seen the other ones. How do they know it's them that scare off the herds?"
"Oh yes, they do! Prater told about it. That man who had returned to his tribe told them they do."

"No way! That man just told the opposite! According to him the other ones do not steel or murder. They are normal people similar to us, and very kind and hospitable. They even saved his life!"
"You see? He was completely under their influence. He started to think like them, justifying their acts. There lies the risk! Be grateful that the other ones will never come here. They would turn you into one of them before you knew it."
Leya smiled sadly. How could someone mistrust other human beings so easily? The journey had taught the friends to be open to everyone. In some exceptional situations people had doubted a moment before inviting them, but only because they felt ashamed when they had no food to offer them as hospitality demanded. Hospitality and sharing food formed the basis of their society, as everybody knew. Unfortunately, these rules could no longer exist if hatred and loathing for the other ones got the upper hand. With their own eyes they had seen how apparently normal and kind people could suddenly turn into bloodthirsty murderers.

It started snowing again during the day as the wind picked up speed. Everyone was glad to listen to Leya that night. She had promised to continue her travel story. Great Narrator was absent. She had been sleeping most of the day. The scarce moments she opened her eyes were spent staring at the walls of the hut. She refused food and even drinks. As far as they could tell she suffered no pain, but she hardly reacted at their questions, as if her hearing had suddenly diminished. Her hands and feet were as cold as stone, in spite of the skins with warm water which Leya had lovingly placed beside her or the cover of soft reindeer calf hides. "Let us hope that spring will come as soon as possible," said her mother. "Only the sun can return the warmth to her body. The sun is good for her."

"Can someone tell me where we left off?" It was Leya who posed the question.

"Somewhere in the South," they called out unanimously. "You had hunted reindeer in Brother's Valley," added someone. "Please, tell us that story again. They tell it time and again around the fires in Brother's Valley. Those were your words. Last night I dreamt that I was with that party."
"If you were dreaming you were there, you don't need to hear it once more," remarked his neighbour angrily. "You already know the details. We on our part like to hear their further adventures. Leya, you had left Brother's Valley with the intention to continue to the South. Tell us about it!"
Everyone clapped appreciatively and roared in agreement with the last speaker.

"I suggest that the majority wins. I entirely agree with you, there is still so much to tell. When we departed from here we did not imagine that the South would be so far away, but everywhere people were willing to help us. Thanks to Ursa's brother we got in touch with the group in Brother's Valley. We passed the winter with them. They invited us to stay, but we were anxious to continue our journey. At the start of spring we said good-bye to Ursa's family. They had gathered with several other families to return to Blue Valley and hunt there that summer. Alternating between tears and bursts of laughter we hugged in realisation that we might never see each other again. They then turned around and disappeared in the direction of Wide River.
Next we had to say farewell to the sister of Durfal's grandmother and her man. They would go westward to collect the precious yellow brown flint. We should not forget, they insisted, to pass on their very best wishes to you. They had such good memories of our family. We really miss them to this very day; their hospitality, the way they mothered us as if we were their children and the good times we had together. At night he would tell us about the Northern Ice Lake and the period he stayed here with us. This farewell was tearful as well.
Then it was our turn to leave. Three families accompanied us because their hunting grounds were somewhere in the

South. For the last time we walked with them to the huge waterfall in Big River, higher and wider than any we ever saw, listened once more to the thundering noise of the gushing water and admired the spume frothing around. In the past winter we visited that spot several times, wondering why the water fell down with such force. We would have liked to stand on top of those rocks in the center of the fall, but no-one was capable of reaching these. The current was overpowering and the water too cold. Krasser chose a pebble, carved a big salmon, kissed it and with a wide arc threw it into the water ensuring that the salmon's spirit would accompany us for the duration of our journey."

"For two days we followed Big River westward until reaching an even larger river coming from the South. We were very surprised. Why was that one not named Big River? But our companions told that it had no name. 'If we walk upstream,' they said, 'we will find good-quality flint for making tools and weapons.' They were absolutely right. The next day we discovered nice flint nodules, as big as a fist, which would produce fine blades and long, thin flakes. We selected the best pieces, which we fashioned on the spot into tool stones* in order to reduce their weight. The first moon of spring had almost passed by the time we reached a lake. Ursa immediately set her mind to fishing, but our friends suggested walking a little farther. 'One more day,' they promised. 'Then you will see another lake, much larger than this one. We call it Long Lake*. There we will hunt and fish.' We wondered: 'Long Lake, is that Southern Water with those beautiful snails?' They laughed heartily. 'Oh no, you will need at least two more summers before reaching Southern Water. It is so far from here that we have never been there. It seems to be much larger than the Long Lake. Wait and see!'
They had not exaggerated. Long Lake was indeed enormous. According to our companions it would take days to walk around it. An immense steppe extended on the other side, where the sun rose in the morning, but they discour-

aged us to go hunting. You would need many people to hunt on that open space and our group was too small for that. On our side the valley narrowed between the lake and the steep western hills, a perfect place to ambush horses or reindeer. We discovered droppings of marmot and goat. At some distance a herd of deer hid between willow and birch bushes. Swans were brooding at the waterside and ptarmigans on the hills, so we could collect as many eggs as we wished. They took us to a favourable spot for the camp, near a narrow strip of water, separated from the lake by a long sandbank. The dogs that followed us had spotted a couple of hares and tried to catch them, but being familiar with the area, their prey managed to escape. Ursa was eager to fish for grayling and burbot. We could not have fared better.

From the traces of earlier campfires, surrounded by flint waste that had been left after tool making, it was obvious that our comrades come there often. The abundance of bone fragments scattered all over the site indicated that this was an ideal hunting ground. We felt glad to have accompanied them. There was enough game for the rest of the spring and we would be able to build up supplies for the rest of our journey. Apart from that, the nights were very cold and the surroundings were practically treeless, so that we had to handle our tent poles and assegais carefully. Finding enough branches for fire was problematic. The immediate neighbourhood had already been stripped bare during previous stays each spring and autumn. Only much farther, on the hills, could dry branches be found."

"Initially the days were sunny and dry, but the weather turned at the end of spring. The first clouds appeared announcing an overcast day and then it started to rain day and night. The other side of the lake could no longer be seen. Everything, our clothing, all hides got soaked. Fortunately, we managed to keep the meat supplies dry, which would otherwise have rotten. We had rarely seen such bad weather before. Each day new streams sprung up on the

hills behind our camp. To add to our misfortune, the lake's waters rose steadily until its edge reached our camp, forcing us to take down the tents in a hurry and flee for safety. We had hoped for a very different farewell!
For days after the drizzling continued at short intervals. In that gloomy environment we trudged wet through to the South, along the rows of hills, advancing with difficulty. Water and mud repeatedly barred our way, forcing us to change our route. Sometimes we sunk in the mire until our knees. The wet provisions on the stretchers we dragged along seemed to weigh twice as normal. We could not shelter in caves or under overhanging rocks. We should have climbed the hills, but under those conditions it was highly questionable if we could even reach these.
There were no dry branches to lay a fire at night. Numb with cold we huddled together below wet hides, chewing a piece of dried meat. More than once we asked ourselves why we had wished to go to the South. But then it occurred to us that you might have to endure even more rain than us. That was a possibility. Moreover, we realised that it had been our own choice to start this journey. 'Never look back,' had Great Narrator told us, 'when you pursue your aim. Think hard before you make any decision, but never look back once you have made up your mind.' This gave us the encouragement to continue walking."

"Not until six days did the sky suddenly clear up. The landscape became visible again and our mood improved by leaps and bounds. That afternoon we reached another lake, that our friends called Large Lake*. On the other side we saw mountains that even at the end of spring were covered with white snow and ice. According to our companions no plants could ever grow there. Even goats avoid that place. We decided to rest a few days so that our clothing could dry.
We finally got time to make new footwear, during the past days all our moccasins had been worn to shreds by rocks and mire.

After that we followed the lake's border to where it ran into a vast river, wider and more torrential than our Big River and also much deeper and with very few crossings. That is why they had named it Deep River. Only here and there you can traverse the river by jumping from one boulder to the next one. Our guides insisted that it was worthwhile to do so. The hills on the other side were strewn with large rocks and thus formed an ideal hunting ground. Moreover, they knew several hideaways which we might use as a bivouac, and reindeer in that region appeared to be larger than elsewhere.
Thus we looked for a suitable crossing-place. We found one in a bend of the river, where the heavy rainfall had produced a landslide of rocks and boulders. The deepest part of the stream was temporarily dammed up. It is true that the swirling and foaming water was making its way between the boulders, but for the time being we could make it to the other side. Durfal and a few young men tested the safety of the route. Some boulders lurched for a moment and then fell back in place. They reached the other side without real difficulty. Next went the children and two pregnant women, and subsequently the stretchers with our provisions. However, the last stretcher went wrong because the stones had gotten wet and slippery."
Leya's expression hardened. She found it hard to continue.

"One of the men skidded, lost his balance and dropped the stretcher. The other carrier was suddenly confronted with the full weight. Desperately he tried to save the provisions, but to no avail. Together with the stretcher he slipped from the boulder and fell in Deep River with a blood-curdling scream. Completely disoriented he managed to come up for air once or twice. Then his head hit a rock and he finally disappeared in the foaming waves. No-one got a chance to react, it all happened in an instant.
On both banks of the river people ran downstream in the futile hope of rescuing him. The rest gathered round a woman who was crying on the ground. She had just lost

her companion. Four days later we stopped the search. Only a tent pole and two assegais had been recovered. At one day's walk part of the meat provisions had washed ashore, but foxes and ravens had seized most of it. We found no trace of the man and imagined that the spirit of his mother would have taken him directly to the womb of the earth. To make sure, Krasser carved the spirit in a stone. The image was passed from hand to hand, and everyone clasped it to his chest. The heavily pregnant widow was the last one to receive the figure. Loudly crying she kissed the fading image time and again and then dropped it into the water. Silent and sad we went looking for a bivouac."

"Slightly further to the east we discovered a fine campsite on the southern shore of Large Lake. The relatively gentle hill sides were flanked to the south by an almost vertical cliff with deep fissures and eagle eyries. Large boulders on the foothills formed hide-outs in case of bad weather, so that we did not have to return to the camp each day. Until the end of summer we hunted and fished there with varying success. We killed ptarmigans and reindeer, and occasionally also a horse or a goat. Ursa and I also taught the children how to snare marmot and hare, or to harpoon burbot and grayling.

At the start of autumn's first moon we returned to Deep River. The stream had removed the boulders, which we had used two months earlier to cross the river, but a long walk farther down, where the river turns to the south, we discovered another crossing place. This time we reached the other side without problems. Here we were able to collect small pieces of flint to repair our weapons and tools or make new ones."

"It was time to say farewell to our friends. They would return to Long Lake and than on to their winter camp, behind the Waterfall in Big River. And so, for the first time in two summers, we were on our own again. We spent the rest of the day looking speechless at Deep River foaming against steep rocks. 'Follow the river,' had been their advice, 'even if it turns to the north. Behind the mountains it will flow to the Southern Water.' The snow on the mountains towering above us inspired us with awe. The first moon of autumn was only halfway through and snow already covered the summits. High above us a solitary eagle glided in silence looking for food.

We could only guess what lay ahead of us. According to our friends there was only a slight chance to come across people, because in winter this region would be quite inhospitable. We decided to continue as long as weather permitted, because our provisions sufficed until the end of the moon. For two days we followed Deep River to the south. The third day it changed its direction streaming straight across a narrow valley to the west. At the end of the day we discovered some caves. We chose the large one, from where we could oversee the area. There was enough space inside for all the huts and tents our camp has here at Big River. Ashes of various fires proved that the last visitors had stayed there many summers ago. We recognised bone splinters of reindeer, red deer, goat, duck and burbot. The entrance of the cave was warmed by the sun until late in the afternoon. The narrow valley of Deep River turned into a much wider one, where reindeer and deer used the countless sandbanks and crossings as drinking places. Ducks, swans and many other birds were swimming in the water. Scattered bushes of willow and birch would serve to approach animals without being noticed, making this an ideal hunting ground.

Under normal circumstances we would never have dared to stay in the cave. Everybody knows that you have to respect the place of other people, but it seemed highly unlikely that anyone would be returning to claim their rights. Since dark clouds in the sky did not bode well, we decided to stay there and pass the night. There was not a breath of wind, but in the distance we heard the rumbling of an approaching thunderstorm. We collected a large amount of dry branches at the bottom of the valley, on the banks of

Deep River, and subsequently dragged these along the brush-covered slope up to the cave. Here we settled for a place at the back.

Before sunset the thunderstorm burst out in great violence, with hail and fierce gusts of wind. Lightning and thunder followed each other in quick succession. Even far from the cave's entrance we did not feel save. Afraid I clung to Krasser, and also Durfal and Ursa held to each other. We listened how wild streams of water ran down the slope, washing away branches and stones. The noise was so terrifying that we feared that the whole rock along with the entire cave might disappear into the depth. In panic I gripped the pouch with the figurines of the spirits of the mothers, hoping they would be able to protect us. They alone could beg the Maker to finish this violence. Our confidence was not betrayed. Suddenly the rain stopped and the wind died down. Only far away did the lightning and rumbling continue a little while. The next day the sun shone in a sheer blue sky and for a moment we thought that the storm had been a bad dream. Large amounts of branches washed ashore proved however that Deep River had indeed burst its banks the night before."

"There was enough kindling for the rest of autumn and part of winter. It seemed as if the spirits wished us to overwinter there. This was the deciding thought; it was wise to stay. First of all we took all the branches to the entrance of the cave, where they could dry. It took several days, having to walk up and down the slope again and again. We collected berries and herbs in the valley, and went hunting, fowling and fishing. At the first snow of winter we had amassed enough meat, fish, berries and honey to stick it out for many moons, thanks to the spirits. A large pile of bones and antlers was waiting to be made into needles, piercers, harpoons and tips for our assegais. We had saved the teeth of deer and other animals for making beads. Claws of eagles and vultures and beautiful feathers served to embellish our clothing.

Contrary to the pessimistic predictions of our friends, goats and ptarmigans stayed in the area throughout winter. One day Durfal and Krasser were lucky enough to catch an elk by surprise. Unfortunately, they could not transport so much meat at once to the cave. Of course, they hid the rest below snow, branches and stones, but when they returned it had already been devoured by a wolf pack."

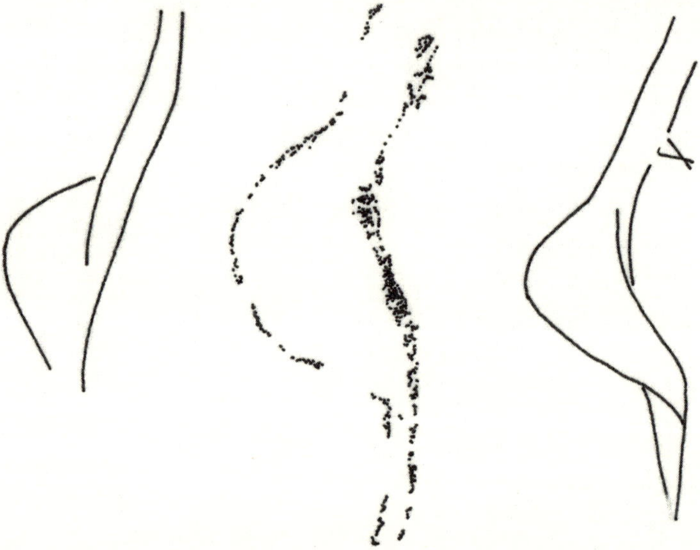

Stylised women of Lalinde-Gönnersdorf type
(spirits of the mothers)

Left: engraving from Gönnersdorf
(Neuwied; after Bosinski & Fischer, 1974).
Center: picture in red ochre from Planchard
(Vallon-Pont-d'Arc; after Bosinski a.o., 2001).
Right: engraving from Courbet
(Bruniquel; after Bosinski a.o., 2001).

Distance between Gönnersdorf and Courbet is 1,100 km, between Gönnersdorf and Planchard 900 km, and between Planchard and Courbet 250 km.

What do we know about our Ancestors?

Many automatically associate the term 'prehistory' with the caves of Lascaux in the French Dordogne or Altamira in Northern Spain, but many more places are open to the public as well. Pay a visit, for example, to the caves of Niaux, La Vache, Bédeilhac and Mas d'Azil in the upper valleys of the Ariège and the Garonne in the French Pyrenees. For those who don't dispose of much time or suffer claustrophobia, the Parc de Préhistoire at Tarrascon-sur-Ariège would be an excellent alternative, although they would miss a unique experience. For instance, the 'Salon Noir' of Niaux is just as imposing as a medieval cathedral. Its enormous dimensions overwhelmed us, so it took some time before we discovered the drawings which are indeed very special, really worth a detour. For good reason reservation is recommended well before your visit. This does not alter the fact that the replicas in the prehistoric park are worthwhile as well, giving us a chance to assimilate our impressions and letting sink in the details.

Neither did we regret our visit to the cave of La Vache, where we got an impression of the daily life of the same people and artists who created the pictures of Niaux.

What strikes us most is the incredible chaos in the cave, the large amounts of waste, here and there more than half a meter thick; residues and ashes of fireplaces, broken tools, broken needles and bone splinters. No wonder that archeologists discover a beautiful object every so often. In between so much rubbish we would easily lose our belongings too! Well, fortunately for us, they sometimes dropped something without tidying up. They did not know dustpan and brush. Brooms had not yet been invented.
This waste not only occurs in the cave of La Vache but at all sites where prehistoric people have stayed. They only brushed something aside if it disturbed them. The distribution of bone fragments suggests that they dropped these on the spot, maybe spitting them on the floor, just as it suited them. Nobody was surprised; they did not know any better. Imagine what their clothing looked like having sat on a carpet of bones and leftovers of meat and grease. The smell must have been terrible, but our ancestors did not mind. Having lived in such an environment from birth, the stench would seem normal and your body gets immune against certain moulds and bacteria.
Moreover, they were followed by an army of foxes, wolves, small rodents and birds, removing all leftovers from the bones. Ravens and gulls, as well as eagles and vultures quickly learnt that humans used to leave behind enormous heaps of rubbish. For those animals the smoke of a fire became a signal that there might be something edible for them.
We should consider us fortunate that our ancestors have left so much waste. Thanks to that we have learnt many details about game and food, the construction and interior of campsites, and the making of tools. Imagine they were tidy, leaving spotless caves. How would we have known they had ever been there? Now we can leaf to our heart's content through an open book. Thanks to that waste we also gain an insight into the social contacts between groups, hunting seasons and game, or the places where they obtained raw material for the stone tools.

Our ancestors were quality-conscious, occasionally covering hundreds of kilometers to collect first-rate flint, but they were practical people as well. Low-quality stones from the environs sufficed for manufacturing more simple tools. They refused to carry heavy stones if this was not strictly necessary.

Their clothes may have been stained with grease and dirt, but they liked to dress up. They were always looking for the most beautiful snails, shells and fossils to fashion jewels, sewing these on their clothes or bearing them as necklaces or bracelets. They would readily make a detour to obtain such objects, or alternatively exchange these precious items with other people. They may have used shells and snails as gift, for example in recognition of rendered hospitality; why not? Imagine someone traveling a long distance in order to find a partner. He would most likely take along some small snails or fossils. They did not weigh much, were easy to carry and were highly appreciated.

Or the visitor may have drawn or made a figurine on the spot as a reward to his future bride or her parents. We do the same thing. You don't like to arrive empty-handed. This might explain the close resemblance of certain engravings discovered at distant sites throughout Europe, as if one and the same artist had made them.

In those harsh and difficult times everyone knew that you could always go to someone for help and hospitality, whether you were ill, lost, wounded, looking for a partner or simply breaking your journey. No-one could refuse a visitor.

This doesn't mean that everybody kept to the rules or that some were not violated. They had virtues and vices just like us. These people were not better or worse than we are. At most they simply displayed different habits, which perhaps astonish us.

It is often argued that they – in contrast to us, modern humans – respected their environment, felt united with the surrounding nature and did not disturb the ecological balance. Is this really true?

The prehistoric hunters of Veyrier in Switzerland or La Vache in France did not distinguish between young or adult animals. In Gönnersdorf and Solutré they killed carrying mares and newborn foals; would you take this as environment-conscious behaviour? Magdalenian hunters did not make a point of the age of the game. They just killed every individual within reach of their assegais. Their hunting parties were not for their own amusement; they killed in order to survive, because they were hungry. That is something we don't always appreciate.

The same story applies to fuel for their fires. Without fire they could not survive, cook, roast or grill their food. They needed fire to warm them or dry their clothing. Where did they collect enough fuel? Most scientists think that those people lived on dry, treeless steppes.

In Southwestern European valleys the problem may have been less pressing, because vegetation there was slightly more variegated and abundant, but trees and bushes were practically absent on the Central European steppes and restricted to a few, local wooded stretches on south-facing slopes along rivers. In most places there grew only dwarf willows and dwarf birches, with extremely thin twigs. You need quite a lot of these for a fire. Where could they collect sufficient fuel for a camp of five or six families, say forty to fifty persons, within a reasonable walking distance? This was only possible by pulling up all bushes, grass and herbs in the surroundings, and even so, they had to move on in the end because there was nothing left. Large groups were unable to stay long in one place. In that harsh, cold climate it took years before vegetation had recovered sufficiently to produce fuel again. They also needed trees and branches to make assegais, tent poles and huts. The appropriate trees and bushes must have been so scarce, that they had to make these last a long time. This explains why they also used bones as fuel. Bones contain fat and burn well. That way they would have solved part of the problem.

They probably did not need fire to keep wolves or lions at a distance. Already 30,000 years ago men could leave this to dogs, which would have defended a campsite as their own territory. No doubt, they still had to be domesticated. Rather think of a love-hate relationship between humans and dogs, the latter mainly living on leftovers and trying to catch part of the quarry.

Some books and films on prehistory spin out stories of periodic meetings of tribes, but it is unlikely that these occurred on a regular basis.
Groups lived much too far from each other. Moreover, their territories of tens of thousands of square kilometers were too vast for a fixed dwelling.
Secondly, they would have had to cross territories of other groups over hundreds of kilometers distance before reaching a hypothetical meeting place; a journey of weeks. They had to eat on the way and for the duration of that gathering. Where would they find sufficient game and fuel for fire? There was good reason for the extensive grounds they hunted on.
Thirdly, no-one could predict where or when large herds of horses or reindeer might appear. Gerd Albrecht and Andrea Hahn, for example, suggest that usually decades must have passed between the successive reindeer drives at Brudertal, in Southern Germany. Our prehistoric ancestors were for good reason nomads, who depended on the seasonal migration of herds, which congregated and disintegrated according to the presence or absence of suitable vegetation that for its part was controlled by unpredictable regional climatic variations.
Of course, families belonging to the same group of hunters may have overwintered together or went fishing and hunting together however it suited them. Robert Gessain has described into detail how the Inuit* of Ammassalik did so less than a century ago in Greenland.
It seems most likely that the same already happened during the Magdalenian period, as shown by the excavations of the Gönnersdorf winter camp, one of the best known examples.

We know that the residents of huts one, three and four hunted in summer somewhere in the north, because they brought along northern flint. The hunting grounds of the family living in hut two were located in the west, where they collected flint in South-Limburg. However, these arrangements must have been without obligations. No-one knew if or when the other families would come.
In contrast to the yearly used accommodations of Ammasalik, the winter camp in Gönnersdorf has apparently been used only once by the Magdalenian hunters. This fits the picture of just four or five families at a campsite, who each year completely depleted the area of its vulnerable vegetation and then had to find a new location.

Today certain animal species, such as saiga in Central Asia or caribou in the extreme north of North America, only congregate in large herds during seasonal migration in spring and fall. In summer and winter however these split up in smaller groups of up to forty animals at most. Something similar will have happened during the Ice Age.
Dale Guthrie described the relationship between available prey and the hunting techniques of African lions. Where prey abounds, as in the south and east of Africa, male lions dispose of a large harem or pride. Female lions do most of the hunting, whereas males - distinguished by large, dark manes - are mainly limiting themselves to defend the pride and their leadership against competitors. In the Kalahari, where prey is less common, especially in the dry season, male lions tend to have a small pride and are forced to help in the hunt as well. The males in that region tend to have smaller, less conspicuous manes than their cousins in the east.
The point is that Guthrie also studied prehistoric cave drawings and engravings of the European cave lion. Struck by the very short manes of the males, and extending the comparison between African lions, he presumed that the cave lion only hunted with one or two females, because for most of the year the availability of prey on the cold steppe was too small.

Why did we bring up this subject? Many scholars suggest that prehistoric hunting and harpoon fishing was reserved for men. Women had to stay at home, caring for children, fashioning clothing and footwear, or collecting herbs and branches for fire. At most they helped with a drive. Even the manufacture of tools and weapons was supposedly men's work.

Why? In large communities this may be a useful division of tasks. However, in the same way that a reindeer herd (their favourite game) split up in summer and winter, humans were likely to have separated in smaller groups as well. Similar to cave lions, men and women had to hunt together, unless the care for new-born babies forced the women to stay temporarily in the camp.

Men hunting alone had to be able to prepare their own meal. They had to ply needle and thread, repairing their clothing. Women for their part were frequently forced to hunt and fish to be self-supporting and to that purpose manufacture their own tools and weapons. Men could stay away for quite some time and get wounded or killed. No-one could be sure if they would return at all. Accidents could happen at any time.

Complete families could vanish from the face of the earth due to famine, illness or accidents. A blazing row with other groups over food or equipment could lead to every last man, woman and child being massacred, as happened in Polish Maszycka. It was not an idyllic society, although we would like to believe so. They did not know about police and judges nor did they handle law books; they depended on the judgment of elders or trusted in the law of the jungle. It certainly would have been difficult for us, modern Westerners, to live in that society.

In spite of the harsh, primitive life those people possessed the same social skills as we have. They realised quite well that their society depended on cooperation, hospitality and compassion; that robbing and murdering one another could only harm it.

Anyway, *Homo sapiens** are not the first human beings who developed social behaviour. On September 25th, 2006, the Spanish La Vanguardia published an interview with David Lordkipanidze, director of prehistoric excavations in Dmanisi, in Georgia. 'I have discovered a fossil,' he said, 'proving that early on mankind already knew about compassion.' Almost two million years ago a man died in the Caucasus. This predecessor of Modern Man has been named *Homo georgicus**. By around his fortieth year this man had lost all of his teeth, except for one canine. Being in a horrible plight due to this severe impairment, he would have starved of hunger at least two years before, if friends or family had not premasticated the meat or given him the softest parts. This is the oldest example of compassion and altruistic behaviour in the history of mankind.
Perhaps an even more moving story has been distilled from thirty skull fragments of a girl, belonging to *Homo heidelbergensis**, living more than half a million years ago near Atapuerca in Northern Spain. She was born with a serious skull deformity that likely affected her mental capacities and physical appearance, but '*early humans did not kill deformed offspring*' stated the British Telegraph in surprise on March 31st, 2009. On the contrary, '*season after season, under unimaginably harsh conditions, her family tended her with callused hands until she died,*' as Michael Cook puts it so aptly in the Taiwan News Online on April 11th, 2009. They managed to keep her alive for at least five and perhaps even twelve years.
These are not the only examples. Also Neanderthals* at Shanidar in Iraq and Chapelle-aux-Saints in France proved 50,000 years ago that they possessed the same human qualities. *Homo sapiens* are not the first and only humans who take care of their family and neighbours!

Our ancestors were, of course, as curious as we are and possessed our adventurous spirit. Conditions permitting they explored ant-like every brook, valley and thicket, studying every potential hide-out over and over again.

In spite of their primitive grease lamps they ventured into deep caverns, walking, climbing or crawling through the narrowest passages over hundreds of meters, leaving behind the most beautiful paintings, carvings, drawings and clay figures.
Social contact around the fire during long winter nights stimulated music, singing and dancing. Drums made from bones or pieces of wood were easily manufactured and they also made primitive flutes. Night was the perfect moment for talking about everyday things, hunting, meeting other groups, life and death, or religious contemplations. Gilles Tosello, inspired artist and prehistorian, has depicted such scenes in superb paintings. We would have been only too happy to listen to them!
Of course, the talent of storytelling was reserved to very few individuals, but gifted speakers will have captivated their audience, just as Homer enchanted the Greeks so many thousands of years later. Some of these narrators may have wandered from one camp to the next, filling long nights with stories, myths and legends, in exchange for food and accommodation. Imagine their audience seated around the fire, listening breathlessly.
The storyteller – in this book we presume that she has been a woman - will not have traveled on her own. She had friends who accompanied her, helped hunting and fishing or kept carnivores at a distance. It was a small group, three or four persons at most, otherwise they would not have been welcome when pleading hospitality. There was a limit to this because food was frequently scarce. The band will have tried to follow existing tracks, along which raw materials for stone tools were transported, or snails and shells for jewelry. A complete network of these tracks must have existed then.
You can expect that they were not afraid to travel large distances once they had set themselves a target. Medieval pilgrims were prepared to walk from all outskirts of Europe to Santiago de Compostela, in Spanish Galicia. Claudine Cohen refers to the book by Richard Lee and Irven DeVore,

in which, amongst others, the South African San are portrayed. San women are said to walk no less than two thousand four hundred kilometers (2,400 km) each year whilst collecting food, visiting neighbouring camps and periodical moves to new settlements. Therefore, it goes without saying that prehistoric people could walk at least five hundred kilometers a year.

Our friends' thoughts will not have lingered about the length of the journey. Young men and women were probably expected to abandon their family, at least temporarily, to find a partner and leave with them. This also strengthened the mutual bond between the various neighbouring groups. In the end, a journey like this was less complicated than we initially imagined. The only condition was finding a few friends ready to join you.

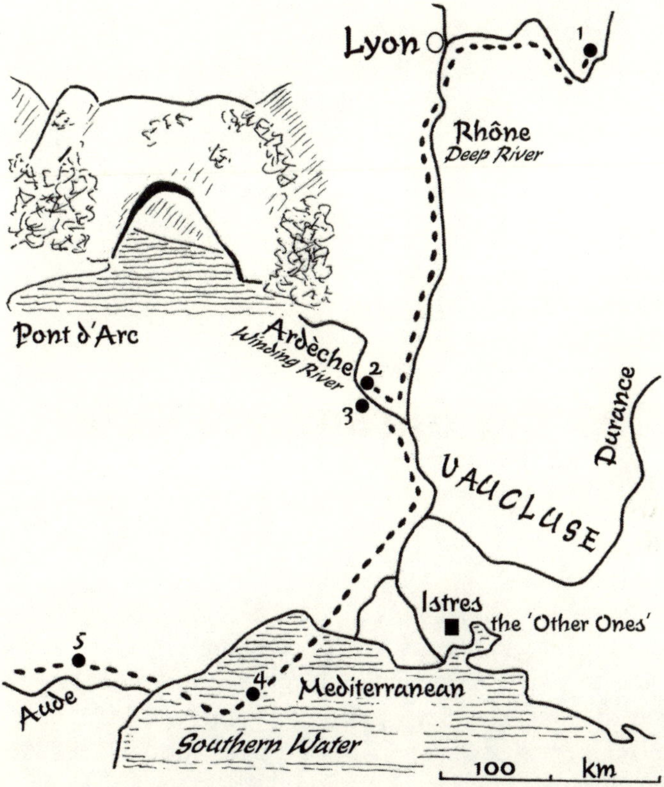

Leya's journey, third summer to fourth spring; from winter camp in cave by Deep River to encounter with Southerners and group of Wild River.

1 – Pierre-Châtel, Virignin (winter camp by Deep River).

2 – Planchard, Ardèche (spirits of the mothers) and Pont-d'Arc (natural bridge spanning Ardèche River, looking like a giant mammoth).

3 – Colombier, Ardèche (summer camp family of Winding River, engravings of mountain goats).

4 – Winter camp family of Winding River on then existing shore of Southern Water (today one hundred meters below sea level).

5 – Tournal, Bize (summer camp group of Turbulent River).

15,000 years ago

Journey to Southern Water

One of the huts in the settlement suddenly collapsed under the load of newly fallen snow. The ice-cold avalanche surprised the sleepers. Screaming they searched for the exit from under the snow and ripped hides. The incident also jolted everybody out of their sleep. As best they could, they removed the snow from the other tents and huts to prevent further calamities. Neighbours offered shelter, but sleep came to nothing. At daybreak, everyone was ready to help repair the damage. They were faced with quite a job, since everything was solidly frozen. Morale did not get better and the slightest thing gave reason for quarrel.
Leya did not get involved. Instead she paid a visit to Great Narrator who had lost her appetite. She even refused the aromatic herb tea, specially prepared by her daughter, and hardly responded to the chatting women. Only when Leya reminded her that she was expecting a child, did a faint smile illuminate her face. Most of the time, she was drowsing away, unaware of the tension in the camp.
Leya decided to continue the account of her journey, in spite of the worry about her grandmother's health. On days like this, people had more need for distraction. Therefore, at nightfall everybody gathered again in one of the huts.

"You know that Great Narrator is not feeling well. She neither eats nor drinks. My mother fears that she may abandon us shortly. She will stay with her tonight, since no-one knows when the spirits are ready to accompany our soul to the womb of the earth."
Everybody nodded in agreement.
"You will remember that we had passed the second winter in a large cave by Deep River. In spring we continued our way along the river, first to the south, then to the north, next again to the south and to the west than again to the south. It became wider and wider as many tributaries joined it. The valley got larger than our Big Valley, and the hills were higher than here. Further southward, the area looked greener. We discovered herbs and bushes, which we never observed here before. Trees were so abundant that we had no shortage of branches for the fire and to replace our tent poles. You should have seen it yourselves! We were convinced that the sky was bluer there and at least during the day it was not as cold as here in the North, so that we could make do with fewer clothes.
We ran into herds of horses, reindeer, roe deer and many, many goats; but there was no trace of a single mammoth or rhinoceros. Perhaps that region is too hot for them because of their warm hide. We humans can take off our clothes, but who has ever seen a mammoth removing its coat?"
This odd comparison made everyone laugh: a mammoth without fur; very funny! But they understood what she meant to say. Mammoth and rhinoceros for good reason migrated northward in summer, because days on the northern plains were not as warm as in the environs of the winter camp. Moreover, they could cool down in one of the many ponds and rivers in that region if the sun was beating down.

"The first moon of summer had already begun, when around a bend of the river we discovered the smoldering rest of a campfire. Drying hides stretched between poles indicated that people had to be nearby. We decided to wait, wondering whether they would be well-disposed towards us. At the end of the day two men appeared, accompanied by five women and several children. One of the women carried a baby on her back. Our presence caught them by surprise. After some hesitation one of the men stepped forward. Krasser did the same, putting down his assegais. Initially he had difficulty in understanding the man, who also had to get used to Krasser's way of speaking. For one moment we feared to have met the other ones. They afterwards told us that they had exactly the same thought. Krasser explained that we traveled to Southern Water in the hope to meet our distant relatives. Our ancestors had departed that region long ago. He opened his pouch and exhibited the figurine of the spirit of his mother. The man's face brightened. He motioned the rest of his family to come closer. They also idolised the spirits of the mothers, in the same way that we do. Then he invited us to share their food.

The family belonged to a group that in summer hunts in the many vales along Deep River. In autumn they move to Southern Water, where they overwinter. Their camp was situated by the mouth of a small tributary, Winding River*, flowing from the west into Deep River. They proposed to hunt and fish together, until it would be time to move to the South; and so we did. The many crossings proved to be excellent fishing places, but Winding River also appeared to be treacherous. After rainfall, it could burst its banks from one moment to the next. At some places the river winds between unimaginably high cliffs, too steep even for a goat. We followed them to a rock shelter that was their summer camp. We helped to collect dry branches for fire and felt happy not to have to pitch our tent.

At night they lit grease lamps and invited us to look at the back wall of our residence. The flickering light brought a complete herd of goats to life. The animals had been engraved in the wall, but in our imagination they emerged directly from the inner-earth. The animal in the center seemed to move his legs in the shadows passing across the wall. 'Here we honor the spirits of the goat,' was their explanation. 'Each summer we add another drawing as a sign of respect. The goat is the only animal to find its way unerringly in the maze of rocks and fissures around us.' We stood amazed; never before had we seen something as beautiful as that. 'Thanks to these figures we know exactly where we can keep in touch with the spirits of the goat. Even in the dark of the night they find this place.' We asked them about the spirits of the mothers. 'Do you carry their image, just like us?' 'No, the spirits of the mothers have got their own place in a deep cave that forms the entry to the womb of the earth.'

It was the first time that someone spoke about an entry to the womb of the earth. Fearing that we had not understood them well, we carefully asked our hosts for further explanation. How could a living human enter the womb of the earth? Only the souls of the dead could do so; that's the way we had always learnt it. For a moment they laughed about our ignorance, since they considered this as self-evident. They explained that the womb of the earth has many holes through which animals and humans had come out, after the Maker fertilised the earth, on the first day. Not only ghosts, they told us, but also living humans and animals enter and leave these holes without any problem. 'Take the bear, for instance. She returns each winter to the inner-earth to have her young. Take us, who visit those places so often. Are we perhaps invisible ghosts? Don't you hear us when we talk to you? Don't you see us eat and hunt?' Their arguments convinced us and we decided to follow them to the cave, where the spirits of the mothers resided."

"The next day we accompanied them to the hole giving entrance to the womb of the earth. On the outside, it looked like all the other caves we had visited before. Nevertheless, we felt hesitant when they signaled us to enter. After a few steps we came upon a wall with only a very small, dark opening. They took out lamps, put grease and bone marrow on it, and stuck a dry juniper twig into it. Someone lit the lamps and taking the first one disappeared into the hole. We followed his example, me being the last one. It was easier than I had feared. In no time I found myself in an enormous space on the other side of the wall, having to get used to the darkness. The rest were invisible, but now and again I observed the shine of their lamps on erratically shaped walls.

One of the women had waited for me. She took my hand, pulling me behind her. I carefully followed her. 'This is the womb of the earth,' she whispered. 'Don't fall in one of these holes!' With the lamp in my left hand and grabbing her hand with my right one, I shuffled behind her. After some steps she halted. I recognised Krasser's voice in cries of surprise and awe. 'What's happening?' My companion pinched my arm reassuringly. 'He has come face to face with the spirit of his mother,' was her answer. 'We have to wait our turn.' 'The spirit of his mother?' I stammered: 'That's impossible. How could she possibly know that we were coming?' 'This place is fixed up to communicate with the spirits of the mothers. Listen! Ursa too recognises the spirit of her mother! It is very easy to meet the spirits, if we just open our heart to them. Distances do not exist to them. They are with us always and everywhere, but especially in a place like this one.' Anxiously I waited in anticipation."

"After Durfal, it was my turn. My companion gently pushed me forward. I trembled with nerves, not knowing what was awaiting me. All of a sudden, I found myself in a small niche. The hand of the woman was gone. I looked around, frightened. And then, in the flickering shine of my lamp, I saw the spirit of Great Narrator's mother. I had never met my grandmother's mother, but I felt, I knew that it was her! Shadows, coming directly from the inner-earth, passed over the wall. In my excitement I tried to cry, unable however, to produce any sound. The lamp slipped from my trembling hand and there I stood in the pitch dark. Countless spirits surrounded me. It seemed to me as if this experience would

go on forever, but according to my companions it only lasted a moment.
One of them kindly touched my shoulder, giving me his lamp. 'Don't be afraid, you have nothing to worry; the spirits are here to protect us. They are delighted with our visit, about the fact that we remember them. They mean us no harm. Here, in the womb of the earth, they are happy together. Forever, they sleep together, caressing and loving one another. The Maker protects them; they no longer suffer pain or fear. Men love their women, and mothers keep their children happy. What's more, the spirits of the animals live peacefully together too.' He picked up my lamp, replacing the lost grease and twig before lighting it again with his flame. Respectfully, I stared once more at the image of the spirit of Great Narrator's mother, the same image in which my friends had recognised the spirit of their mother, or their mother's mother. In the end they slowly took us back to the entrance.
Deeply moved and happy we walked outside, where the sun was shining, just as every other day. We felt as if we had woken up from a dream. Only after listening to all the details of my friends' experiences, did I understand that it had not been a dream. We really had entered the womb of the earth! Afterwards, we have entered many other holes in the South that open onto the inner-earth. Each time, we were highly impressed when we visited those places. But that first time was something I will never forget!"

Her audience clung to one another while Leya was talking about the womb of the earth. They even closed their eyes, afraid of the shadows she was describing. In the end they heaved a sigh of relieve, after understanding that there was nothing to fear about.
After all, the spirits were happy forever! They would harm no-one and the Maker protected them. They felt especially relieved when Leya and her friends left the cave again. There was no time however to dwell upon this, because the story continued.

"We did not know that another surprise, at least as marvelous, was coming. While we descended the hill to Winding River along a different path, Durfal suddenly roared in excitement. He pointed at a giant rock spanning the river, and then Krasser, Ursa and I understood why. An enormous mammoth was standing in the river. His forelegs stepped on the bank on our side, whereas his hind legs were still on the other. The giant trunk seemed to be groping for food halfway the hill that we just had descended, although we could not observe any motion. He stood there, petrified, immobile, transformed into a giant rock. Maybe he had been standing there since the first day, since the moment he had left the womb of the earth. As if he was in charge of protecting the Valley of Winding River; we will never know. We told our companions what we were seeing, but they did not understand. They had never heard about mammoths, let alone that they had seen one. In vain Krasser made a drawing in the sand. In order not to disappoint us, they politely looked at the picture, at something they could not understand. In the end they reacted with a shrug, turned to the river and went to fish."

"In the autumn we moved with them to the South, where Winding River splits up in several small rivers and brooks with various crossing places. It was a lush region with many herbs, trees and bushes. We suggested our friends to use the occasion and go hunting. The vegetation had to attract abundant game. They refused however to do so. 'Absolutely not! These swamps are the hunting grounds of the other ones!' 'The other ones?' 'Yes, of course, the other ones! Don't tell us you don't know who the other ones are! They live in these swamps!' 'How do you know this if you never have been there?' 'Of course not,' was their irritated reaction. 'Be happy that we never did! They are beasts, bloodthirsty man-eaters! You are lost if they spot you. We don't go there. Those who did never returned. No-one escapes from their claws, we stay at a safe distance. From time to time we observe a plume of smoke above the woods, a sign that they are devouring their prey, in the same way lions do.' 'Lions never build a campfire. Only humans do so.' They began to get impatient and snapped: 'They are half human, half animal. We should stop talking about it. This will come to nothing!'

We did not meet the other ones and can't add anything about them. Maybe these were just rumors. Remember Prater's story. He had never seen the other ones. Nevertheless his fellow tribesmen refused to accept the words of the only eyewitness; even worse, they accused the man to have changed into one of them. We did not dare to touch the subject again. We should not upset our hosts, who were treating us so well. Anyhow, we avoided the swamps and reached Southern Water some days later."

"We could see Southern Water long before we reached the shore. It gave off a peculiar scent that we smelled from a distance. Beholding Southern Water with our own eyes had been one of the aims of our journey. That last day, on our final approach, we danced rather than walked towards it. We had made it! All our efforts had not been wasted. When we reached the shore, we dropped everything and ran to the water. You have never seen it, but believe me, it was so overwhelming. The water tasted like tears so that we spat it out immediately. They had warned us about this, but we did not care. Moreover, it was not as cold as any water we had ever seen before.

Everywhere, we discovered the most beautiful shells and snails exhibiting a wide variety of the most incredible forms, some smooth and gleaming, others with ribs and thorns, but all with wonderful colors. In no time we had collected more than we could carry. Our companions smiled while observing our efforts. 'You will learn. You can't take it all.' They were quite right, but this did not stop us. We collected everything hoping to select the best specimens at the end, but we were incapable of making any selection at all. Moreover, we missed the pink snails. 'They don't live in Southern Water,' explained our friends. 'They live underground, not far from the shore. Come on, we will show you where.' And there we finally collected these beautiful snails, a gift for the people we hoped to meet later on during our journey, and a proof to you that we really had seen Southern Water."

"I don't remember how often we walked the shore, looking in vain across the lake for the other side. Our hosts insisted that it did not exist. Day after day we listened to the sound of the waves rolling to the coast; usually quiet and calm, but sometimes wild with white spume. For the first time in our life, Ursa, Durfal and I saw the seals, which Krasser had described to us so many winters before. He showed us how to catch them by sliding and writhing like worms along the ground, with a hood on our head to resemble the beasts. It sent us into a fit of giggles, but it worked well. The animals looked at us curiously, while we approached them and had no chance of escaping into the water, where no human can follow them. The skin and fat of these animals are extremely useful, but we can't say so about the meat. The taste is disgusting. We prefer fish or a fine reindeer quarter!

We got acquainted with other families, all friendly and hospitable. They even invited us to stay, because several men and women wanted to court us. Imagine if we had responded to their advances; we would now be sitting on the shore by the Southern Water, where winter turns into spring after only five moons. I shall not deny that we felt flattered, but we would not have been happy there. The desire to know the South of our ancestors urged us to move on. Early in spring we said farewell to our friends. Following their advice we walked westward along Southern Water, but that is something I'll tell you tomorrow."

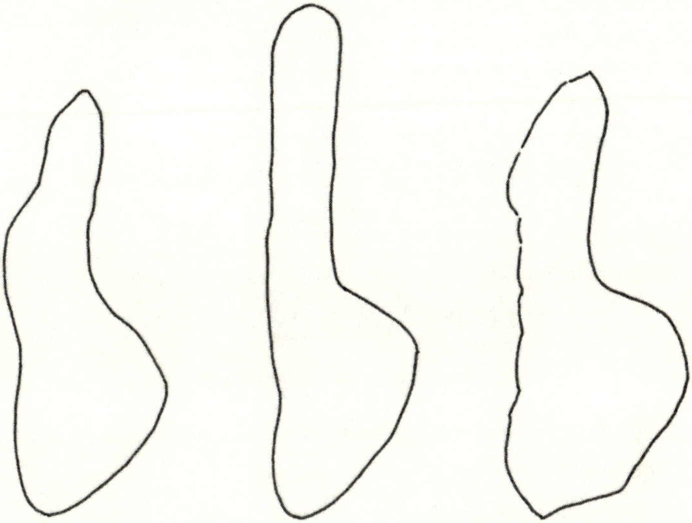

Figurines of stylised women of Gönnersdorf type
(spirits of the mothers)

Left: shale statuette from Gönnersdorf
(Neuwied; after Bosinski, 1982).
Center: pebble statuette from Oelknitz
(Jena; after Bosinski, 1982).
Right: flint statuette from Wylczyce
(Cracovia; after Fiedorczuk a.o., 2007).

Distance between Gönnersdorf and Oleknitz is 300 km,
between Oelknitz and Wylczyce 650 km.

Reconstruction of a Journey across Europe I

Do we have concrete indications that people could travel across Europe 15,000 years ago? That was the first question we posed ourselves, when we began to think about the story of our narrator. They may not have had the intention to do so, but prehistoric people left their virtual footprints in the form of all kinds of objects, so that we are able to reconstruct the routes they went.

We suggest that our friends' journey should start in Gönnersdorf near Neuwied, since this is one of the best documented Late Magdalenian campsites in Central Europe, conveniently situated by the Rhine. This settlement included at least a few large huts and several tents and was pitched at the eve of an extremely rapid temperature rise at the onset of the Late Ice Age. Residents of similar encampments may have experienced in person the dramatic consequences of this major climate change. We know that some families arrived in Gönnersdorf at the end of autumn, whereas other groups turned up late in winter.

Eighteen stone and ivory figurines of stylised women and

an enormous quantity of shale engravings make this a unique, unparalleled site in Western and Central Europe. More than four hundred stylised female silhouettes and almost three hundred animal images have been carved in stone. Gerhard Bosinski mentions dozens of horses and mammoths, and also rhinoceros, cow, mountain goat, saiga, roe deer, red deer, reindeer, elk, wolf, bear, lion, wolverine, frog, fish and all kinds of birds, among which goose, swan, crane, bustard, raven and ptarmigan.

We are especially puzzled by the engravings of seals and sea turtles. How could artists create such accurate depictions at five or six hundred kilometers distance from the sea? Don't forget that sea levels were one hundred meters lower than today, and one could walk across Doggerland (the then dried up North Sea area) from the Netherlands to England. Did the artists work from memory, or did these animals swim up the Rhine until the environs of Bonn? The river then discharged into the Channel River that for its part ran into the Atlantic somewhere north of present-day Cherbourg, far from the place where the drawings have been made.

Of course, seals can swim six hundred kilometers upstream, but would a sea turtle do so as well? Bosinski therefore suggests that people have observed and perhaps hunted these animals on the shores of the Atlantic coast. The depictions of a turtle don't allow us to identify a specific species, but perhaps they have tried to recall a chance encounter with a washed ashore leatherback, the only sea turtle capable of foraging in water as cold as that of the Barents Sea.

These pictures prove that Gönnersdorf people must have traveled far beyond the hundred to hundred and fifty kilometers long supply routes of flint and other raw materials for tool making. They would most likely have needed several years to bridge the distance from Gönnersdorf to the mouth of the Channel River and back. It clearly indicates that yearly meetings of these families at a fixed location were not very likely.

Our virtual band had two options on their way to the South. The first route follows the Rhine and the Aare upstream, passing Lake Neuchâtel and Lake Geneva, and then goes downstream along the Rhône until the Mediterranean. This is the shortest road and we imagine that it has been used from time to time.

Our friends decided however to follow the Rhine until the environs of Mannheim, where Late Magdalenian hunters have bivouacked at the time. From there they went along the Neckar and the Jagst to the Nördlinger Ries and the German Jura, also known as Suabian Alb. The engravings of stylised female silhouettes from Hohlenstein, one of the caves in the Nördlinger Ries, north of Ulm, are exact copies of similar ones from Gönnersdorf. Perhaps one of our friends was an artist, leaving his marks at both places, proving that people traveled from Gönnersdorf to Hohlenstein or around.

The Suabian Alb must have been an attractive hunting ground as suggested by the remnants of more than hundred Late Magdalenian campsites. In Gönnersdorf, the Nördlinger Ries and the German, Swiss and French Jura, from Hohle Fels in the Vale of Blaubeuren near Ulm up to the cave of Pierre-Châtel in the Rhône Valley, people have left fossil shells, which had been collected in the environs of Mainz. That is another indication that supports the here suggested route along the Nördlinger Ries and Suabian Alb. We imagine that one of the members of our group was a skilful carver of bone, ivory or jet figurines, because archeologists have excavated an ivory statuette of a stylised woman in the Lone Valley, north of Ulm. It closely resembles similar figurines from Gönnersdorf and Petersfels, in the extreme south of the Suabian Alb. At the latter location people have carved these figurines in jet. This fossil wood lends itself much better than ivory or reindeer antler for the reproduction of the female curves. It resulted in a slightly different form. Most interestingly, they have later discovered exact copies of the Petersfels jet figurines at Monruz, by Lake Neuchâtel in the Swiss Jura.

Fossil snails, collected near Steinheim in the northern part of the Suabian Alb, were abandoned or lost farther southward in the Lone Valley, the Vale of Blaubeuren, at Felsställe by the Danube, in the Brudertal, at Schweizersbild in the outskirts of Schaffhausen, and also at Monruz. They form another track that can be followed.

Stones, which have been used for tool making, provide worthwhile information too. Certain flint stones of Monruz, for example, had been collected in the northeast, near Olten by the Aare and Singen near the Brudertal, whereas other pieces came from the southwest, from Bellegarde and Seyssel by the Rhône. We should be grateful to our ancestors, for all the waste they left us. It helps us to reconstruct the routes they followed.

From Monruz they went to Veyrier, on the foothills of the Salève, by Lake Geneva, where part of the flint stems from the environs of Bellegarde and Seyssel. The route along the Rhône between Veyrier and Pierre-Châtel, near Virignin, was equally familiar to them. This is deduced from the presence of the same species of Mediterranean snails and shells at both locations. We may thus conclude that our friends traveled from the Brudertal in the southern Suabian Alb, along Aare, Lake Neuchâtel and Lake Geneva, to the Rhône Valley.

The route along the Rhône from Lake Geneva to Lyon has been used by several Magdalenian bands that hunted in the valleys across the French Alps and Jura. Our friends will have been surprised by the variety of trees at sheltered, sunny places, including oak, and elm, at the time unknown farther northwards.

They will have looked in vain for mammoth, rhinoceros and bison that had disappeared from Southeastern France some thousand years earlier.

The friendly relations between the groups of the Rhône basin and those in Central Europe are easily demonstrated by the many sites with Mediterranean shells and snails, which have been transported along the Rhône to the north, up to Gönnersdorf and Andernach.

The Rhône groups also kept in touch with people in Southwestern France, as indicated by the style of drawings and engravings in the caves along the Ardèche, maintaining however their own character as can be deduced from stone tools and art. We therefore must accept that these connections were less intensive. Frequent visits to and fro Central Europe and Southwestern France were apparently out of the question. These connections must have existed however, because shells and snails could not have been sent by post!

The same holds for a stylised female silhouette in the cave of Planchard by the Ardèche. It has clearly been copied from similar models occurring elsewhere throughout Europe. You can therefore safely assume that our virtual friends covered the Rhône Valley until the Mediterranean, on the way paying a visit to people camping by the Ardèche.

They could have admired the female depictions in the cave of Planchard, at only a few hundred meters from the famous Pont-d'Arc*. This must have been an unforgettable experience for them. It was perhaps the first time in their life that they observed such images in a cave. Thanks to investigations by Gerhard Bosinski and Petra Schiller we can imagine the details of that visit. They entered the cave through a wide porch. Ten meters farther they went through a small hole in the wall, just half a square meter. They lit the grease lamps, hoping that these would hold long enough, and crept inside. Behind it was a very large space and it remains at least doubtful whether the lamps could illuminate the entire room. The gallery to the right is a dead end, so they turned to the left. They carefully avoided some enormous holes in the floor, with a diameter of two to three meters.

Ten meters farther – that must appear much longer in the darkness – they reached some sort of niche, delimited on both sides by stalagmites. On the back wall, at eye level, they descried a red ochre drawing of a stylised female silhouette, absolutely similar to engravings they had seen before in Gönnersdorf. There was not enough room for two persons, so everyone quietly awaited his or her turn. And then after by-passing another hole in the floor, they discovered ten meters farther on, almost at the end of the cave, where they had to stoop and crawl due to the low ceiling, a second niche with a similar image. This time somebody had retouched the natural relief of the wall in order to accentuate the shape. A few scratches, red dots and a heart-shaped vulva are the only other signs in this cave.

A special cave for the spirits of the mothers, as if they wanted to be as near as possible to the spirits, which lived in the womb of the earth! Those depictions in the cave of Planchard were meant as an aid to experience their closeness. In this particular case they may not have been interested to get into touch with the spirit of an abstract, nameless mother, but with the specific spirit they recognised in that image. Perhaps the spirit of their own (dead) mother, or the spirit of their mother's mother; in short, the spirit of someone they had a very strong tie with in their lifetime, someone who would certainly help them.

Everyone had, of course, his or her own preferences. The residents of the overhanging rock shelter of Colombier, for instance, at one kilometer from Planchard, only carved mountain goats in the wall, whereas their neighbours depicted all sorts of animals.

Did our friends really recognise the outlines of a huge mammoth in the silhouette of the Pont-d'Arc, the natural arch spanning the Ardèche? Daniel André and Michel Chabaud believe they did. The forelegs of the beast are standing on the northern bank of the river and the hind legs on the southern one.

Although mammoths had disappeared already from Southern France towards the end of the Magdalenian period, they continued to live in the environs of Gönnersdorf, where their images have been engraved in shale. Our friends may thus well have imagined that the shape of Pont-d'Arc represented a giant mammoth; the largest one that ever had lived on the earth and petrified in a distant past. Naturally, they will have had difficulty in explaining this to people who never had seen a mammoth in their life!

It is a shame that we can't study the remnants of their Mediterranean winter camp, because these are nowadays covered by one hundred meters of water, due to the sea level rise since then. As you will remember, all this water had once been locked up on land in the form of kilometers thick ice caps, primarily in Scandinavia and North America. It will therefore take quite a long time before someone will be able to study the site. Nevertheless, we should be safe in presuming that these campsites existed. Our friends will have avoided the swamps of the Rhône Delta, the domain of Eastern Tribes as we have established before.
Our narrator and her friends must have been very impressed by their first view of the Mediterranean, an endless lake with no other side. What will have been their reaction to the salty taste? Imagine also their enthusiasm when they discovered the shells and snails on the beach. They will have started to make large collections until it became clear that they could not carry it all. The same happens to us when we walk along the beach, especially after a heavy swell.

The tiny pink snails of *Homalopoma sanguineum*, occurring in many archeological sites across Europe, have not been found on the beach, because the water of the French part of the Mediterranean was much too cold for them. Thus our friends must have collected fossil snails from older beach deposits! This made these an even more precious gift.
These snails put us back on the right track of our narrator. We can follow her steps along the Aude River to the cave of Tournal, near Bize in the Minervois, and from there to the vales along the upper course of the Ariège.
In spring the band will have walked westward, along the Mediterranean shore up to the mouth of the Aude, where

they may have had a chance encounter with rabbit hunters who normally lived in the coastal regions south of the Ebro. In autumn they went to the upper course of the Ariège, where people hunted for goat and ptarmigan until spring. Their winter camp was built in front of the cave of La Vache and from there they paid visits to the nearby Niaux Cavern with those superb drawings of bison, horse and mountain goat.

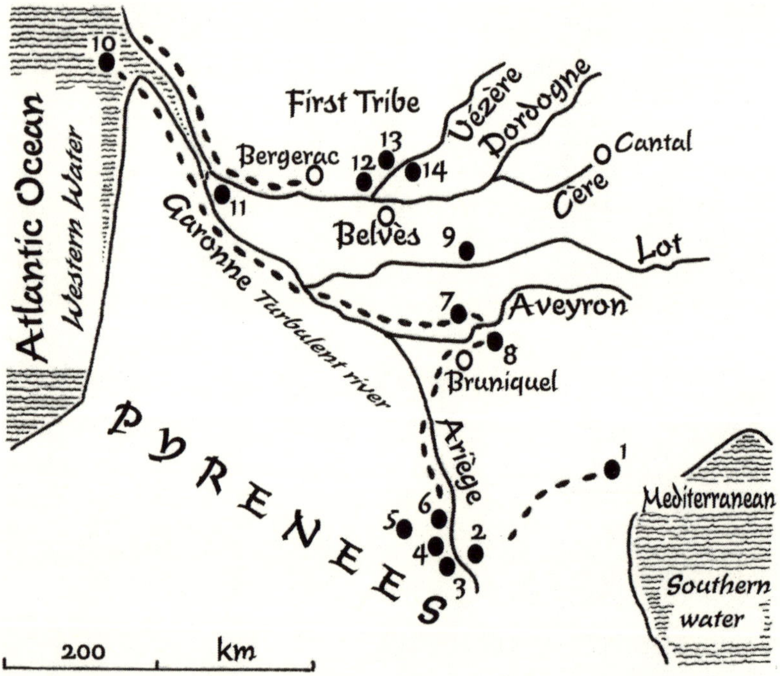

Leya's journey, fourth summer to sixth spring, from summer camp of group of Turbulent River to territory of First Tribe.

1 – Tournal
(Bize, summer camp group of Turbulent River).
2 – Les Eglises (Ariège).
3 – Niaux
(Ariège; cave drawings group of Turbulent River).
4 – La Vache
(Ariège; winter camp group of Turbulent River).
5 – Mas d'Azil (Garonne)
6 – Bédeilhac (Foix, Ariège).
7 – Courbet, Magdeleine, Montastruc
(Aveyron; spirits of the ancestral mothers).
8 – Fontalès (Aveyron).
9 – Carriot (Lot).
10 – Gironde
(winter camp of groups from Garonne and Dordogne basins, which went to fish and hunt together, among others seals and Great Auk*; today one hundred meters below sea level).
11 – Faustin (Dordogne; residence First Tribe).
12 – Gare-de-Couze, Lalinde, Limeuil
(Dordogne; residence First Tribe).
13 – Laugerie, Madeleine
(Vézère; residence First Tribe).
14 – Combarelles, Comarque, Saint-Cirq-du-Bugue
(Vézère; caves with images of spirits of the mothers; First Tribe).

Bergerac, Belvès and Bruniquel: flint deposits.

15,000 years ago

Time of Great Change

It had stopped snowing, when they woke up next morning, but a dense fog forced them to stay in the camp one more day. The children threw snowballs and organised a competition between those who passed the summer on the northern plain and the rest that came from the west. The outcome was predictable, because most children went northward in summer. The adults discussed the weather, grumbled about nothing and returned to their hides, which protected them against the cold.

Leya got up too, but only for a short while. Fortunately, the sick feeling had not returned. As always, the first visited Great Narrator. Her mother did not need to say a word. Her grandmother did not show signs of improvement, on the contrary. She lay there, ash-grey, with her eyes closed and a gaping mouth. Only a soft rattle and at times a sigh indicated that she was still alive. The spirit of her mother should be ready by now to take away Great Narrator's soul. She did not react when Leya called her name.
Leya looked at her mother. For so many winters and summers she had been tending Great Narrator, cooking the

finest pieces of meat and fish, and saving the bloodiest liver as well as nutritious marrowbones. Leya observed despair on her face and knew that the end was forthcoming.
"Can I be of use?"
Her mother looked up sadly. "Who can help Great Narrator? I am afraid that she is already seeing the spirit of the mammoth. We have done everything possible; you know that. Go back to Krasser; don't forget him, even though you are expecting a child."
"What about tonight? What shall I do?"
"You have to entertain them, they are counting on you. They are able to momentarily forget their worries thanks to your stories."
She nodded, embraced her mother and walked back to the hut, where she rapidly pulled the hides over her head, cuddling up to Krasser. The warmth quickly returned into her body.

In spite of the dejected mood in the camp, they all gathered around the fire. Everyone understood that Great Narrator was dying, but they were able to put this and their worries about kindling and food aside. Leya saw herself surrounded by merely cheerful, expectant faces. As soon as everyone was seated she got up to speak.
"This morning I could not imagine that we would assemble this night, here around the fire, fearing that Great Narrator was already looking at the spirit of the mammoth. At this very moment he may be carrying her soul to the innerearth, because the verge of life and death is frequently as invisible as the difference between a normal cave and the womb of the earth. My mother will stay with her tonight." She gulped, staring absently in front of her, and then remembered her mother's words: 'They count on you!' She should not let down her friends and family!

"In the fourth spring we walked westward along the waterside. The days were pleasantly warm when the sun was shining, but as soon as the wind came from the north, it could be bitterly cold. Fortunately, this rarely happened. Without any problems we crossed several brooks running from the north into Southern Water. After spotting snow-covered mountains in the distance, we decided to follow a narrow stream that came from the west. 'Go westward,' had been their advice, 'and you will meet people.'

The first people we met at the mouth of that river did not live there. They were strangers, just like us, and initially we had problems understanding each other. Together we put up camp.

It took a while to explain where we came from. After much talk, they finally understood that other groups like ours were living north of the North they were familiar with.

They for their part had arrived from the South, a full summer's walk from behind the snow-covered mountains. Last summer they had abandoned their territory. The rare game still living there had died or disappeared due to the long-lasting drought. Many relatives had died of starvation. The survivors split up in small bands, which looked elsewhere for new chances. They had moved northward along the shore of Southern Water in the hope of joining other groups, but all their efforts had been unsuccessful.

We were surprised. Did this mean that people in the region did not keep to the rules of hospitality? 'Of course, they do,' was their answer, 'but only for their own family, for members of their own tribe. They treat us as the other ones, as inferior Southerners*, since our group is living south of Southern River.' 'South of Southern River? How is that possible?'

They explained that their family initially lived in the North, north of the place where we were at the moment. However, long, long ago, at the Time of Great Change, their ancestors had decided to move to the South, behind the snow-covered mountains. Soon after, some families crossed Southern River, the stream that up to then had bordered their territory, because the group had become too large to feed. This was a completely wrong decision. The southern region was arid and unattractive, devoid of reindeer, saiga, aurochs or bison, while horses were rare. Their answers to our questions made clear that they had never heard talking about mammoth or rhinoceros."

"Can you imagine that we should have to live there on rabbit, deer, and occasionally a goat or a seal? 'Why do they treat you as the other ones? Your ancestors were members of the same tribe.' 'Because we speak differently and use words they don't understand.' 'But we do that too,' was our reaction, 'and nobody takes notice.' 'Well, here they do! They refuse to believe that our ancestors once belonged to their tribe. Even so, they shouldn't have made the stupid decision to cross the Southern River. No normal person would ever do so! Being their children's children we had lost our right to return and cross Southern River to the north again.
Moreover, it had not been raining for long, so that due to an extended drought, game had become scarce in the territory between Southern River and the snow-covered mountains. Famine was already lurking; another reason for not accepting us in their group.'
Nobody had ever used similar arguments to us and we could not understand why people could think like this.
Yet again we asked them if they might have misunderstood the wording, but they sadly shook their head. Oh no, that was discounted. They had once more explained to them that their family had become too small to survive, but the other group had chased them away with sticks and stones. If they would dare to return, more drastic actions would be taken, no-one would survive. All contacts had ended in a similar way.
We carefully observed them once more. They had a funny accent, that was true, and they dressed differently; but so did every group we had met so far. They seemed to be nice and honest people, and yet we were the first ones who invited them to bivouac together without having been asked."

"We were completely perplexed and worried about the unpleasant surprises that perhaps awaited us. Was it really possible that the inhabitants of this region would drive us away? We didn't get much sleep that night. The thought of not being welcome kept us awake. The next day however, the sun shone and it was pleasantly warm. We went hunting together with our new friends. They were skilled seal hunters, whereas we showed them the advantage of fishing with harpoons carved out of reindeer antlers. Their harpoons were made from deer antlers and only possessed minuscule barbs. We had plenty of food that night and were in an elated mood. It was fantastic to sit there on the beach by Southern Water!"

"The day after, we went to fish and hunt again at the mouth of the river and had a great time, until they suddenly froze. They pointed cautiously to the bushes behind us, from where a large group of men and women, all armed with assegais, emerged. They did not look friendly and approached us slowly. It was pointless to run away as the river and Southern Water blocked our way out, especially for the small children of our friends.
Durfal motioned us to take it calmly. He laid his harpoon on the ground, stretched his arms and showed his empty hands. The other group halted. Their leader also dropped his arms and stepped forward.
He began with a hot-tempered talk that rapidly turned into shouting. The man was speaking so fast that we could hardly follow his words, but the intention was clear. This was their territory. We had to leave immediately. Durfal let the man finish his outburst, and then patiently explained that we had come from the North. His relatives of Deep Valley had suggested us to pay them a visit. Every day we had laid a fire in order to draw their attention to our presence without ever seeing smoke in reply. Durfal kindly suggested that their habits to make contact might differ from ours, habits unknown to us. In that case he would like to offer him our most sincere apologies.

The man looked bewildered and calmed down. 'Forgive us the way we approached you. You are naturally welcome here. We initially feared for our lives, because we had mistaken you for the other ones.' 'Why?' 'Well, most of you are dressed like the other ones, like Southerners!' He pointed at our friends, who had been listening breathlessly. 'They are family,' was our subtle comment. 'Their ancestors were born in our tribe.' The man consulted the people around him. Then he decided: 'They come from the region south of Southern River; they talk differently, dress differently and think differently. They are sneaky Southerners, lurking for a chance to kill us! How dare they say that their ancestors were our relatives! Let them prove it!' He defiantly looked at us.

'Can you prove the opposite?' asked Durfal. 'That's not so important!' shrieked the man angrily. 'They are different, that's what matters! They even use words that no-one understands.' 'We have a different accent too. That's normal for people living that far from one another. The important thing is that we understand each other. We have met them some days ago and set up a camp together. They share our food and are our friends. The rules of hospitality make our friends yours too.'

He did not know how to answer. Yet again they deliberated with abrupt gestures, and then the man addressed us once more. 'You are right; your friends are our friends. I suggest that we eat together and postpone further decisions until tomorrow.' I heard our friends heave a deep sigh of relief. They approached the group and offered two seals they had killed that morning. Broadly smiling the man accepted their offer, tapping them kindly on the back. Tension was over. The newcomers put up their tents next to ours. We made fire, collected herbs and prepared fish and seals. We had a real party. Everyone was singing and dancing. Completely exhausted we went to sleep."

Leya had to swallow, her voice faltered. She exchanged a knowing glance with her fellow travelers who knew already what she would tell. She continued with her voice down.

"Cries of despair woke us in the middle of the night. It took a while before we realised that something was going terribly wrong. Then we rushed outside. The tent of the Southerners was all ablaze; the uproar originated there. The newcomers were standing around. We heard them howling. Everybody was awake, walking to and fro. All of a sudden two or three figures came stumbling out of the tent, burning like torches. People rushed towards them, to help them we thought.
In a flash we saw clubs being smashed against the figures, which twisted and whimpered on the ground. At that very moment we realised that they were being murdered! Our new companions revealed themselves as coldblooded murderers!"
Her voice betrayed cropped-up rage. The furious look in the eyes of Krasser, Ursa and Durfal was obvious too. With growing indignation her audience was listening incredulously to her description of the horrible facts.
"Some other shadows dashed out of the tent before we could react. They met with the same fate. Krasser and Durfal tried to intervene but were brutally knocked aside. 'Stay out of this! Do you want to die too?' Durfal was hit by a stone and silently fell down. Krasser started back, lent down and grabbed Durfal, dragging him to safety. Ursa and I were screaming with terror. What would become of us? One of the women broke away from the group and pushed us back into our tent: 'This has nothing to do with you. We are only interested in the other ones! Stay here, don't try to interfere!' The moaning and lamentations did not last long. We heard the rest laughing and whooping while the flames slowly went out. Only the smell of burned flesh and hair still lingered in the air."

"They went to sleep as if nothing had happened. We kept silent, in mortal fear of them; afraid they might change their mind and intend to burn down our tent. Durfal came groaning to his senses. Ursa took care of the wound on his head that was not too serious after all. We spent the rest of

the night between sleep and wake, our weapons at hand. Not until daylight dared we to go outside. The remnants of our friends' tent were still smoldering. It was impossible to identify the completely carbonised corpses or to tell whether these had belonged to adults or children. Heavily mutilated, half-burned corpses were scattered around the spot. We almost simultaneously vomited the previous night's food on the ground.
The noise awoke the people in the other tents. Unperturbedly they came closer, and judging the situation, spat on the bodies whilst counted them, making sure that no-one had escaped. Then they turned to us. They had not intended to involve us into the nightly massacre. They insisted: 'If we had not killed the other ones, they would have murdered us and you as well. That's beyond all doubt. You should be glad that we solved the predicament!'
They decided to depart immediately and take us with them as hospitality demanded. They left the bodies on the ground. 'Grant the vultures, foxes and ravens a pleasure, although we doubt that they like Southerners.' They shrieked with laughter at this joke. We decided not to react, though we had our doubts about their arguments. Was it really thinkable that people we had believed to be our friends the previous night, who had shared our food, would have intended to kill us? We could ask them no longer."

"It took little time to pack. Everyone wished to leave the scene of the massacre as soon as possible. We did not glance backward, although we would like to have seen Southern Water once more. We feared to see the black-burned bodies and felt guilty, without knowing why. The memory of that terrible event is haunting us until this day. We do not know what spirit had taken their souls to the womb of the earth. We had not spoken about this, having known them only so shortly. We wondered whether they had idolised the spirits of the mothers.
Our new companions preferred instead to entrust themselves to the spirits of goat, bison, aurochs, deer or horse.

These spirits had gotten a preferential place in the caverns of the womb of the earth, as they would show us later. They even saved a space for the spirit of the ermine, since he can take the souls through the smallest holes. Some people had chosen the spirits of lion, wolf or bear, but no-one entrusted himself to the spirits of the mothers."

"Leya, why do these people not worship the spirits of the mothers, just like everyone else? They too have a mother." One of her nieces posed the question.

"Initially, we too were very surprised, that's for sure. Only much later, during our stay in the South of our ancestors, a region north of our companions' territory, did we understand why. We can talk about it some other day."

"Why can't you tell us just now?" questioned her niece. Krasser's brother agreed with her. "Come on, Leya, we like to hear the details." The rest of the audience clapped to support the demand.

"No problem, but don't be angry if I forget where I left off."

"Don't worry, Leya, we won't."

"People have told us that all humans once lived in the South of our ancestors, the centre and most beautiful place of the earth. Winters were short and there was no snow. Everyone was happy since there were plenty of game and countless trees and bushes for tent poles and fire. The region was visited by large herds of mammoth and rhinoceros, animals that no longer live there. Rivers were teeming with fish that could be caught so easily. Every family found shelter below one of the many overhanging rocks and there were no conflicts. Holes forming the entry to the womb of the earth existed everywhere, and there was space for all spirits. That was the Time of Prosperity*.

And then came the other ones! They came from the East and the South, without being noticed. They were jealous of the happiness of our ancestors, since no game was living in the East or South. They pretended to be humans in order to gain our ancestors' trust and copulated with them; but their children were malcontent and malignant beings, who sowed discord and conflict. They killed the game, chased herds away and burned down all trees and bushes. Famine struck the tribe and winters became colder and longer, thus ending the Time of Prosperity.

Eventually, the humans decided to chase away the other ones and their children. A fierce battle followed. Sometimes, the other ones seemed to be winning, but at other moments the humans had the upper hand. So many were killed on both sides that it was feared that no-one would survive. It did not get to that stage, however. The intervention of the spirits of rhinoceros, lion and mammoth decided the battle. The other ones were forced back to the region south of Southern River and to the inaccessible mountains in the East. However, through cunning and guile they managed to seize part of the game as well as trees and bushes.

The Time of Prosperity did not return to the South of our ancestors; the centre of the earth according to them. They were in desperate need of branches and twigs for fire, assegais and huts. Mammoth and rhinoceros had fled to the North. Finally, the pinch of food scarcity ended in fierce rows. That was the beginning of the Time of Great Change*.

The eldest concluded that the tribe would be better off if some people followed the animal's example, and look for new hunting grounds. However, no-one was prepared to go. Who could be sure that life was better elsewhere, or that the spirits in those new regions would take the souls to the womb of the earth? Many doubted aloud that leaving would be wise, in spite of the fact that the shortage of food was killing their children. The eldest started yet further deliberations."

"After long consultations they came with the following proposal. 'No-one knows if we will find enough game elsewhere, nor if the spirits of the animals in these unknown territories will be willing to take all souls of the dead to the womb of the earth. However, each of us has a loving and tending mother. Let us beg the spirits of the mothers to protect us and take our souls to the inner-earth.' Many families, especially those planning to move to the North and East, felt comfortable with the thought. How could the spirit of a mother deny anything to her children, when in life she had lovingly cared for them through so many summers and winters?

Other people took a different view, preferring to entrust themselves to the spirits of the animals that had protected them from immemorial times. They wondered how the spirit of a mother might be faster than the spirit of a horse or stronger than the spirit of a bison. They argued that everyone should be free to choose. 'Some trust the spirit of a mammoth, whereas other persons prefer the spirit of a salmon or the spirit of a lion. Many of us beg various spirits for help. It is good to honor the spirits of the mothers and implore their protection, but everyone should be free to make his own choice, even here in the South.' Everyone agreed about that."

Her audience nodded in approval. Leya had explained it very well.

"Well, if you are satisfied, I can continue my story. After the massacre of the other ones, we followed our new companions to the west, to the fast-running Turbulent River* that originated somewhere in the snow-covered mountains. In a deep valley, in the foothills below these mountains, they built their winter residence, in front of a cave that was used as shelter."

"Leya!"

She looked up and saw her mother entering the hut, her eyes red and tears rolling down her cheeks. She immediately knew what had happened.

"Leya, Great Narrator just died. The spirits of the mammoth and her mother have carried her soul away!"

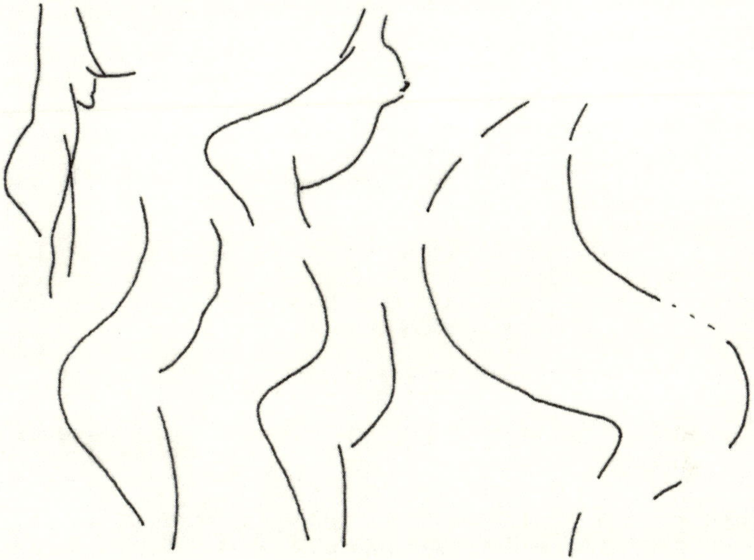

Engravings of stylised women of Lalinde-Gönnersdorf type

(spirits of the mothers)

Upper left: image from Gönnersdorf (Neuwied; after Bosinski a.o., 2001).
Upper right: image from Combarelles (Les Eyzies; after Duhard, 1993).
Lower left: two images from Fronsac (Vieux-Mareuil; after Duhard, 1993).
Right: image from El Linar (Alfoz de Lloredo; after Bosinski a.o., 2001).

Distance between Gönnersdorf and Combarelles is 1,000 km, between Combarelles and Fronsac 90 km, and between Combarelles and El Linar 500 km.

Prehistoric Camps of 15,000 years ago

In 2007, the winter in the Netherlands was not as cold as usual, a consequence of the greenhouse effect according to general opinion. This phenomenon was unknown in the Ice Age, when winters were extremely cold. Fortunately, people discovered early on how they could insulate the floor of their dwellings against the rising damp and cold from the ground. They probably slept on a layer of stones and/or branches and twigs, covered with grass and sedge. Sand or clay may have been added to preserve the floor against the continuous trampling of the inhabitants, as it was done 23,000 years ago in Israel. The partly charred remains of these floors have been unearthed by Dani Nadel and his collaborators at Ohalo, a campsite of fisher-hunter-gatherers on the shore of the Lake Galilee. They may have finished it off with a cover of hides.

Very wisely, people only insulated the floor of the sleeping place and not the entry or the fire place. Maybe they pulled off their dirty footwear (presumably moccasins and some sort of boots) at the entry, crawling barefoot to their place on the hides. They reserved a space for tool making. Stone splinters fallen on the hides were thrown away outside the

hut or the tent. Their dwellings were very functional, and floor insulation is not a modern invention!
What more do we know about those campsites, what did they look like? According to Gerhard Bosinski, the large Gönnersdorf dwellings resembled a jaranga*, the tent of the Chukchi* people, relatives of Eskimos and Inuit, in Northeast Siberia. Nowadays, walrus hides cover the vertical walls and cone-shaped roof, resting on a central supporting pole, but at the time people will have used horse hides. Many long poles are however needed for these structures. Just imagine a jaranga of five to eight meters diameter, fit for six to eight persons. You need dozens of long poles. Were these easily found on a treeless steppe? Large bushes won't do. Smaller dwellings with a diameter of only three meters, fit for five or six persons, have been discovered at Étiolles and Pincevint near Paris, and Schweikhuizen near Sittard. It is highly doubtful whether these resembled teepees of North American Prairie Indians, as suggested by some reconstructions, since you need several meters long poles for their construction.
Most dwellings will have consisted of circular to oval, dome-shaped brush huts, similar to the wigwams or wiki ups built by the Apaches in Arizona at the end of the nineteenth century. You only needed a few days to erect these. San* or Bushmen continue to build similar structures in the African Kalahari, into present times. Fresh flexible branches and twigs of willow and birch will have sufficed. These may have been more widely distributed on the steppe, especially by the river-side. A cover of hides protected against rain and cold.
Cold Ice Age winters also had a positive side. Large amounts of food could easily be preserved because of the months-long frost. To this end Siberian Chukchi cut out an uveran*, a hole in the permafrost for the conservation of provisions. You only need a cover of some heavy stones to keep out any uninvited scavengers. It's as simple as that! During the Late Ice Age however, it could abruptly start to thaw in the middle of the winter.

These winter thaws were new to them. In the middle of the cold season, from one day to the next, they had to deal with bad meat and fish, and unforeseen food shortage. Our generation will not be the first one to live through the consequences of a climate change!
Our ancestor's thoughts will not have lingered long about the question why thaw occurred in the midst of the winter. They rather looked for practical solutions to guarantee their food supply. Initially, they will have searched for game in the environs, but, as a final resort, they abandoned the campsite and split up in small groups, which tried to survive elsewhere.
Of course, the weak, sick and eldest - those unable to set off - had a serious problem. What could their relatives do when they were running out of provisions? It was not an option to stay with them, as they might all starve to death. Naturally, everyone will have promised to return with fresh food as soon as possible, but in practice this was rarely feasible. It might be too late for those staying behind, even if the other group returned. We can only guess at the number of casualties. Those moving to other areas were well aware of the fact that nobody could guarantee them to be better off. As we have seen before, these may only have been golden times for scavengers.

15,000 years ago

Burial Rituals

Most people did not get much sleep that night. Great Narrator's death had touched all of them. Although old and fragile, she had been the last link to a distant past. In the course of time they had all come to her with their questions and problems.

Drawing on her considerable experience she had been able to offer sound advice as well as indulgence to those who had made errors of judgment. Her own youth had not been flawless either.

Winter after winter she had filled the long nights around the fire with her stories. Everybody called her Great Narrator. No-one remembered her real name. She was old, had lived a good life, but her children, children's children, and their children as well, felt sad and distressed.

Leya spent the night in the hut of Great Narrator, wailing over her death together with her mother and other relatives as tradition demanded. They powdered the body with red ochre, painted face and hands, dressed her up as beautifully as they could, and put on the necklace of pink snails. They finally placed the body on a litter covered with the hide of a bear.

The men in the camp got together as soon as the sun rose above the hills. In silence they walked to Big River, removed snow and ice, and laboriously hacked out a shallow hole in the frozen ground, using reindeer antlers. No-one said a word when they returned to the camp, where everybody stood ready to accompany Great Narrator's body to its last resting-place. Then they carried the body to the grave. All the signs and symbols of her dignity were laid down by her, together with the images of the spirits of the mothers and the mammoth. They filled the grave and covered it with lumps of frozen earth and stones. Fortunately, it was not snowing very much.
Krasser engraved the image of the spirit of a mother on a large slab of shale. Everyone knew that is represented the spirit of Great Narrator. One of the women sang a song, an ode to the spirit of Great Narrator. A man took it over, begging her spirit for protection against famine and snow.
The rest of the day, Leya and the eldest stayed with her mother and uncle. She warmed water and prepared tea, trying to improve their mind. The slab of shale with the picture of the spirit of Great Narrator was leaning against the central pole of the hut, illuminated by several grease lamps. Outside the hut snowfall continued unabated. People were really worried by now. This should not go on for long. They were running out of supplies. It was high time to go hunting and collect branches for fire.
It was already getting dark, when her mother looked at Leya: "Have you been thinking about the story you will tell tonight?" "Euh? I forgot all about it! I don't feel in the mood for this."
"Nor do I, but don't mourn too long. It makes you depressed. The men and women in the camp need distraction. Continue your story. It will cheer them up. I too shall be there."
"I am feeling so miserable," sobbed Leya. "How can I live without her? She inspired me; without her I am no-one."
"Her spirit is here with us. You know that. She will prompt the right words into your head. Great Narrator had once

been through the same emotions when her mother died. I was still a child, but I remember it well. After the burial she cried more than you. She seemed inconsolable. The eldest approached her, begging to tell a story that night to cheer people up. She answered just as you did, and yet she was sitting by the fire that night. She knew that it was right to do so. The spirit of her mother strengthened her. She spoke better than ever before. Even now, after all this time, I can hear her voice. You may feel heartbroken, that's normal, but life goes on. People need your voice, not your tears!"
Leya looked at the tear-stained face of her mother and nodded.
"You are right. I shall do it."
They hugged each other.
"You are a wise woman," she added softly.

The rapid mood change of the audience astonished her while she listened to the cheerful voices, as if nothing had happened, as if this was a day like all other days. How is this possible, she wondered, how can people forget so soon?
Her mother was sitting in the place that had been reserved for Great Narrator, next to her uncle, Great Narrator's brother. She gave Leya an encouraging nod. Leya secretly clasped the pouch with the ivory figurine she was always carrying with her, knowing it now represented the spirit of Great Narrator.

"This was a day of sorrow, as it should be, but does it occur to you that we are privileged, having been able to bury Great Narrator? We all have lost relatives during hunting expeditions; beloved persons who disappear and can't be buried. It happens everywhere. During our journey we have lived through it several times. Last night I told you that our new companions from Turbulent Valley refused to bury the charred bodies of our friends, because they were other ones who lived somewhere south of Southern River.

It is about the worst thing that may happen to you. The members of the group of Turbulent River were quite aware of the fact that we have to bury the dead and honor their souls. It is the wish of the Maker.

If someone vanishes however, this is impossible. I remember that we were hunting reindeer by Turbulent River. Summer had almost passed and soon the animals would move to the plains north of those mountains. As usual, we had split up into small bands. Our group was lucky enough to spot a young animal that we killed without further problems. In turns we carried it on our shoulders down to the camp. It meant meat for everybody and we were in a cheerful mood when we butchered the beast. Even a dense fog, suddenly hiding the mountains from view, could not diminish our morale, since practically all hunters had already returned to the camp.

Only one tent remained empty. Nobody doubted that the residents were sheltering somewhere and would be waiting that visibility improved the next day.

'What a pity for them,' laughed some-one. 'We will eat their portion too.' Of course, we put the best quarters apart for them.

The next day the sun shone and the fog had dissipated, but our friends did not come back. We began to worry. One of them might be wounded or they had lost their way. The following day we organised a search; and so we did for several days; but all in vain. We screamed ourselves hoarse without getting an answer. We continued to hope against better judgment, but in the end we had to accept the crude reality. Our friends had vanished without leaving a trace.

There were three of them, a man, a wife and her son. Our dismay was enormous. They had to be dead by now, no-one doubted it. Perhaps they had fallen in a deep fissure, landing straight into the inner-earth. That would be the best for them. We all hoped that the other ones had not seized them. We feared that the Southerners had wanted to avenge the dead who had been murdered in spring by Southern Water."

"There was also a possibility that they had been devoured by bears, wolves or lions. Lions frequently wandered through that region, especially on the foothills of the mountains, where the plain began. They had explicitly warned us about them. One day we observed with our own eyes how lions, two females and a male, caught a large bison by surprise, an adult bull in the prime of his life. He was drinking from a pool, unaware of any danger. We were thinking how we could possibly kill him when we noticed the lions. They approached him in silence, slipping closer and closer until the bison got wind of the male. He showed no fear, turned around and aggressively stepped forward to the lion that kept at safe distance from the sharp-tipped horns. He was unaware of the females, coming from behind, until it was too late. They suddenly bounced forward and clawed their paws in the hind quarters of the utterly surprised bull. The wounds were unimportant, but the hefty blow threw him off balance, his hind legs giving way. He tried to gore his aggressors with a wild wave of his formidable head, but at the same time the male lion leaped forward and seized the bull's muzzle in a firm bite. It did not take long before the struggle was over. It's with good reason that we make a detour when we spot lions. Due to his tremendous paws and teeth, some people in Turbulent Valley entrust themselves to the spirit of a lion."

"We discovered no signs whatsoever to solve the mystery, no remains of their weapons, no scraps of clothes, no torn parts of a body, and total lack of footprints, as if giant vultures had carried them away through the air. We were dominated by feelings of impotence and despair. We left the tent where it was, although nobody believed that they might still be alive. We deposited some pieces of dried meat under a few heavy boulders, although no-one thought they would need it."
Her audience was listening with closed eyes. Everyone had lived through similar situations, losing family and friends. The uncertainty about their fate was the worst part.

They remembered Prater's story about someone who had returned many winters later. Everything was possible, of course, but how to explain this to surviving relatives?
"We did not speak much on our way back to the main camp. It is true that we carried meat and a hide, but no-one felt proud of it. Everybody noticed at once that three persons were missing. Questions remained unanswered, whilst the harrowing cries of the relatives reverberated through the valley. There was no time for mourning, just like here. They had to catch salmon and the first goats were descending from the mountains.
One of the men put himself to work selecting a piece of reindeer antler. He carefully smoothed the surface, just as Krasser does before making an engraving. Some parts were left out, at least that's what we initially thought, but against the smooth background the silhouette of a reindeer became visible. The head was a bit large, but possessed beautiful antlers. Krasser too was astonished, because he had never seen this technique. In the same way, behind the animal, three shadows came into being, shadows of a man, a woman and a child; no doubt the souls of the dead. In contrast to our tradition the images were in the possession of a head, although without eyes, nose or mouth. The spirit of the man clearly carried two assegais to hunt somewhere in the inner-earth."

"That night everybody gathered around the fire against the back wall of the cave. The antler with the scene of the souls and the reindeer had gotten a place of honor amidst us. The eldest woman of the group respectfully held the antler in her hands while one of the men dug a little hole in front of her feet. She carefully placed the antler in the hole. Someone covered it with a reindeer quarter and the rest put stones on top of it.
'Now their spirits know that we will not forget them,' said the woman. 'They will protect us whenever we ask for it.'
Many families in the South of our ancestors sustain the same tradition. It is a good thing to hold on to traditions,

but we don't have to adopt these here, since our traditions are just as valuable.
Then it was our turn to honor the dead. Krasser took a pebble and engraved the silhouette of the spirit of a mother. Next everybody sang and danced, in the same way that we have done this morning in honor of Great Narrator."

She fell silent. Her audience had something to think about. She looked up at her mother who signaled that it had been enough for this night. Everyone was tired, a good time to go to sleep.

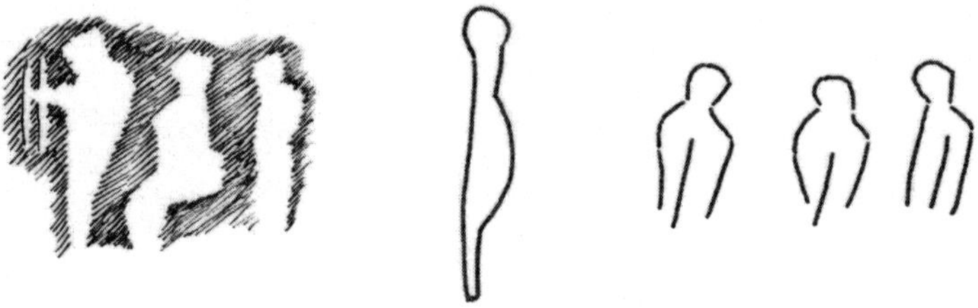

Late Magdalenian human silhouettes

Left: La Vache
(Alliat; after Duhard, 1993),
bas-relief on reindeer antler (part of a hunting
scene with reindeer).
Center: Fontalès
(Saint-Antonin-Noble-Val; after Duhard, 1993),
bone figurine.
Right: Raymonden
(Chancelade; after Brigitte and Gilles Delluc, 2003),
engraving in bone (part of a scene showing human figures
around a boned bison.

The remarkable presence of a stylised head distinguishes these figures from the spirits of the mothers. These silhouettes typically occur in Southern France. In Leya's story, they represent spirits of men, women and children who had disappeared during hunting expeditions (note the vaguely indicated assegais). By then, the tradition of depicting a head already existed ten thousand years earlier in Gravettian times.

Distance between La Vache and Fontalès is 200 km, between Fontalès and Raymonden 200 km, and between La Vache and Raymonden 350 km.

Reconstruction of a Journey across Europe II

We ensured for good reason that our narrator and her friends made a stopover at the cave of La Vache near Alliat. The excavations have yielded the remnants of 4,566 ptarmigans and 1,831 mountain goats, as well as 147 reindeer and 85 chamois. These numbers might suggest that those people had never known food shortage.
It is an enormous amount of meat, but we have to bear in mind that these numbers must be spread over three hundred years. If this was a yearly hunting camp, they will have killed six goats and fifteen ptarmigans each year, and every two years one reindeer or chamois. Archeologists suggest that the hunters usually occupied the campsite from September or October to April. This implies slightly less than one goat and two ptarmigans each month; a real let-down for people living on a meat diet. About ten percent of the goats were very young animals of less than a year, and slightly more than half of the adults are females. An adult female weighs forty to fifty kilos, including bones, hide and hair, and a full-grown male about twice as much.

On average, they disposed of one to two kilos meat a day, depending on the proportions of the butchered animal. Now you can calculate for yourself that the group could not be too large.
Of course, they caught fish as well. Late Magdalenian people ate a lot of fish. Harpoons with a double barb, fairly common at La Vache, were outstanding weapons for spearing salmon. It is possible as well that most animals were butchered and eaten outside the cave. In that case all our calculations are useless, since we only dispose of the bones within the cave. Maybe they lived outside the cave as long as the weather permitted and only used it as a shelter. It just shows that many questions remain unanswered in spite of all these investigations.

Until now we have only been talking about food, but we should not forget the hides they needed to fashion clothing, footwear and blankets, or as cover for tents and huts. This aspect is often overlooked. Primarily moccasins and boots had to be frequently replaced.
No wonder that in La Vache a few hundred complete and broken bone needles have been unearthed. Making new footwear and repairing clothes must have been daily routine for prehistoric people, but despite this, not many needles were broken.
Over a three hundred year period this implies that each season they only lost one needle, given that they will have pierced holes in the leather beforehand. Even so, one needle for converting six hides into footwear and clothing is not a bad average. They were less wasteful than we at first thought.
There was plenty of time for other activities as well, such as the decoration of tools and other objects. Apart from the many animal teeth, shells, snails and fossils, which have been used as adornments, they also produced real masterpieces of art. Perhaps the artist of our virtual band left his marks in the picture of an animal or the silhouette of a stylised woman.

In spring our friends continued northward to the Aveyron Valley. This can be deduced from the fact that the group of La Vache collected part of the flint for their tools in the Vère Valley. At Bruniquel this brook flows into the Aveyron, a tributary of the Garonne, as is the Ariège.
No doubt, they have visited the mysterious women in the cave of Magdeleine. We are talking about partly natural reliefs, their shape having been accentuated and completed by someone about 17,000 years ago. Although invisible from the outside of the cave, they catch enough daylight to be admired without the help of lamps. The two recumbent figures, each with the unspecified head resting on a backwards bent arm, recall some of the nudes painted by Amadeo Modigliani.
These images already existed some two thousand years before our friends visited the place. They for their part left a limestone with four stylised women in front of the cave.

The families in the Aveyron Valley not only used flint from the Vère Valley, but also from locations much farther away along the Dordogne, at Bergerac and Belvès. The easiest way from Bruniquel goes downstream along the Aveyron, the Tarn and the Garonne to the Gironde, in which the Dordogne discharges too. The various groups of the Garonne-Dordogne basin may have gathered yearly on the shores of the Gironde estuary, where they hunted together for seals, as is suggested by the many depictions and remnants of these animals in this area. Jordi Serangeli even mentions coldwater species, such as harp seal and ringed seal, which prefer Arctic regions today.
Step by step we follow our narrator's trail from La Vache northwards. To tell the truth, we never imagined that this would be that easy.
We daresay they breathlessly saw the sun sinking in the Atlantic, night after night. We are unable to follow their footprints on the beach, because the then existing shores are now covered with one hundred meters of water. Doubtlessly, they will have noticed that the water of the

Atlantic was much colder than that of the Mediterranean. At the time, the warm Gulfstream did not exist and icebergs drifted from the Hudson Bay in the direction of Europe. This explains why ringed seal and harp seal occurred in the Gironde estuary.

Yet again they must have walked the beach, collecting snails to fashion ornaments. They have carried these land inwards along the Dordogne to the Vézère Valley; another trail we can follow thanks to the winkles they lost at Laugerie-Basse near Les Eyzies.

The Vézère Valley is also called the 'Valley of Mankind' because of the many prehistoric sites, among which La Madeleine, where Gabriel de Mortillet defined the Magdalenian*, and Laugerie, where Henri Breuil described the Late Magdalenian*. Here started the mass migration to Central Europe 16,000 years ago, and here were the family roots of our narrator.

The Late Magdalenian groups in the Vézère Valley were no true nomads, since most of the year they caught sufficient game in the immediate surroundings. This must have surprised our friends who were used to roam long distances; in the same way all the groups did, that they had met thus far in Germany, Switzerland and in Eastern and Southern France. By their standards, the Vézère Valley must have been a land of unprecedented abundance. The game hunted along the Vézère is very impressive indeed: reindeer, horse, bison, red deer and roe deer, saiga, mountain goat, chamois, boar, wolf, hare, rabbit and snow fox, not to forget countless birds and fish, including salmon, trout, ale, carp and pike.

Such lists may be misleading however. How many wolves and boars have been killed? It happened only occasionally. They were and remained reindeer hunters and salmon fishermen, who from time to time killed a horse; the rest was irrelevant. This does not mean that the other animals were uncommon. Perhaps they preferred reindeer for the meat and because the hides were the most suited for clothing and footwear.

Naturally our friends went to visit Combarelles, a cave at a few kilometers from Les Eyzies, where they engraved the silhouettes of stylised women in the wall, and also Saint-Cirq-du Bugue, a hamlet near Les Eyzies with a small cave that is really worthwhile to visit. The latter one is renowned for the image of a man with hands and feet, a face with eyes, ear, nose and mouth, and large, eye-catching genitals. He is known as the 'sorcerer of Saint-Cirq'. When our friends visited the cave, that image was already two thousand years old! They must have seen it, wondering who made it and why. Spirits of men were not depicted then, let alone a figure with a complete face, hands and feet. During their visit to this cave they engraved two stylised women in the wall, so that we can't lose their tracks. The figures at the entrance of Saint-Cirq are much older. They had been carved some four thousand years before Leya's arrival. We have puzzled over the question why in this cave only three times images have been left behind, at intervals of two thousand years, particularly because the cave is situated at only a few kilometers distance from Les Eyzies, where people were living practically all the year round.

The next part of the journey led them straight across the volcanic region of the Auvergne, along the summits of the Cantal and other volcanoes, which had been extinct for millions of years. 15,000 years ago, this region was hardly accessible and largely covered with snow and ice. Even in the midst of summer, the few routes were rarely passable. They will have needed the help of a guide, someone who knew the region quite well. We can reconstruct the journey in broad outlines. They will have followed the Dordogne and the Cère upstream, by-passing present-day Aurillac. Behind the pass in between the summits of Cantal and Puy-Marie, they reached the rough valley of the Alagnon, flowing seventy kilometers further northeastwards into the Allier. During the Magdalenian, this route has been used several times, as indicated by stone tools at Molompize, which had been made from flint collected in the Cère Valley.

Remnants of several bivouacs in that area prove that the hunters were not afraid of setting up a camp at eight hundred meters above sea level, even if this was not a regular practice. This path next led them to Enval, east of Clermont-Ferrand and Puy-de-Dôme, where people hunted reindeer and horse from spring to autumn.

One might expect that prehistoric men would have avoided that area because of the then active volcanoes. Names that spring to mind are that of Tarteret, Thiolet, Goules, Nugère, Barme, Côme and Marais that erupted 12,000 – 15,000 years ago. No doubt, this list will grow longer, and yet we know a dozen campsites of the same age, one of these, Neschers, being situated on the flanks of the Tarteret.

Those people were not afraid of volcanoes, because most of the time the volcanic activity in that region has been limited to some rumbling in the subsurface. Centuries went by without any eruptions. Even a smoking volcano may not have frightened them. They will have wondered, of course, what was going on; trying to invent an explanation after their own fashion. In general, a serious eruption did not last long, and the possible damage was limited to a rather restricted area. Only in exceptional cases were western winds able to blow volcanic ashes eastwards over a distance of hundred and fifty kilometers. For example, the centimeters thick ash layer covering the camp of Enval originated from an eruption of the Nugère. Jean-Pierre Daugas and Jean-Paul Raynal take it for granted that events like this obtained a place in the prehistoric myths and legends.

The figurine of a stylised woman from Enval proves that the devotion to the spirits of the mothers was not limited to the groups in the Dordogne-Garonne Basin, but also took hold on the other side of the mountains in the Loire-Allier Basin. This impression is reinforced by an engraving at Saut-du-Perron, south of Roanne.

The hunters around Clermont-Ferrand and Roanne collected a large part (in some cases more than two thirds) of the flint for their tools in the north.

The journey from Enval to the flint sites around Le-Grand-Pressigny and Saint-Aignan and back was almost three hundred kilometers long; and much longer to and from Saut-du-Perron. Our friends too will have traveled the flint route from Enval to the region southeast of Tours. In winter, they and their guides pursued the northward moving herds to a region abounding in water with countless brook valleys running to the west or northwest, which in winter offered shelter against the cold northern winds. In summer however the area was infested with mosquitoes and flies, forcing the herds to return to the higher situated territories near Clermont-Ferrand and Roanne. Each season again people had to go after their food supply. The search for flint was less important; being a welcome bonus, of course.

The guides took our friends to the overhanging rock of Roc-aux-Sorciers, a shelter embellished by their ancestors with superb reliefs. After their previous visits to the caves of Magdeleine and Saint-Cirq, this was the third time they could admire similarly old expressions of art. Naturally, they were unaware of the fact that these had been made two thousand years earlier, during the Middle Magdalenian. We can pick up their trail once more because of the engravings of stylised women.

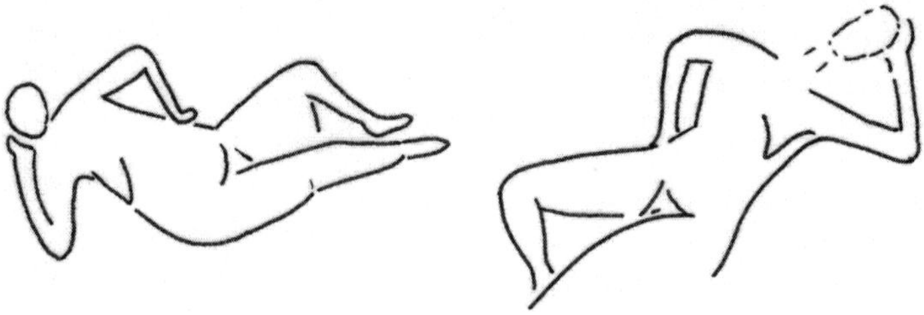

Bas-reliefs of female figures of Magdeleine
(Penne-Bruniquel, Aveyron; after Duhard, 1993)

During the Middle Magdalenian, some 17,000 years ago, the artist has improved the natural relief of two opposite walls in the cave of Magdeleine, portraying two about one meter large women. In Leya's story they play a part as the spirits of the ancestral mothers, invoked for fertility and procreation. The same role is attributed to female torsos with a prominent vulva at Roc-aux-Sorciers.
These depictions of the spirits of the ancestral mothers in the cave of Magdeleine are the only ones with a vaguely indicated head.

15,000 years ago

Meeting the First Tribe*

With combined forces they built a wall of snow around each hut and tent. This protected the dwellings against the storm. Leya was not permitted to help because of her pregnancy. She accepted her new role without complaint. She knew that it always had been like this; a tradition that never would change. It gave her a chance to reflect on the continuation of her story.
Two or three times during the journey she had encountered images of the spirits of the ancestral mothers. She had confided in them her misery of never having been pregnant, her deep wish to get a child someday. She had invoked their help to become a mother, but summers and winters had gone by without any visible result. She feared not to be predestined to become a mother; and yet, she was finally expecting a child! The spirits had shown great wisdom by waiting to fulfill her wish until she had returned to Big River. Here she could safely bear her child. She decided to say a few words about the subject.

The group was depleted due to the departure of several hunters who had set out to look for game.

They needed food, as soon as possible. The whole day people had been talking about it. Would the scouts be successful? Would they find their way back to the camp in the snowstorm? The rest had gathered around the fire, waiting for Leya's story.
"Who knows how many winters had passed when we traveled northward across Turbulent Valley?" Leya's voice sounded as casual as possible. Secretly amused, she observed the frowning faces around her. Counting posed a serious problem to most of them.
A cousin waved his arms enthusiastically: "I do! ¿May I say it?"
"I wonder whether you have the right answer, go on and tell us!"
"Four!" was his resolute answer. He took hold of the little finger of his left hand and started counting: "The first winter you passed with the group in Brother's Valley, after the reindeer drive. The second winter you stayed in that cave by Deep River, and the third winter you collected those beautiful snails on the beach by Southern Water." He got hold of his forefinger and raised it: "In the fourth winter you went to hunt with the group of Turbulent River; where that family got lost, a man, a woman and a child."
"Fantastic! You have been very attentive!"
The boy beamed with joy. "It was not that difficult. I think it has been a wonderful adventure!"
"You are quite right," confirmed Leya, "it is something we never will forget.'
"Let's hope that it will keep snowing the forthcoming days," added somebody. "Otherwise we will have to wait too long before you continue the story. Go on, there is no time to lose!"
"I shall do what I can; but not before I have had some tea!"

"As my cousin has already confirmed, four winters had gone by since our departure. At the start of the fifth spring, we accompanied several families to the north. They had sons and daughters who were looking for a partner.

They maintained good contacts from way back with the groups along the many tributaries to Turbulent River, and hoped to meet them somewhere. I forgot the name of the river, but I remember very well that we received a warm welcome. Those people live in a rather deep valley, as deep and twisting as Winding Valley, that place I have already talked you about, where we met the spirits of the mothers. We did not have to put up our tent because of the many caves and overhanging rocks. There was plenty of game and fish so that we decided to stay for a while.
Each night, we listened to each other's stories and sang together. They were no less devoted to the spirits than us. What's more, they idolised the spirits of mammoth, rhinoceros and musk ox, so that we really felt at home. They taught us how to make finely decorated spear throwers from bone and reindeer antlers."

"Summer had already begun when one of the women got pregnant. They celebrated this in the same way that we do it here. The currant juice we were drinking that night intensified the fun.
Whilst everybody was singing and making music, one of the women observed my breasts attentively. She asked me cautiously if I had ever been pregnant, and I responded sadly that I had not. 'Why don't you invoke the help of the spirits of the ancestral mothers?'
'Where can I possibly find them?'
'You are lucky. We have devoted a special place to them that can only be visited by women. We can go tomorrow.'
Of course, I would like to do this! 'Can we take Ursa with us? Her two children died shortly after they had been born. It's a pain that never fades way.'
She immediately agreed."

"Next morning she took us to a small cave, high above the river. Our eyes had to get accustomed to the dark, but then, just in front of us, we detected a small niche with the spirit of a horse. Slightly further to the right, the spirit of a woman, showing the symbol of fertility, was awaiting us. 'This is the helper,' explained the woman, 'the spirit of a girl who had never slept with a man. She is the helper of the spirits of the ancestral mothers. No man is allowed to approach her. All the girls of our family come here before they will sleep with a man. She helps them find the right partner; a problem that you solved already.' She had to laugh at this. She signaled to a dark space at the left. 'Follow me.'

It was not as dark as we expected. We noticed the spirit of a resting bison and, just above it, the spirit of an ancestral mother who had already breastfed a child. The complete body was represented, including arms and legs. We had never before seen such a huge image of a spirit. She lay on her back, seemingly asleep, the head leaning on her left hand. She was so enormous, dear friends, so impressive, so strong.

We kept gazing at her admiringly until noticing that she was not asleep at all. She seemingly wondered what we were doing there.

'Can we tell her the reason of our visit?' The woman nodded: 'Of course, but why don't you tell this to both of them? She has a twin sister!' She pointed at the wall behind us. In our excitement we had not seen her. We turned around, and yes, there she was, the twin sister. She looked at us too, although she had no eyes, ears, mouth or nose. We clearly felt that they both were watching us in the way that only spirits can.

We went down on our knees, fervently begging them to fulfill our wishes, to make us pregnant. I don't remember how long we have been there, but when we left the place, the sun was setting behind the horizon. 'This is the perfect moment for invoking the help of the spirits of the mothers as well,' remarked the woman very wisely. 'If the spirits join forces, your hopes will be answered.' She helped us to find a stone, in which Ursa and I carved the spirits of the mothers. We dug a small hole and buried the stone, making sure that they would answer."

"Well, you all know the end of this story. I don't know exactly how many summers and winters went by since then. I had almost forgotten that I had ever visited the spirits of the ancestral mothers and lost the hope to get pregnant; but now look at me! I am expecting a child! New life is growing somewhere in my belly. The spirits were much wiser than I shall ever be. They knew I still had many summers and winters of travel ahead, that it would not be a good time to get pregnant. They have waited until this winter, until I could rest amongst my family, here by Big River. This teaches us that the spirits do well not to act immediately on each and every wish, even if we don't understand their wisdom. Nobody but they and the Maker can look into the future. If it is their wish, Ursa too can be a mother again."

Leya turned to Ursa whilst she said this. Everybody noticed her radiating eyes and the rosy cheeks. She took another sip of tea before she continued.

"In the autumn we traveled downstream again along Turbulent River, into the direction of Western Water*. It is as large as Southern Water and nobody has ever seen the other side. Every night the sun sinks into the water, as Krasser had already foretold; nobody understands why, but we ourselves have repeatedly observed it. Krasser had warned us that the water was undrinkable, similar to that of Southern Water, and yet it was a peculiar experience when we checked it ourselves. Western Water is much colder than Southern Water, where we could swim in sheltered places. Western Water is as cold as our Big River, summer and winter alike. Autumn storms sometimes produce high waves which can easily wash you away. In winter however the lake is calm and smooth, and covered by large ice floes, primarily near the mouth of Turbulent River, which is even wider than Great Lake, where we hunted for reindeer.

Each winter, all families gather by Western Water, where they fish and hunt together, seals being their favourite game. There live so many seals that everybody got sufficient hides for new clothing. At the end of the winter new visitors invaded the shores: birds as large as a goose, but wingless so that they can't fly. In the water they swim faster than fish, but on land they go slowly and clumsy. It had such fun to observe their movements. It was easy to come within reach and kill them. People told us that they have occasionally met mammoth, rhinoceros and musk ox, but we did not see them and don't know whether these stories are true."

"Just before the beginning of the third moon of that winter another group arrived. Everybody had obviously been awaiting them, because the sight of their campfire's smoke caused great merriment. They were given a very warm welcome.
'These are the descendents of the First Tribe*,' explained our friends. 'All families in the South, the North, the West and the East are their relatives. Your ancestors have once been born in their territory; and ours too!'
They all hurried towards them and we observed tears of recognition and joy, whilst they greeted and hugged each other. They exchanged presents as a token of friendship. The members of the First Tribe gave every family a nicely cleaned tool stone, a highly appreciated gesture.
Initially, we kept in the background because we had never seen them before. The woman, who had taken Ursa and me to the cave of the ancestral mothers, took us by the hand and introduced us: 'These Northerners* have been looking for you for many summers and winters. The past summer we had the opportunity to listen to their stories. We have learnt a lot from them, because they have proven to be excellent fishermen and hunters.'
She kindly pushed us forward and the next moment they hugged us as old friends and said: 'It's always great to meet distant relatives. We have met people from the North before. They needed two summers to arrive here. What about your family, how far do they live from here?'

I raised my hand, spreading the fingers: 'We have needed five summers, a handful as you can see.'
'We rejoice already to hear all the details. Days are short and nights are long. As soon as we have erected our huts, there will be plenty of time for talk.'
That's how we came to know our relatives in the South. It felt as if we had known them from birth. We immediately connected with each other. They proved to be very charmed by our accent, because they don't pronounce words in the way we do, and use expressions unknown to us.
'Perhaps that's the reason why your ancestors traveled northwards,' they laughed, 'because of some misunderstanding!'
'That's one of the things we would like to know. Have you any idea why they decided to go away?'
They answered with a shrug: 'Our narrators sometimes speak about the end of the Time of Prosperity, about famine and illness that almost destroyed the First Tribe; about families in the Time of Great Change that went looking for game in all wind directions. We don't know the details. Our stories mention disaster and bad luck, battles with the other ones, enormous massacres, heroic deeds, love and compassion. It would be great if you can add new stories.'
'Do the stories tell you about the spirits of the mothers?'
'Of course, they do! The spirits of the mothers have a preferential place in the womb of the earth. Perhaps you like to see it next spring, when we return to the Valley of the First Tribe.'
Naturally we wanted to do so. This had been one of the aims of our journey: to get acquainted with the South of our ancestors, the South of the First Tribe!"

"At the beginning of the sixth spring we accompanied them eastward. They took their time, making many stopovers to present us to members of their family. To our amazement, they knew exactly where each group was staying. We wondered why they did not move around.

'Why should they? There is sufficient game in the environs. Most families in the Valley of the First Tribe tend to stay at the same place. There are caves and overhanging rocks serving as permanent shelters for everyone. The main reason for our journeys to Western Water is the contact with other families. Hunting and fishing together help to prevent misunderstandings. It also provides an excellent opportunity to listen to new stories and to exchange news, while our sons and daughters get a chance of meeting other young women and men. You have seen yourselves how important this is.'

'Why did our ancestors leave the Valley of the First Tribe if game abounds there? Why do so many families live outside your valley?'

Our questions amused them.

'There is only space for a limited number. Young people have to abandon the valley before their family grows too large. There is sufficient game for a small group, but not for everybody. The eldest decide who can stay or has to leave. That's the way it always has been, since the end of the Time of Prosperity.'

'Will we be welcome?'

'Of course, we always reserve a place for guests and especially for guests who have come that far.'

They did not exaggerate, on the contrary. We received everywhere a warm welcome.

Throughout summer and winter, many kinds of game live in the valleys and on the steppe; with the exception of mammoth and rhinoceros. Most people however prefer to hunt reindeer. For the first time in our life we spent the autumn at the same place where we had passed the summer. We really had to get used to it! We worried about the forthcoming winter. Would there be enough game for us all? They reassured us: 'Don't worry. Wait and see! As long as game will stay here, so do we.'

They were right. The herds did not leave. We had never disposed of so much time for the embellishment of clothing and footwear. Each night we were listening to their stories.

We have learnt so many tales! As soon as the account of our journey is completed, I shall tell you some of these."

"What have you learnt about the Time of Prosperity? You should tell us, Leya!"

Everybody turned to the man who had interrupted the story. Normally, Stille spent the day without saying a word. He felt deeply ashamed for his interruption.

"I, well, perhaps it is a stupid question, but I would like to know if people have told you something about it." He looked embarrassed, but to his surprise the rest of the audience agreed with him.

"You are right, Stille," roared someone. "I wanted to ask exactly the same question!"

"I have to disappoint you," answered Leya. "There are no stories about the Time of Prosperity; although, one day an old man approached us. He was perhaps as old as Great Narrator. In spite of his great age, he was still alert and kept a brisk pace. Living on his own, he did not appear to be very talkative, but he always listened to our stories with much interest.

'I have noticed that you are always asking about the past of the First Tribe. If you wish, I can show you something very peculiar. The members of my family have never seen it, and you must promise me not to say a word to anybody. I only share this secret with you!'

His words aroused our curiosity, so we promised him to maintain the secret. A few days later he took us to a hill with an overhanging rock, not far from the place we were staying. Owls, crows and jackdaws were nesting in the many holes and fissures. There was evidence of an old camp that had been abandoned many summers ago. We had seen similar sites before, so we gave him a questioning look.

'Since childhood I occasionally come here looking for eggs, initially with my mother, later with wife and children; and for many springs alone. You rarely find goats here, whereas horses and reindeer stay in the valley below.

This explains why no-one visits this place. Look, the remnants of this camp already existed, when I was a child. Nobody bothers to come here.'
We could easily imagine why. We never would have gone there if he had not insisted so much. Then he told us enthusiastically: 'Our ancestors have been here! They discovered an entry to the womb of the earth. Here they have honored the spirits in the Time of Prosperity!'
We started to our feet.
'In the Time of Prosperity,' had been the old man's words. How could he possibly know this? Yet again he smiled: 'Wait and see! Do you see those jackdaws up there in that hole?' He pointed at a small hole in the rock face. 'As child I was looking there for eggs. I had to roll this boulder below it in order to reach it, but there were no eggs.'
He stepped on the boulder and nimbly pulled himself up. Then he signaled us to follow his example. Krasser and I joined him, while Ursa and Durfal kept waiting below, because there was not enough space for everybody."

"Immediately to the right of the entrance we noticed the spirits of a bison and a horse. The man took a lamp, adding grease and a juniper twig; then lit it. On hands and feet he crawled deeper into the hole. On our left, another spirit of a horse became visible, ready to disappear in a narrow fissure in front of him. The man resolutely continued and we followed him, feeling our way. All of a sudden he rolled on his back and whispered: 'Come here!'
We moved nearer. Two spirits of bison emerged from a crack in the wall. Only the heads were visible, and they looked at us with large round eyes. Cautiously, the man held up the lamp again and pointed with great emotion at the ceiling immediately above his head. It took a few moments before we saw it, but then we got as excited as he was. He stammered: 'The Maker! Our ancestors dared to portray the Maker! Did you know this?'
We had never seen the Maker before, but there was no question about it. He was absolutely right.

This was the Maker, with arms and legs, hands and feet; with a head and face I shall never forget. The left ear was clearly visible, and also the mouth and the nose. We felt his searching glance while he wondered about the reason of our visit. He proudly showed us his member that had fertilised the earth on the first day.

The old man rolled on his right side and we did the same. At arm's length of the Maker, a second face emerged from the wall, staring unflinchingly at the spirit of a bear.

'This could be the face of the first human being,' whispered the man respectfully.

'Why has no-one told us this before?'

'Nobody knows this place. I told my mother about my discovery, but she refused to believe it. According to her, no man or woman would ever dare to portray the Maker. She forbade me explicitly to enter this hole again or to speak about it to other people. Perhaps she feared that I might have been mistaken, making a fool of myself. So I never dared to speak about it with anybody. You are the first persons who see this. Of course, my mother was right. Nobody would nowadays dare to depict the Maker, but ages ago our ancestors did. You have seen it yourselves!'

'This really must have been a long time ago,' remarked Krasser thoughtfully. 'You are right; these figures may have been made in the Time of Prosperity.'

'That's my opinion too,' answered the old man. 'These images stem from the Time of Prosperity. In this cave the spirit of the Maker and the spirits of humans and animals are always present. I can feel it very clearly.'

'It should be a good thing to have the spirits of our mothers here as well,' suggested Krasser. He took out the flint graver and carved the silhouette of the spirit of his mother in the wall, just below the head of the bear.

'Please, lend me the graver too, Krasser.'

Now it was my turn. I cautiously squeezed my way deeper into that space; the ceiling got lower and lower. Then I held the graver with my right hand and carved two lines in the rock above me. As by a miracle the spirit of the mother of

Great Narrator emerged from the darkness. I felt that she once more reassured me that she would protect us on our journey; in the same way that she had done it in that cave by Winding River."

Leya heaved a deep sigh as if she was awakening from a trance.

"Well, that's what I can tell you about the Time of Prosperity. We have seen the Maker as well as the spirits of the first humans and animals, and I know they accompany us until this day."

"Terrific!" said Stille. "Thank you for this explanation."

Leya nodded and continued.

"The members of the First Tribe were very interested to hear our stories about our life here in the North, and about the mammoth and rhinoceros. They listened with rapt attention to our tales and songs that we had to repeat again and again.

Our stories appeared to be completely different from theirs, even if we belong to the same tribe. We got on very well together and the eldest urged us to stay with them. It was an offer you can't refuse and I admit that we have seriously considered it. To become members of the First Tribe was something we could only dream about!

'Never again wandering around,' pondered Durfal. 'Imagine all that fish and game in front of your hut!'

'I would really miss the mammoth,' mused Krasser, 'and the rhinoceros. Will their spirits find us here in this region?'

'I think so,' reasoned Ursa. 'Don't forget that we have seen their images in several caves; and also the figures of the spirits of the mothers.'

She wanted to stay, but I hesitated.

'I'm not so sure. Our friends of the First Tribe honor the spirits of the mothers, that's true, but they don't value them in the way that we do. Do they carry their image? Thus far I have not seen it. They secretly laugh at our devotion. They suggest that we exaggerate.'

'Let us follow their example!' The idea was uttered by Ursa.

'We should adapt ourselves to their traditions, invoking from now on the protection of the spirits of horse and reindeer.' She thought that this was a matter of give and take. 'We have to be willing to renounce a very small part of our devotions, if we really want to stay with the First Tribe. Why should our traditions be better than those of these people? I completely agree with Durfal. We have to adapt ourselves or leave.'
'What about our own identity?' argued Krasser. 'What's the value of our traditions if we forget who we are?'
Over many days we pondered the arguments for and against.
'To never roam again and never again smell the scent of our northern steppe,' Durfal suddenly put forward. 'Will we miss it? The winter will have passed by and we continue to stay here on this very spot. It sounds so boring to me. At this moment the stories are new, to us and to them, but next winter, what will you tell them, Leya? Have you thought about it?'
He clearly wanted to leave. Durfal was right. We had to part. He had convinced us.
It hurt us to tell our decision to the eldest, but they sympathised with us and repeated: 'Of course, we will miss you. To us you are like brothers and sisters. Never forget that we always hold a place for you in the Valley of the First Tribe.' We felt happy and sad after these cordial words."

"In this way the seventh spring too began with saying good-bye to all these men and women, who had treated us as brothers and sisters. Many tears were shed, because everyone knew that it was not very likely that we would meet again.
An experienced hunter accompanied us. Three summers earlier, he had come to the First Tribe, looking for a girl that might want to share his bed. They had offered him hospitality, but equally to us he had become attached to a traveling way of life. Together with his smiling wife and newborn son he was going to return to his family on the eastern side of the mountains.

Bursting with impatience he went ahead, urging us to hurry up: 'We still have a long way to go, there is no time to be lost!'
He knew the way better than anybody else, never hesitating at yet another tributary. He kept on saying: 'Straight ahead, straight on upriver to the East!'
At the end of the second moon of spring, the valley became narrower and deeper. All of sudden, he made a halt and studied the environs. 'Three summers ago I made a bivouac here to rest a few days. I suggest we will now do the same. There may be goats in the area. Let's try to kill one, so that we have sufficient food for the next moon. Around this bend the valley will rise rapidly. Do you see those snow-covered summits at the horizon? No, a little more to the left. Look there, to the northeast, that's where we are heading for. From here it seems more difficult than it really is. If we are lucky, the passage up there will be free of snow. The valley passes left of that highest summit. Along the way we will collect flint as a present for my family.'
Naturally, we agreed to everything. There were no alternatives! His wife was glad to rest a few days, because the women of the First Tribe did not travel long distances. He only laughed: 'This is nothing. Wait until winter and then you will really learn to walk!'
Together with Durfal and Krasser he went to hunt. Ursa and I stayed with the woman and her baby. We collected berries and eggs, snared a few birds and some meager marmots. 'It's better than nothing,' was our comment.
The hunt turned to be a success. Four days later the men came back. Long before we saw them, we could hear their cheers. In turns they bore a goat on the shoulders. We took our time in preparing the meat and hide, whilst our guide told about his family. His enthusiasm proved infectious. In the end we all were bursting with impatience to continue as soon as possible."

"Upstream the valley was harder to go. Herbs, bushes and even the goats had disappeared. Repeatedly, we faced thick ice sheets with treacherous cracks that had to be crossed one way or another. A thin layer of slippery snow frequently masked the edges, so that is was quite dangerous to leap them. The wind was blowing increasingly stronger and it got colder as well. Fortunately, the wind came from behind. It took us six days to reach the highest point of the valley, where we had a breathtaking view of our surroundings. The valley behind us was marked by a seemingly uninterrupted white line of snow and ice, reflecting the sunlight. We could no longer detect the cracks, or the site where we had collected the flint. To our left and right, snow-covered summits towered high above us. We were lucky that we did not have to climb them! The valley ahead of us descended again in a straight line to the northeast, ending up in a wide plain that was vaguely discernible in the distance.

'Look! That's the territory of my people,' explained the guide, his face shining with pride. 'Within a few days you will see the beauty of this region for yourself, the loveliest place on earth! Nowhere else you find so many herbs and bushes, and nowhere are these as large as there.'

Initially, the descent posed more difficulties than the way uphill. A number of times we slipped away in deep ice cracks, having to pull each other up with long ropes. Two days later however we finally set up our bivouac at an ice-free place, which showed the first blades of grass. We were covered in bruises, cuts and bleeding wounds and our clothing was badly torn too.

'I don't think that we should repeat this experience,' remarked Durfal. 'We have been very lucky. Thanks to the spirit of the goat we have arrived here without broken arms or legs.'

We all agreed with him. Our guide fully endorsed his words: 'Only very few persons would have dared to travel this way. I think that we have been the first, since I went up this valley three summers ago. Look at these flint tools I left at the time.' He pointed at the remains of an old camp.

Awestruck and incredulous we asked him if he had made that journey on his own.

'Of course, I did; what else? One of the eldest incited me to this journey. I can't remember how often he related the story how he, being a young man, had found his partner on the other side of the mountains.
He convinced us that we too would find there the most beautiful women, and then he pointed at his own wife. For him she was the prettiest of all, who gave him four children. She was beautiful indeed and I adored her. She was my mother's mother. I always carry the figure of her spirit with me.'
He touched a small pouch of marmot fur that hung from his neck: 'Long ago I made this, shortly after her death.'
The figurine was as small as a bone in my finger, but we recognised the attractive round buttocks and sturdy hips of the spirit of his grandmother.
'The knowledge that she had traveled that journey with her man inspired me. She was expecting her first child, my mother. Now look at my wife; she is as beautiful as my grandmother.'
The first moon of summer had already passed before we met his family. They had pitched camp on the hillside of a narrow valley, by a northward winding river. Our guide had been right. Herbs and bushes were greener and larger than elsewhere; no wonder that game was plentiful there. We asked them why this might be and they proudly pointed at the mountains on the western side of the river.
'When the earth gets a cold or becomes ill, she starts coughing and clears her throat. The ground below us trembles and clouds of dust rise above these mountains. Nobody understands why, since we have never spotted an opening into the inner-earth, but herbs and bushes grow greener and larger in all places where this dust settles. Our ancestors recognised this phenomenon early on.'
They brought us to a well in the vicinity and said: 'Taste the water.'
We did so and discovered that the water tasted like tears, equally undrinkable as that of Southern and Western Waters.

'The eldest believe that this has been produced by the tears of the earth. There are more surprises. Follow us!'
We went with them to the river and climbed a steep slope.
'Do you see the color of the water welling out of this crack? It looks like blood. Put your hand into it and note the warmth. According to our storytellers, this is the warm blood of the earth, flowing out of an old wound. Don't drink it; it produces terrible stomach cramps.'
We were really impressed by the tears and warm blood of the earth, the dust-producing mountains - albeit that we had yet not seen this ourselves - and the vibrant green steppe around us.
Occasionally, we noticed that the ground below our feet trembled slightly, sometimes so hard that stones rolled down the hills. The first time we were scared to death, but people there did not know better and shrugged their shoulders: 'After a while you don't know any better.' That was easier said than done, especially when the tremors were accompanied by a thundering noise in the distance.
In the autumn, a cloud appeared above one of the mountains, just as they had predicted. 'These are the dust clouds,' was their explanation. The ground kept shaking whilst a rumbling noise, like a severe thunderstorm, emerged from the inner-earth. Believe me that we wished to have been elsewhere. Our guide worriedly examined the mountain. The dust cloud was getting bigger and bigger and slowly moved into our direction. A rain of dust, like the ashes of a fire, descended on our camp and covered the steppe. All the animals ran startled away.
Finally, the complete mountain exploded, vomiting stones and fire. I already told you the rest. We dropped everything and ran into all directions, but in the end our curiosity got the upper hand; primarily because we noticed there was nothing to fear. Stones and fire fell back on the mountain; at least two days walk from the place where we were. For several days we kept watching the spectacle until the mountain suddenly calmed down. The dust cloud faded away and the earth no longer trembled, but the animals did not return.

Our guide explained that they had moved northwards to the region, where they normally pass the winter. He told us that each autumn his family followed the herds, and he invited us to go with them. Naturally, we accepted his offer, and began with fresh courage a new stage of our journey.

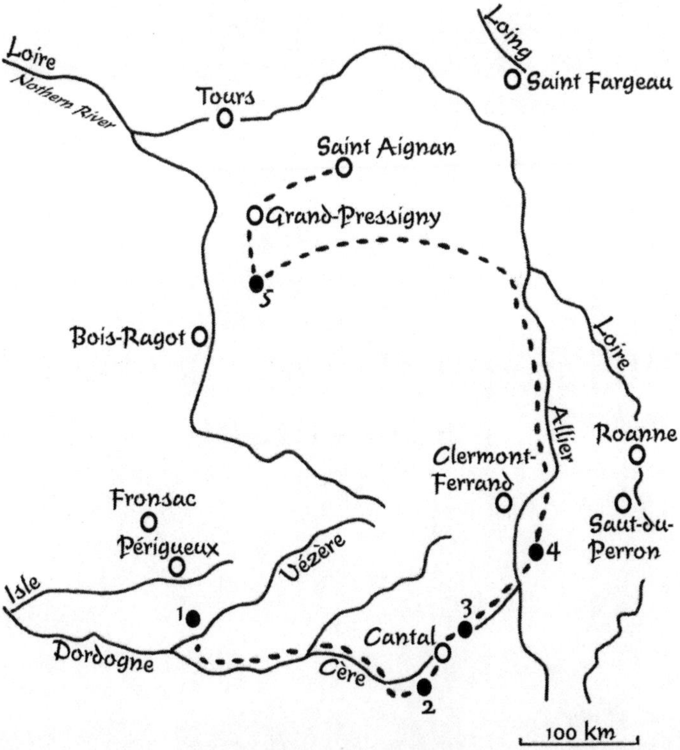

Leya's journey, seventh to eight spring, from Valley of First Tribe to winter camp of the guide's family

1 – Laugerie (Les Eyzies; residence First Tribe).
2 – Manhès-Ouest (Saint-Mamet; bivouac southwestern flank of Cantal).
3 – La Tourille-Celles, Cusers-Neussarges, Le Cavalier-Molompize (Alagnon; bivouacs northeastern flank of Cantal).
4 – Enval (Vic-le-Comte; from spring to fall camp of the guide's family).
5 – Roc-aux-Sorciers (Angles-sur-Anglin; rock shelter with Middle Magdalenian reliefs; during Late Magdalenian winter camp of the guide's family).

Bergerac, Grand-Pressigny, Saint-Aignan and Saint-Fargeau: flint sites.

Reconstruction of a Journey across Europe III

One might wonder to what extent the distances covered by our virtual friends are exaggerated or not. Current research suggests that the bands along Allier and Loire covered three to five hundred kilometers each winter. That's not a figment of our imagination!
In some cases prehistoric people completed even longer journeys. Take the Gnirshöhle as an example, a small cave in the Brudertal near Engen, at a few hundred meters from Petersfels, where a small band bivouacked 15,000 years ago. They most likely traveled deliberately in the winter. It will have been much easier to walk on the hard frozen ground and cross frozen rivers, especially if they had to carry large supplies, weapons and tool stones. Among their possessions were fossil snails from the vicinity of Reims, and tools made from flint that somebody had collected in the environs of Paris, both places situated at six hundred kilometers from the Brudertal. They also carried dog whelks from the Atlantic coast, at least eight hundred kilometers from the Gnirshöhle.

To cap it all, they carried a fossil from Kirchberg-an-der-Iller, near Ulm. If they collected all these objects themselves (and why not?), they must have covered a distance of at least one thousand kilometers before arriving at the Gnirshöhle.

Thousand kilometers may seem an enormous, perhaps even unbridgeable distance, since most of us, modern humans, do not walk that far. However, look at the journey of that family traveling to the Polish Maszycka Cave during the Middle Magdalenian. They were in the possession of Ukrainian flint, from three hundred and fifty kilometers to the east, and flint from the environs of Ulm, eight hundred kilometers to the west, and they used special bone knife-handles (so-called 'navettes'), proving they originated from the Dordogne.

All in all we are talking about a journey of at least two thousand kilometers! A similar knife-handle has been unearthed at Veyrier near Geneva, meaning that they moved from the Dordogne to Lake Geneva. From there they traveled to Kesslerloch near Schaffhausen, where they carved a musk ox head on a spear thrower. Thanks to Carole Fritz and Gilles Tosello we know that they must have learnt the therefore required technique in Northern Spain, the Pyrenees or the Dordogne. From Kesslerloch they marched along the Danube, making a stopover in the environs of Ulm to collect tool stones. Even after so many millennia, we can rather accurately reconstruct their journey.

In Austria, the Magdalenian hunters may have met a family belonging to the Eastern Tribes that for its part originated from Hungary. This may be concluded from evidence found at Grubgraben near Kammern, where flutes made from reindeer bone have been discovered. Thomas Einwögerer and Bernadette Käfer reconstructed the flutes and tried them out.

The Austrian Academy of Sciences has produced a CD, appropriately named Knochenklang (sound of bones). Perhaps the encounter has been celebrated with songs and dances,

whipped up by flutes and rhythmic instruments. At the time nobody could foresee that the journey would end with a massacre!
Near present-day Bratislava they came upon the Carpathian outliers, having the choice to continue eastward along the Danube or northward along the March or Morava. They went along the Morava up to the Becva Valley, and from there eastward along the northern flank of the Carpathian Mountains until Maszycka, north of Cracovia. These examples show that prehistoric men were really road maniacs!

We last left our friends in the environs of Roc-aux-Sorciers, Le-Grand-Pressigny or Saint-Aignan, at the end of the winter season. From there their traveling companions returned to the territories along the upper reaches of Loire and Allier. On parting they recommended our narrator to go further northwards. They may have known the groups, which lived there. This explains the presence of flint stones from Étampes and Saint-Fargeau at the site of Saut-du-Perron. Walking to the northeast, our virtual friends came upon the Essonne or the Loing, two tributaries of the Seine. Going downstream, they must have discovered one of the many campsites that have been excavated for the past fifty years, for instance Tarterets or Étiolles.
We for our part would rather take Étiolles near Paris as an example, because of the rather detailed reconstructions of daily camp life at the time. Besides, we know that many fossil snails and shells from that location had been collected in the vicinity of Reims, so that we can easily follow their footsteps upstream along the Marne.
It is only a stone's throw from Reims to the Meuse Valley in the French and Belgian Ardennes, where fossil snails from the environs of Reims and flint from the Loing Valley occur. Apparently, one and the same group hunted in spring around Étiolles and in summer in the Ardennes. They may occasionally have overwintered further westwards, near Saulges in Mayenne, where the Margot Cave has yielded

engravings of horse, rhinoceros and birds as well as the image of a stylised woman.

Anyhow, this has been one of the most extended Magdalenian hunting territories, suggesting that living conditions were less favourable in Northern than in Southern France. The vegetation may have been relatively scarce and needed more time to recover after the passage of herds. This forced the animals to forage over larger distances in the successive seasons. The hunters had no choice but to go after them. We in turn can easily follow their trail.

Our ancestors will have preferred to camp in the valleys due to the accessibility of water, a vital necessity. However, the campsites in the Seine Basin were frequently flooded; a disaster for those people, but a welcome opportunity for archeologists. We are able to get detailed information about the design and function of successive camps and huts, tools and weapons, and more or less successful hunting seasons and game. In the valleys of the Belgian Ardennes they found shelter in the many caves by the rivers.

One site deserves a special mention: Roc-la-Tour, on the northern slopes of the Semois Valley, slightly north of Charleville-Mézières. The site is situated at two hundred and seventy meters above the river, a quarter of an hour walk. It consists of two very small rock formations, each one with a surface of only a few hundred square meters. Magdalenian hunters made their bivouac on the eastern platform, where three rocks offered a perfect outlook in all directions. Today, this view is partly blocked by trees. Farther down, the Semois flows into the Meuse. Abandoned slate quarries indicate how people made a living in these valleys less than a century ago. Today it is a perfect place for visitors like us, for cyclists and hikers.

Why did a small band of prehistoric hunters (ten to fifteen individuals) select the top of a hill for their bivouac, a place without water? You have to walk some six hundred meters to the nearest well. They must have had powerful reasons to camp right there and return again and again, each time carrying pieces of shale they had collected somewhere down in the valley. The ground dries very quickly after rain, that's an advantage. They could find ochre, a then very popular item; and it was an excellent outlook, especially in a treeless environment. We for our part would have chosen to stay down in the valley near the water, where vegetation (including branches for fire) and game were more abundant, rather than having to haul it all uphill.

Colette and Jean-Georges Rozoy believe that they preferred Roc-la-Tour because of its magic appeal: the 'place of the spirits'. Many pieces of slate were used to engrave images of horse, bison, mammoth, bear, deer, wolf or dog, lynx and fish, stylised women without a head and other human figures. They also carved hundreds of signs and symbols in these stones, among which peculiar zigzags. The latter ones are distributed across Europe; just as the figures of stylised women. Comparable zigzags were recognised in Saaleck in Germany, six hundred and fifty kilometers eastwards, at Fornols-Haut in the eastern Pyrenees, thousand kilometers to the south, and from there another thousand kilometers to the southwest at Siega-Verde on the Spanish meseta. These are all open-air sites surrounded by rocks. Should we ascribe these zigzags to shamans who may or may not have been in a hallucinogenic trance, or do we have other explanations?

The homogeneous style of the images, signs and symbols of Roc-la-Tour suggests that these were made by one and the same person or group of persons, belonging to a band that thirty to forty times bivouacked at this site. Starting from the idea of one bivouac a year, we are talking of thirty to forty years; less than a human life time. It is thus well possible that only one artist made all the engravings. Did he or she encourage the members of the band to return here at least once a year, to perform some sort of ritual? It is an acceptable hypothesis. Maybe, this person was indeed a shaman. Afterwards no-one has bivouacked here again. Had the magic lost its force? Had the artist passed away? Did the group no longer exist, had it moved to another territory? All these questions are still waiting to be answered!

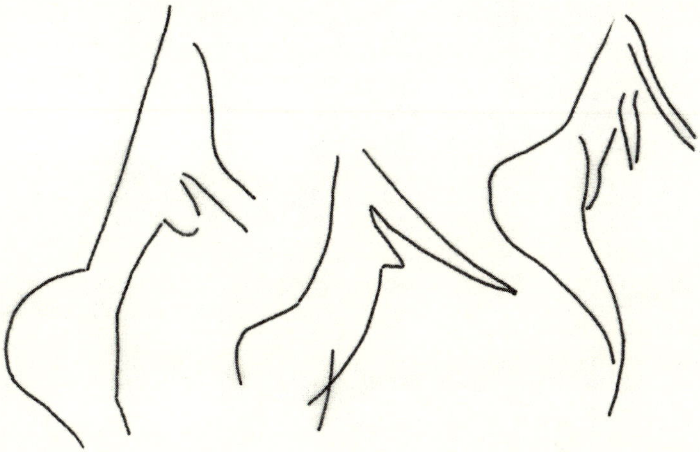

Engravings of stylised women of Lalinde-Gönnersdorf type
(sprits of the mothers)

Left: Gönnersdorf (Neuwied; after Bosinski a.o., 2001).
Center: Pestillac (Montcabrier; after Sentis, 2005).
Right: Gare-de-Couze (Couze-et-Saint-Front; after Duhard, 1993).

Distance between Gönnersdorf and other locations is 1,000 km, between Gare-de-Couze and Pestillac 50 km.

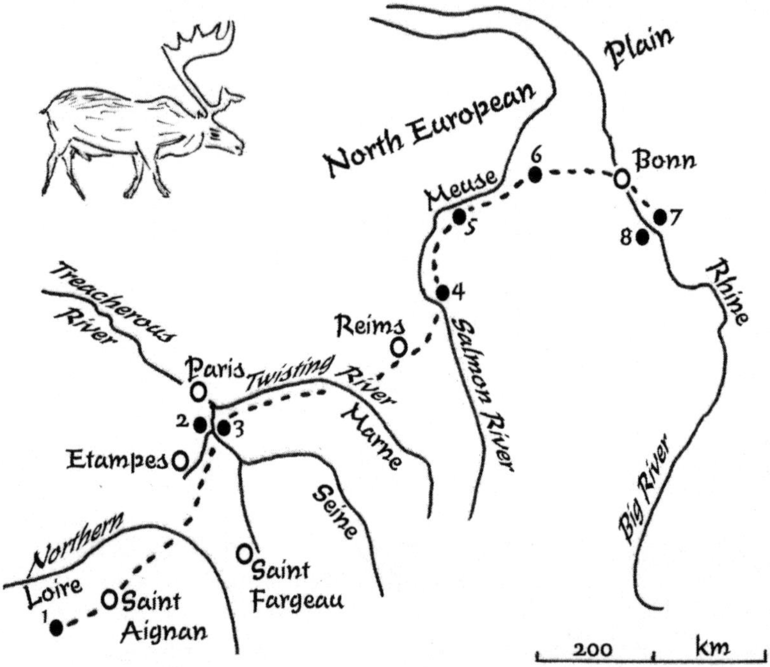

Leya's journey, eighth spring to eighth winter, from winter camp of the guide's family to winter camp of Leya and Great Narrator

1 – Roc-aux-Sorcier
(Angles-sur-Anglin; rock shelter with Middle Magdalenian reliefs; during Late Magdalenian winter camp of the guide's family).

2 – Tarterets
(Corbeil-Essonnes; at high water flooded camp of Northerners).

3 – Étiolles
(Corbeil-Essonnes; spring camp of Northerners).

4 – Roc-la-Tour
(Semois; summer camp Northerners).

5 – Goyet
(Mazet; summer camp Northerners).

6 – Eyserheide
(South-Limburg; fall camp of Krasser's brother).

7 – Gönnersdorf
(Neuwied; winter camp Leya and Great Narrator; only few kilometers from Niederbieber where two thousand years later people of the Federmesser Culture carved stylised women in a piece of sandstone).

8 – Andernach
(Rhine; western camp of Leya after flooding of the Rhine).

Saint-Aignan, Saint-Fargeau and Etampes: flint deposits. Environs of Reims: site of fossil snails and shells that were used as ornaments.

15,000 years ago

Finally Home Again

"The wind is shifting, Leya, and it's not snowing so heavily any more. Maybe we have seen the worst. With a bit of luck, we may get nice weather tomorrow. It's about time too! We are running out of supplies."

She nodded thoughtfully. "Be patient, Krasser! You keep staring at the horizon in the hope of spotting one of the scouts. They only left yesterday, they need time. Be patient, they will be back!"

"Perhaps they are lost; or worse!"

"Don't be so pessimistic! Give them time to do their job. They are experienced hunters! Your brother is with them!"

He had his doubts: "I don't know. It was a stupid decision to stay here."

"Nonsense! We need good men here in the camp, don't forget it!"

He agreed with a sigh: "You have always been an optimist!"

"With good reason, since the spirits of the mothers and the mammoth have never let me down!"

He smiled. "All right, let us wait until tomorrow. I am happy that you can entertain our people with the next account of our journey. They are very impressed by our adventures.

Try to finish the story tonight. If the weather really changes, there will be no more time for stories this winter."
"I shall try."

"I have promised Krasser to keep it short this night. With some luck we can finally hunt tomorrow. This means that in the forthcoming time we won't be able to gather quietly around the fire."
"But we need to eat!" objected someone. "You can continue the story while we are eating!"
"Thank you! You like to eat and listen whilst letting me starve!"
The speaker bowed ashamed his head: "Sorry, it did not occur to me."
"Yeah! I have to eat even more than the usual," added Leya, softly touching her belly. "Krasser is right. I better recount the last part of our journey."

"Last night you have heard that we left the valleys near that fire and dust vomiting mountain in the seventh autumn. Our guide said: 'In winter this place is too cold, and it snows too much, even for the animals. Each fall we therefore follow the herds to the north, where they overwinter.' Krasser, Durfal and Ursa will fully endorse that it was a long journey. It was very easy to follow the trail of horse and reindeer, even if we had lost sight of the game. 'Don't worry,' remarked our guide, 'we know the region they are heading for. By the end of the autumn we will run down the stragglers.' New families joined us on the way, who all appeared to be close relatives of our guide. Beaming with pride he presented them his wife and child. It took us a full moon to catch up with the herds that by then had been distributed over many valleys in the undulating landscape. For the first time in many winters we saw mammoth and rhinoceros. 'In this region it rarely snows in winter, in any case much less than on the steppe we have left behind us. The animals will find enough to graze here,' they assured us."

"Halfway the second moon of winter we found shelter below an overhanging rock. Their ancestors had adorned the back wall by carving figures of the spirits of bison, horse and goat. Each figure seemed to emerge straight from the wall and was nearly as large as a living animal. The sprits of the ancestral mothers had a preferential place amidst all those animals, and that's how it should be too.
They had selected this place with much care. Throughout the day the rock wall was warmed by the sun, whilst the cold northern winds had no grip on it. We built a long hut against the wall, large enough for us all. Long ago someone had made holes in the wall for fixing hides, giving every family its own space. They offered us the central room where the spirits of bison and ancestral mothers kept watch over us.
Other families chose the rooms with the spirits of horse or bison to our left, spaces that from the early morning were warmed by the sun. Our guide's family preferred the right side where the spirits of goats played a leading part. 'We always choose this part,' said our guide, 'because so many spirits are here united. Look here to the left, the spirit of a bison, and there, below that young goat, the spirit of an ancestral mother. The large male in the center clearly is the leader of the herd. He shares this special position with the spirits of lion, reindeer and horse, which have been carved below. We have also found a place for the spirits of the dead.' To our utter amazement we noticed two human faces with eyes, nose and mouth. 'Why do these spirits have a face?' we asked. 'We didn't think spirits needed it' He laughed: 'You are quite right, spirits don't have a face. We know it. But the people who made these drawings preferred to remember their loved ones as they were in life. They really must have loved them, I guess.'"

"In our room too, someone had drawn the face of his loved one in the wall, just above the spirits of the ancestral mothers. In the flickering light of the fire his eyes stared down at us. We did not know his name, but we felt that he was watching over us. Of course, below all these images Krasser added a stone too, depicting the spirits of the mothers. That winter we would be safe, benefiting from ample protection. We stayed there until the end of the third moon. From the top of the rock we could easily survey the surrounding area and especially the valley south of us that narrowed just in front of our camp. The deep river and strong current prevented the game to escape. Thus, we always drove our quarry in the direction of the camp where the hunters awaited to kill them."

"Next we moved slightly further northwards to collect flint stones. The valleys in that region sheltered the animals against the ice-cold northern wind. We could not complain. Halfway the winter's fifth moon our supplies were large enough to continue our northward journey. Our friends too were preparing their way back, in the hope to reach the southern territories before the thaw set in. We had decided not to wait until spring, since the many rivers might burst their banks. Everybody rejoiced to be on the move again.
However, the night before our departure a heavy snow storm surprised us. This was unprecedented in that region, according to our friends. In no time our tents were buried by snow flurries. I can assure you that it was as bad as it is now. The storm lasted two days and two nights, and then the wind changed and it stopped snowing. We removed the snow with great difficulty and recovered our supplies. All around as far as the eye could see was white and beyond recognition. However, the southwestern wind made the snow vanish very quickly and the valleys turned green again. Everywhere, water ran from the hills to the brook below us that got wider and wider and finally turned into a swirling river. Fortunately, our camp was situated high enough, outside the reach of that wild water. The surroundings of the camp however had changed, yet again, into a vast quagmire, in which our feet got bogged down. It became impossible to traverse the mud. We had to postpone our departure until the ground dried.

The dogs around the camp had disappeared, and ravens and gulls too. They had obviously discovered a carcass. Wolves and lions were disputing carrions in the distance, while more and more eagles and vultures were gliding through the sky. We went to size up the situation and found that the steppe was strewn with the dead bodies of animals that had not survived the snow storm. The carcasses were too numerous for all the wolves, wolverines and vultures that had gathered there. Never before had we seen so much dead game. We collected hides, long bones and the best quarters of meat as quickly as possible.
A few days later the cold returned. We immediately left, walking northeastwards across the frozen ground. Only the dogs followed us. The guide had already warned that nobody would be prepared to accompany us. 'Every winter we come here, and never go farther. We don't feel at home in the territory of the Northerners*, north of Northern River. We don't visit each other nor exchange partners. They rarely come here in our territory, and we for our part respect the boundaries that had been established ages ago. I have met them a few times; they behave differently, dress differently. I can't imagine that they would be related to your family, but perhaps they can help you further.'
Our journey went smoothly. The westward flowing rivers were all frozen, so that we could easily cross them, just as they had told us. We finally came upon a brook that ran northwards, a sign that we had reached the territory of the Northerners.
Ages ago, people had called us Northerners too. We had considered this a loving nickname, since we came from the North. What could we expect from these Northerners? Would they be kind and hospitable? It would be wise to let our presence be known. We pitched our tent and made a big fire with lots of smoke, but waited in vain for an answer. Apparently, nobody was dwelling around there.
The beginning of thaw heralded the spring, the eighth one of our journey. We followed the brook until it joined a wide river that flowed through a broad valley towards the north-

west. At the bottom of the slope, on our left hand, we discovered the remains of two abandoned huts. The encrusted mud indicated that the river had recently flooded the banks, driving the residents away. We had no idea whether they would return and decided to stay there.
It was a nice place. Flowering herbs covered the steppe. We could once more feast on the succulent leaves of bistort, chive, wormwood and dandelion. In between all that green vegetation, we discovered again and again the partly eaten carcasses of animals, victims of the snow storm that two moons earlier had hit us. Wolves, foxes, martens, ravens and vultures were chewing the bones and pecking away at the meat. We also saw some bears that had recently awoken from their winter sleep. Our presence seemed not to bother them.
Every day we built a fire to make ourselves known, until four days later we noticed smoke in the distance. Somebody was answering our signal! The next day, the Northerners reached our camp, keeping the dogs at a distance with assegais and stones, since these had no intention to admit those strangers into their territory.
We left our weapons deliberately on the ground. Two men stepped cautiously forward, an assegai in each hand, giving us a questioning look. The rest kept a safe distance. It was quite obvious that they were not used to meeting strangers. Durfal for his part stepped forward too and did the talking. They looked surprised when he began to speak and then appeared to be relieved. They could understand us without any difficulty! Durfal explained who we were and what we were doing there. Then he pointed at our fire and invited them to sit with us. They briefly considered what to do, put aside their weapons and called the rest, who could no longer restrain their curiosity. They ran nearer, casting eager eyes over the food that we had laid out. It had been a good idea to offer it, because they looked weak and in bad shape. They urgently needed new clothing and footwear. They helped us with the fire and soon the campsite smelled after roasted meat that we eagerly wolfed down.

It was dark before everyone was satisfied. Only the next day did we get into conversation.
They had indeed escaped from the rapidly rising water. Due to the thaw after the heavy snow, the ice in the river had suddenly broken up. In the middle of the night, they had heard the ice breaking and subsequently floes were gliding on top of each other with tremendous violence. The next moment the river they called Treacherous River*, had burst its banks and flooded the huts. They only managed to escape by the skin of their teeth, loosing all the supplies. The past two moons they had been wandering around, eating the meat of the carcasses. They had been very surprised to see the smoke from our fire. As far as they knew no-one else was living in their territory. They tended to overwinter in a gorge, somewhere in the West; where the sun sets. Several caves in that region were connected with the womb of the earth, the residence of the spirits. In spring they hunted reindeer along Treacherous River, but this time all their provisions had disappeared. Fortunately, we disposed of a large pile of hides, which we gladly shared with them. We moved the camp to the opposite bank, where a small brook ran from the north into Treacherous River. There we had everything near at hand: stones for the fire and large pieces of flint to make tools and weapons. The brook valley with its many willow and birch bushes was a perfect place for a drive. Within just a few days we came upon a mare with her young and a stallion.
Through cunning and patience we managed to drive them slowly into the valley, where the hunters were awaiting with their assegais at hand.
A few days later we had the chance to kill an adult reindeer and a bison. Whilst the meat was drying and we were dressing the hides, the children came dragging a mammoth bone. From early morning till late at night they drummed on it with stones and antler pieces. They could not get enough of it.
We did not stay long. At the beginning of the second moon of spring they proposed us to accompany them eastwards,

where they knew several sites with splendid snails and shells. From there we would go northward to hunt for reindeer. It did not take much persuading.

The day before our departure one of the women brought a very peculiar stone to the camp.

'Look what I found,' said she trembling with emotion. 'Have you ever seen something similar?'

It was a big, flat, curvaceous stone.

'It is a woman's body,' exclaimed one of the Northerners. 'I see a lovely waist and nicely rounded hips!'

He grasped a piece of charcoal and drew a triangle on the stone.

'Now it looks like the spirit of an ancestral mother!'

'You are really right,' agreed Krasser. 'This looks like the spirit of an ancestral mother, but wait a moment.'

He turned the stone and drew a few lines with the charcoal.

'What do you see now? These are the spirits of the mothers!'

He earned a warm applause. The spirits of the ancestral mothers and the mothers on one and the same stone, a better protection was unthinkable. We made a little hole in front of our tent to put the stone upright. The woman who had discovered the stone was beaming with pride. That night she was rewarded with the biggest long bone to suck out the marrow."

"The next day we came upon a river running from the east, that they called Twisting River* because of its many bends. Without hesitation, they showed us various sites, where countless snails and shells are living underground. Unfortunately, they always die as soon as they are touched by the sunshine. We never saw living specimens. We have made some beautiful ornaments from them.

The summer had started already when we came to another valley, at two days' walk to the north. The many bends in the river reminded us of the Twisting River we had left behind, but the hills were almost as high as here, around our winter camp.

They told us that they usually passed the summer there and claimed: 'There are many caves and rock shelters for our bivouac and abundant game as well.'
They were right. We discovered many fresh tracks of horse, reindeer and goat, and a few tracks too of a donkey and a bison. According to our friends, there also lived bears, foxes and wolves.
We saw large salmons swimming in the water, which immediately attracted Ursa's attention. 'Look at all that fish! There are at least as many as we normally see in the Salmon River*, where your brother took us, Krasser.'
The Northerners looked surprised and proclaimed: 'Our ancestors already used that name for this river. This is the Salmon River! Could this be your Salmon River too?'
Krasser gave a shrug.
'I don't think so. The valley where my brother and I grew up was shallow and wide, and the hills were low.'
'This may be the same river. After half a moon walk, the hills will get lower and the valley broader; but that is beyond our territory.'
Krasser's eyes started gleaming.
'Perhaps that is the region where I was born! My brother may be hunting there at this very moment!'
He suddenly was in a hurry and wanted to move on. Our companions sympathised with his feelings and offered to travel into that direction. We naturally embraced their offer!"

"Before departing they wished to propitiate the spirits as they always did. They took us to a place, where we could cross the river, and on to a tributary flowing from the east. In front of us was a large hill.
'Up there we always beg for rain. As you can see, the herbs on the slopes around us are withering already, so that game will not stay here very long.'
Initially we wondered if the spirits would go to the top of a hill, as we believed that they resided in the inner-earth. The Northerners however assured us that they had discovered several entries to the womb of the earth.

'Moreover, we are closer to the clouds that might bring us the rain,' they argued.
Uphill we noticed several deep cracks in the rocks that might well be entrances to the inner-earth. We had to repeatedly walk up and down the hill, because there was no well near the top and the slopes were devoid of any tree or bush. Even the pieces of shale we needed to get into contact with the spirits had to be carried to the top."

"Every day we called the spirits by engraving their image in the stone, similar to how we do this here. After just a few days the first clouds appeared in the sky. We were very pleased to see the rain pouring down in abundance, in the end even more than we had expected. In fact, we did not know that it could rain so much and so long in summer. At the start of next moon, the slopes of Salmon Valley had turned completely green, but we did not find much game. Apparently, only a small number of animals had survived that heavy snowfall in the past winter. There were more herbs than ever before, but the herds stayed away. We had to content ourselves with a stray aurochs and a few reindeer. Fortunately, Ursa captured as many fish as we needed. We had hoped not to arrive empty-handed at Krasser's brother, but we were unable to amass sufficient meat and hides; with the exception of herbs of course!"

One of the eldest interrupted the story.
"We have had exactly the same experience. Last summer it had been raining heavily here in the North. It never happened before, as far as we can remember. You are right, the plains were indeed lush and green, but there was not much game to hunt."
All the audience sided with the speaker. Everyone tried to make clear to Leya that the past winter and summer had been really disastrous for the group. They all wanted to have their say at the same time. Leya hardly understood a word, but she could easily read the concern on their faces. She decided to finish the story as soon as possible.

"At the onset of autumn we saw that the Salmon River was bending again to the north. We had to say goodbye to the Northerners. They went along a tributary that flowed from the south, while we continued our northward journey.
Two days later Krasser recognised the environs, where he in his childhood had learnt to make his first tools. Ursa, Durfal and I vaguely remembered having been there some day. We made a big fire with lots of humid leaves so that the smoke would be visible in the distance. Just before dark another smoke column appeared at the horizon. The next day Krasser finally met his brother again."
Leya looked at Krasser and his brother's family. Yet again she noticed the tears in their eyes; just as in the past fall.
"Well, you all know how this story ended. Krasser's brother had had a poor hunting season too, but in spite of this we celebrated our reunion for several days. Only one thing went terribly wrong. We lost the snails and shells we had collected by Twisting River. Somewhere on the way, we apparently forgot the bag with the ornaments. We all know that this happens from time to time."

She fell silent and emotionally squeezed the hands of Krasser and her mother. She felt the warm hands of Durfal and Ursa patting her back and looked at the radiating faces around her. Everybody joked about the fact that they had forgotten the ornaments. Leya was right; these things could happen now and again.

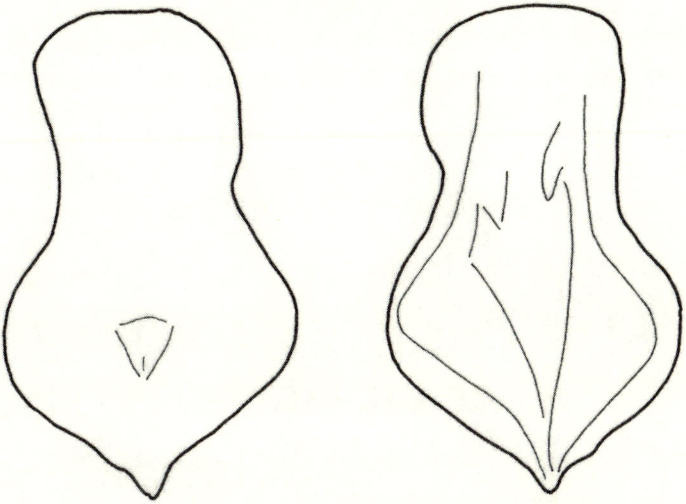

The flat stone of Étiolles (Corbeil-Essonnes, Seine; spring camp of Northerners by Treacherous River)

The possible meaning of this stone (well over forty centimeters) has been extensively analysed in a publication by Nicole Pigeot. She and Marianne Christensen draw the attention to the female curvatures and compare these with the outlines of two stylised female silhouettes 'facing' each other, similar to those observed at Lalinde and Gönnersdorf. Krasser's charcoal drawing (right) has been inspired by Pigeot's and Christensen's example.
Yvette Taborin highlights the location, where the stone has been discovered, suggesting that it was intentionally placed there. She recalls that Magdalenian people frequently used the natural outlines of stones and rocks in expressing their mythological thoughts. One of the Northerners has done this as well by drawing a vulva on the left image.
Gilles Tosello however questions the correctness of these interpretations that in his view are going too far.
Unfortunately, any possible charcoal drawings by Krasser or the Northerners (as imagined by the authors of this book) have vanished completely in the course of time, so that nobody knows who is right.

Reconstruction of a Journey across Europe IV

Eyserheide is a small hamlet, romantically situated on a flat hill, north of Eys, about halfway between Aachen and Maastricht. Time seems to stand still here and the panoramic view over the hills and valleys of South-Limburg makes this a privileged place to live. It is one of our favourite walking areas, where we regularly return.
In 1990, someone discovered here the remnants of a small Late Magdalenian bivouac, but the finds were rather disappointing. Only stone tools and some ochre were unearthed, because the acid groundwater had dissolved possible bones and traces of vegetation. Some of the tools were used to work hides and antlers, but we can only speculate whether a reindeer has been butchered on the spot or if the hunters carved into naturally shed antlers. Nothing can be said about the vegetation, due to the absence of pollen and charcoal.
The location of the bivouac on top of the hill suggests that it served as an outlook for spotting game. From there, they could survey the Eyserbrook Valley to the south, the dry

Krakelberg Valley to the north and the Geul Valley to the west, because at the time no trees or bushes will have barred their view. The limited dimensions of the site suggest a single brief stay.
They must have made a well-considered choice when they opted for this strategic site. Each individual hunt was carefully planned. Perhaps they drew rough maps of their surroundings on the ground, including the course of the streams, the hills and the exact position of the spotted game, whilst discussing the best way to approach the quarry. You may object that this is pure speculation, but Pilar Utrilla and her colleagues recognised similar maps on stones in the cave of Abauntz in Northern Spain! According to her, comparable sketches were also made some 25,000 years ago in various places across Europe. It is further evidence that our prehistoric relatives possessed the same mental powers as our own.

First-rate flint occurs everywhere in the vicinity; very easy to make tools and weapons as those people were well aware. At the end of the winter they have carried with good reason a flint supply to their winter camps in Gönnersdorf and Andernach in the Rhine Valley. Jos Deeben and Eelco Rensink mention similar bivouacs from elsewhere in South-Limburg, the neighbouring Lower Rhine region and the Peel area. Some of these have yielded stones, which had been imported from the Middle Rhine Valley (between Mainz and Emmerich); an indication that hunters traveled regularly back and forth between the Rhine and Meuse valleys. We therefore imagine that Eyserheide was only one of countless bivouacs in a vast hunting territory that may have stretched from Mainz and Luxembourg up to the mouth of the Channel River into the Atlantic. This hypothesis explains the drawings of seals and sea turtles in Gönnersdorf and Andernach, as well as the presence of fossils, which had been collected around Mainz and Luxembourg.
People from the Paris region hunted in the French and Belgian Ardennes, but did not collect flint in South-Limburg.

Apparently, they knew that this area belonged to a different territory, but this boundary will not have formed an obstacle for our fictitious travelers, who followed the Meuse downstream as far as South-Limburg.
In our imagination they bivouacked at Eyserheide and carried flint stones from that vicinity to their winter camp in Gönnersdorf by the Rhine; a distance of one hundred and fifty kilometers. This is the last trail we have to follow. Thanks to the extremely detailed information, we can tell you exactly that they resided in hut number two of Gönnersdorf.
They arrived there late in winter or early in spring, just after the birth of the first foals. They did kill them, as we have noticed earlier. Perhaps they arrived just in time to meet the residents of the other huts, who were already preparing to depart along the Rhine to the north or the south. Harald Floss and Martina Sensburg enumerate the precise locations, where our friends had collected the flint. Some flint tools stem from Simpelveld, a few kilometers east of Eyserheide, and were later abandoned in huts one and four of Gönnersdorf; as if they were meant as a special gift for their family.

A trip in the midst of an Ice Age winter from South-Limburg to Gönnersdorf may seem odd to us, but it was the best thing they could do. Remember those people who resided in the Gnirshöhle near Engen. They arrived there in winter and stayed just a few weeks, long enough to hunt, replace their supplies and repair their clothing and footwear.
The hunters of Allier and Loire traveled in winter too, collecting flint stone around Saint-Aignan and Le-Grand-Pressigny.
Winter was perhaps the best time for traveling on the frozen ground and crossing frozen rivers. As soon as the ground was thawing out, people had to slog through the mud. Besides, they knew from experience that spring was the season of breaking ice and flooding rivers.

Whatever the case may be, our friends' arrival in Gönnersdorf at the end of winter or beginning of spring, makes clear, that they must have spent autumn and part of the winter in South-Limburg. This perfectly matches a spring camp in Étiolles and a summer stay in the French and Belgian Ardennes; thus closing the circle! And so, after a journey of eight years, they finally returned to the place of their departure.

15,000 years ago

Difficult Decision

The wind had changed in the past night. The air was less cold and it had stopped snowing. For the first time since the end of the winter's fourth moon the sun woke them up. There was not a single cloud in the deep blue sky. As far as the eye could see, everything was covered by a thick layer of glittering white snow that might soon disappear now that thaw had set in. There were no tracks of any game. The silence was only disturbed by a pair of croaking ravens, which glided high above their heads looking for something edible; but even they could not find anything to their taste.
In the camp, people were milling around. They started with the daily ritual of removing snow on and around the huts and inspecting the strongly depleted kindling. Nobody knew how to replenish it, because all the vegetation lay invisible below the snow. No-one had expected that the snowfall would last that long. It was the umpteenth time now that they looked for a possibly forgotten food stock; once again they had to admit that practically all food was gone! Even the dogs had abandoned the camp, since all the bones were used to keep the fires burning. If they wanted to get something to eat, they had to go hunting immediately.

Prospects were unfavorable. The snow had wiped out every possible trail and in many places they sank down to their waist in it. The hunters had been out looking for game and had yet to return. They might have lost their way in the snow storm, being unable to find the camp. Impatiently pacing up and down, people repeatedly scanned the horizon hoping for a sign of life. They had rarely been so worried and irritated. It came as quite a relief, when a small speck became visible on the other side of Big River. It rapidly became larger and they ran into its direction. It appeared to be Prater, one of the men from the East, who wildly gesticulating neared the camp.
"We have spotted mammoths," he shouted excitedly, "three females and a young! We discovered them yesterday; at a day's walk from here. They look exhausted and move slowly northward. Tomorrow or the next day they may arrive in the area, unless they change their route. Krasser's brother is tracking them. Quick, there is no time to waste! Let us get ready! We can ambush them. This is our best and only chance!"
Everybody started cheering: three mammoth cows and a calf, all exhausted! It meant sufficient food until spring if they could kill these. That would be a tremendous relief. Only Ursa refused to share their joy. She looked at Durfal who like the rest rejoiced at the news that food was on the way.
She nudged him saying: "We never hunted mammoths! Why do we have to now? There are only so few! These may be even the last ones! Can you imagine a steppe devoid of mammoths? Why don't we wait for the other hunters? They have perhaps spotted horses or reindeer. There must be plenty of them. There is still food for a few more days."
Durfal looked surprised.
"Do you know what happens if no reindeer is found; no horse, no bison and no saiga? We will be facing real trouble! Our stocks are depleted! Remember Leya and the other pregnant women. Should they and the children starve to death?"

A third one came into the discussion.
"Ursa is right, Durfal. We never killed mammoths. How will our souls find their way to the womb of the earth without the help of the spirits of the mammoths?"
"In the East we eat rhinoceros if we are hungry," commented Prater. "There may be more mammoths than you are aware of."
"I completely agree with Prater," intervened a fifth person. "It's them or us, don't forget that!"
The cheering subsided. Everybody followed the discussion that got more and more passionate.
"Take it easy," Krasser said. "Why should we be quarreling now? Let us list all the arguments and submit these to the eldest. Let them decide for us. That's the way we have always abided by."
"I don't see the point," argued someone. "The eldest will keep brooding and wavering. Next, the mammoths disappear and we will have nothing to eat. We have to act at once!"
Krasser shook his head.
"You are speaking like a fool! Our group will break up if everybody decides for himself without listening to the eldest. Do you prefer to hunt alone on the steppe, without the support of the rest, without sufficient people? Who will look after your wounds? Who will search herbs if you get ill? Who will help your wife giving birth to her children? Who will breast them if she has no milk? We have to stay united!"
The other person interrupted him: "Nonsense! Don't be foolish! Without food we will die. What do the eldest contribute to the hunt? I only see them eat our supplies. Without them we would have food for everyone! Keeping united is senseless if there is no food! How can the spirit of the mammoth help us if we all die?"
Krasser became enraged, pushing the man aside: "Enough! Last winter snow was worse than now and then thaw set in. We found dead game everywhere; enough to survive. Why should this be different now? Why can't we wait for a few

more days? Should we kill the last mammoths for no other reason than that you are unable to wait a few days?"
"And what happens if we don't find any dead game?" The other one was really angry now, emphasising his words with wild gestures.
The hide at the entrance of the principal hut was pushed aside. Leya's mother and the rest of the eldest appeared. They had heard the uproar and discussions. To them it came as no surprise. They had been deliberating for days before they ordered the hunters to track for game. They all could see the concern on their faces.
Leya's mother straightened her back and stepped forward. She raised her left hand showing them a piece of shale with the white outlines of the spirit of a mother. Everybody recognised the image.
It was the figure made by Krasser after Great Narrator's funeral.

The last speaker stepped involuntarily backward. Being face to face with the eldest he did not know what to say. She kept looking hard at him. He tried to evade her glance, bowing his head down to the ground. She approached him slowly.
"Am I greatly mistaken if I say that you entrusted yourself to the spirit of the mammoth? You can tell me if I am wrong. Nobody will hurt you. Come on! Do you fear an old woman who eats your food?"
He did not answer. He preferred to become invisible below the white snow. Ashamed, he tried to step backward, but failed because Krasser was standing in the way. Finally, he admitted: "I can't remember what I said. My mind was only focused on food, nothing else."
"We are worried too; long before you were. We hoped that the spirits would help us in finding a solution."

"Perhaps they did!" It was Leya's voice. "Is it possible that Great Narrator's spirit has sent us those mammoths to solve our problem?"

She heard a sigh of relief rising from all those throats. Had the spirits sent the mammoths? Had the Maker got mercy? Was he prepared to sacrifice the last mammoths to save them?

Her mother turned around, examined the faces of the eldest and noticed their doubts. Then she directed herself again to her audience. "I am afraid that this matter can't be solved by the eldest alone. Everybody should have a chance of saying his piece. Our future is at stake. Let us deliberate together. There is still time. I suggest that the majority decides."

Drastic Changes

The Stingenberg in Bonn-Oberkassel is an idyllic place, where the locals take their dogs for a daily walk. The usual route passes by 'the grave with the dog,' a place where a hundred years ago the skeletons of a man, a woman and a dog were unearthed. A bill board at the entrance to the former basalt quarry marks the spot of this peculiar find; the remnants appeared to date from the Late Ice Age.
They are now exhibited to the public in the Rheinisches Landesmuseum in Bonn. We doubt if it matches the intention of the people who committed these bodies to the earth. There are many more things that they could not imagine. Otherwise, they would perhaps have looked for another place to bury their beloved ones; but would this have been effective? Sooner or later the skeletons would have been uncovered; that is a given.
What will this place look like in the next fifty years? Will it be covered with apartments, or will people like us be musing in front of this bill board? Fortunately, we can't see the future, no more than our prehistoric relatives.
Try for a moment to imagine the landscape of 15,000 years ago; devoid of houses or roads and practically without trees and bushes.

Our distant relatives dug a shallow hole at the feet of the hill, wide enough for two bodies and space for a dog, as can be seen on that reconstruction in the museum in Bonn. To the west, they overlooked the Rhine Valley that has changed only little since then. The shape of the Stingenberg was different however before the basalt quarry came into being. Moreover, 15,000 years ago the level of the Rhine was fifteen meters higher than today. This means a yearly deepening or incision of the river bedding with one millimeter. One millimeter a year may not impress us, but the final result is spectacular. Fifteen meters is equivalent to the height of a four to five story building!

Every river flows from high to low, from the mountains or hills in the source area to the lowlands around a lake or a sea. In the highlands the force of the currents produces erosion that deepens and broadens the valley. The river carries the erosion material in the form of gravel, sand and clay. As soon as the current slows down, these products will settle again; firstly stones and gravel, then sand and finally clay. In the western coastal region of the Netherlands, the Rhine has locally deposited up to twenty meters of sediment through the past fifteen thousand years.

This process continues into present times. Enormous amounts of money are spent with good reason on dredging, in order to maintain the water depth of the lower courses of the Meuse and the Rhine. We try to force natural processes to our will, keeping rivers under control or making them run in the desired direction. It works rather well as long as we are ready to pay for it.

Sometimes, it may be wiser and cheaper to adapt to the circumstances or anticipate events and restructure or even move complete seaports and cities. Complete villages had to make way for the German brown coal quarries near Mönchengladbach and Erkelenz, whereas one and a half million people had to move for the construction of the Three Gorges Dam in the Chinese Changjiang or Yangtze River.

Naturally, other options are possible. The Foz Côa reservoir project in Portugal was stopped in the very last minute because the government attached more importance to the recently discovered prehistoric heritage. The move of cultural-historical monuments, such as the Nubian temples of Abu Simbel, one of the principal tourist attractions in Southern Egypt, has proved to be another option. We have the knowledge and the means to realise these projects. The question is if we want to do it.
Residents in coastal regions will get hit twice. On the one hand they have to resolve the problem of sediments brought by the rivers, and on the other they are facing the raising sea level. This must be really worrisome, especially in the lowest regions.
Every Dutchman has learnt about the flood disaster of 1953 or the Saint Elisabeth Flood of 1421. These could have been prevented by early reinforcement of dikes and dams, by increasing their height and pumping out or draining away the excess of water. The same holds for the Katrina Flood that hit New Orleans in 2005.

A sea level rise of dozens of meters seems something inconceivable, and yet this is what happened since the last Ice Age. 20,000 years ago, sea levels were at least one hundred and twenty meters below the current one. All the water that evaporated from the oceans was deposited on the land in the form of snow. Due to the low temperatures in the Ice Age, this snow did not melt in spring or summer but was piled up into kilometers thick ice sheets, similar to those on Greenland and Antarctica. So much water was extracted from the oceans that the sea finally lowered one hundred and twenty meters. Shorelines moved and almost the entire North Sea became a dry area. The Thames, Rhine, Meuse, Scheldt, Somme and Seine discharged into the so-called Channel River that for its part ran through the actual Channel into the Atlantic somewhere north of present-day Cherbourg. Only 20,000 years ago, this process came to an end.

Subsequently, ice sheets started melting again. Five thousand years on, sea levels had risen considerably, up to one hundred meters below the current one. Rapid global warming subsequently marked the start of the Late Ice Age. In Leya's story, this process began in the seventh winter of our friends' journey. Sea levels increased sixty meters within four thousand years. At the beginning of the Holocene*, they were forty meters below the current level. This implies an average rise of one and a half meter per century, in any case much more than the sixty centimeters by the year 2100, which have been predicted by the ICCP in 2007. Vast regions were rapidly flooded, among which the North Sea and the Bering Strait. We have discussed this before. In the past few thousand years however, this ice melting process has slowed down as has sea level rise.

Of course, things could have been different. 125,000 years ago, during the penultimate interglacial period, global temperature was much higher than today and sea levels were six meters above the actual ones. A large part of the Netherlands was covered by the sea. We may consider ourselves fortunate that this has not or not yet happened, since the ice caps on Greenland and Antarctica won't last forever. Humanity has been lucky that this enormous ice melt has been simmering for so long. Otherwise, seaports like Rotterdam, New York and Hong Kong would never have reached their present-day prosperity.
In fact, it is amazing to think that our prehistoric relatives were flexible enough to survive all those changes at the end of the Ice Age. The relative speed of processes like sedimentation, erosion and sea level rise, that are measured today in millimeters, centimeters or decimeters per century, was then far more important. Bare steppes turned into wooded areas and their favourite game disappeared. Their tremendous vitality made them overcome all these setbacks and disasters. They had, in a manner of speaking, to adapt to new changes every day. In practice, it would take some five hundred years before the Magdalenian civilisa-

tion had disappeared from Europe; new cultures and techniques did not come into being at once. However, our ancestors put their knowledge and means to good use, to master the new conditions, coming through all those challenges.
We can do that as well! Salomon Kroonenberg came right to the point: '*Why would we, with our highly-developed technology, be incapable to master a sea level rise of about one meter, if stone age people with bear coats and stone axes managed to survive a complete Ice Age?*' Climate and landscape are subject to continuous changes, with or without our doing. History teaches us that the speed of these changes can be extremely variable and even unpredictable. Yet again, with our knowledge and means we can decide how to handle in each situation.

The mourning group at the Stingenberg was not concerned with these problems. They had gathered there to bury their relatives and were plunged into grieving. The age of the man suggests that he was one of the eldest of his family, with grandchildren and perhaps a first great-grandchild. The young woman in this grave may have borne him one or two children as well. Who knows?
All in all, the band around the grave may have been rather large, saying farewell to the patriarch of their family, a man with the experience of three or four generations. One of them will have carefully placed the bone hairpin, with a roe deer head carved on top, in the hair of the woman; a last loving gesture. One hundred years ago, this hairpin was discovered below her skull. The presence of a dog in that grave will forever remain a mystery.

Only two graves from that period have been described in Central Europe. In Wylczyce, in Southeastern Poland, some nine hundred kilometers east of Bonn, the bones of a stillborn or an at most a few days old baby have been unearthed; a girl according to DNA analysis. 15,000 years ago, people must have buried her below the floor of a hut.

Wylczyce is renowned for the discovery of several dozens of bone, ivory and stone figurines of stylised women without a head, almost exact copies of similar figures from Gönnersdorf; evidence that the spirits of the mothers were idolised in Poland too. In Prater's story, this location was situated in the northern territory of his family, where they hunted ptarmigan in autumn and early winter, and also snared fox and hare because of their white winter coat.

In addition to the skeleton of the baby, the researchers found eighty pierced fox teeth. Did these belong to a necklace, or were they originally sewn onto a fur, in which the girl had been wrapped? This fur or necklace must have been prepared well before her birth; a sign that prehistoric women fostered the same illusions as any expectant mother in our days.

These graves, which can't be compared with each other, serve as a model for countless other ones that still have to be discovered. Doubtlessly, our narrator and her friends have mourned by similar graves, with similar feelings and emotions.

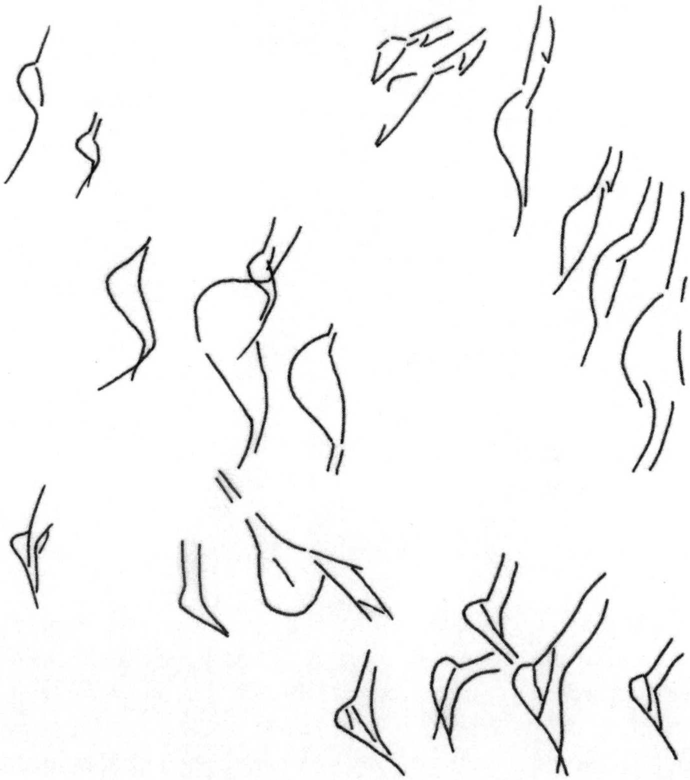

Engravings of rows of stylised women

(Spirits of the mothers)

Upper right: row of six figures from Gönnersdorf (Neuwied; after Bosinski a.o., 2001).
Upper left: row of six figures from Hohlenstein (Nördlinger Ries; after Bosinski, 1982).
Below: part (eight figures) of a group from Lalinde (Dordogne; after Duhard, 1993).

Distance between Gönnersdorf and Hohlenstein is 350 km, between Lalinde and the other two locations is 950 km.

15,000 years ago

Adapt or Perish

The thaw had indeed continued. Many people, among whom Prater and Stille, Leya and her friends, Krasser's brother and his family, were on the west bank of the river, when breaking ice and rapidly raising water cut off the way back to the winter camp. Big River had been changed into a giant lake of rapidly streaming water. They had set up a temporary bivouac.

It was unlikely that they would meet their family and friends again before the next autumn. They could not swim to the other side because of the strong current and cold water.

Those staying in the winter camp at the moment that Big River burst its banks, would move northward as usual and pass summer on the edge of the plains. Leya, Krasser, Durfal and Ursa had to make a decision as soon as possible. They could join Prater's group and look for new hunting grounds on the northern plains. Perhaps it had not been snowing very much in that region, so that they would find abundant game. They also could accompany Krasser's brother and move to the hills and valleys along Salmon River in the west.

The heavy snowfall had created a slaughter among the game, even worse than last winter. Primarily young animals and bearing females did not survive. Carcasses were scattered everywhere; a feast for the large groups of scavengers and carnivores, but for humans too. Everybody was busy, collecting and preparing the meat and hides for the forthcoming time. Nevertheless, they worried about the future. The herds had been drastically depleted. They doubted if there would be enough game next summer to feed everyone and make provisions for the winter.

The atmosphere in the group had been seriously damaged. After a most tumultuous meeting, in which fear of famine had prevailed, they decided to kill the mammoths. Two days after the slaughter however, whilst everyone was still occupied in dragging the meat and hides of the mammoths to the camp, the first bodies of horses and reindeer emerged from below the melting snow. Krasser had been right. Killing the mammoths had been unnecessary, if only they had accepted to wait a few more days. There had been many words between them; especially Leya got it in the neck. Her suggestion, that Great Narrator's spirit might have sent the beasts, had played a major part in the heated arguments and finally decided for them. Now she understood that it had been better to keep her mouth shut. She bitterly blamed herself. Even the encounter with a living mammoth bull and two cows did not change her feelings. Mammoths should not be killed. Ursa had made it very clear!

"This is not the moment for quarrels," said Krasser's brother. "What's done is done. We urgently need to take a decision. What will we do?"

"Fish will have survived the cold," commented Ursa. "Let us go to the brooks around Salmon River."

Durfal doubted. "But what about horse and reindeer in that region; what's your opinion?"

Krasser's brother pondered the question. "Last summer, the hunt did not bring in that much. We clearly noticed that many animals had died in winter. It may be even worse this time, but we have no choice. Too many families are moving to the northern plains; so that's no option as far as we are concerned."

Krasser looked thoughtfully at Leya who had kept out of the discussion. "What would you do, Leya?"

She hung her head in shame: "Why do you ask me? My opinion doesn't count. I am to blame that the eldest made the wrong decision, when the fate of the mammoth was at stake. Please, don't ask me to get involved in this."

"Everybody can be mistaken. It happens to me too. Stop blaming yourself! We took that decision together. Your opinion is as important as every other one!"

Leya hesitated. "If you really want to know my feelings, I fear that we have no future here. Right now, there are more dead bodies scattered all over the steppe than we and all the wolves, lions and eagles can eat; that's for sure. Next moon however, things may be quite different. Besides, if so much snow falls in the next winter, the rest of the animals may be killed off. Not only the last mammoths will die, but also all horses and reindeer. What will we do then? We won't be able to hunt enough to live on."

"What are you trying to tell us? Do you want to leave? Where should we go? You are pregnant."

"I know I'm expecting a baby! It is a horrible thought too that I have to abandon my mother and the rest of the eldest. I was born here by Big River. After our journey through so many summers and winters I had hoped to get old and die here; but if conditions don't change, we will die of starvation. Soon, the spirits of the mothers will roam around here in vain, incapable of finding anyone who needs them. We have to look for a better place!"

"We can try our luck further northwards," suggested Prater. "I have already explained this to you. I am sure that we will find game in abundance on the northern plains."

"No!" disagreed Krasser's brother. "I don't believe so. No-one has ever seen large herds there. Let us assume however that they exist; what will you do to surprise and catch the animals on an open plain?"

"Perhaps we can improve our assegais, or fashion new weapons?"
"I'll see before I believe it!"
"We might move to the south," said Ursa, "to my family in Brother's Valley."
Leya sat up. "This may be an option! Why not?" She gave the rest a questioning look.
"Their group is already too large," remarked Durfal. "Do you really believe that they need us?"
Krasser's brother intervened again. "What about the First Tribe? You told that you would always be welcome there, that you were like brothers and sisters. Maybe we should go to them. Besides, I would like to see Western Water again!"
They looked at each other and nodded. Nobody had considered this possibility.
"It is a long way," was Krasser's reaction. "Do you truly want to travel that far with two pregnant women? Will your wife and Leya be able to complete such a long trip? Is there no better choice?"
"If the women believe they can do it, we should go!"
"Who can assure me that it will be better in the South than here," sneered Prater. "You have told about all that snow in last winter, about all that dead game. Perhaps all animals have already died there. Look who's talking! Stille and I will explore the northern plains. No-one will stop us!"
The majority assented. "You are right, Prater. We will follow you!"
"What happens to the eldest in the winter camp?" It was Durfal who posed the question. "Who will look after them if everybody parts?"
"They can fish and snare hares," stated Ursa. "That's what they have always done. And perhaps, someone may come around to share his supplies."
"What about their food stocks for next winter?"
"With the help of the Maker, Prater's group will return with a big catch. The spirits will protect them. Remember us, we were only four persons and we survived all those winters. They should be able to do so as well."

"Leya is right," said Krasser. "We have no future here. We have to leave, the sooner the better. We know the way to the South of the First Tribe. They assured us that we could always return. We must take the risk. As Prater has said, it is senseless to stay here any longer. Only the Maker knows if we will succeed, but at least we should try our luck. Perhaps we can reach that magic place, where we spent last winter, before the children are born. Come on, let us do it!"
Leya jumped on her feet. "I am feeling fine! I will go with you!"
Krasser looked at his brother and then at the rest of the group. "I agree with you. Let us move southward. Fortunately, we already have sufficient supplies."

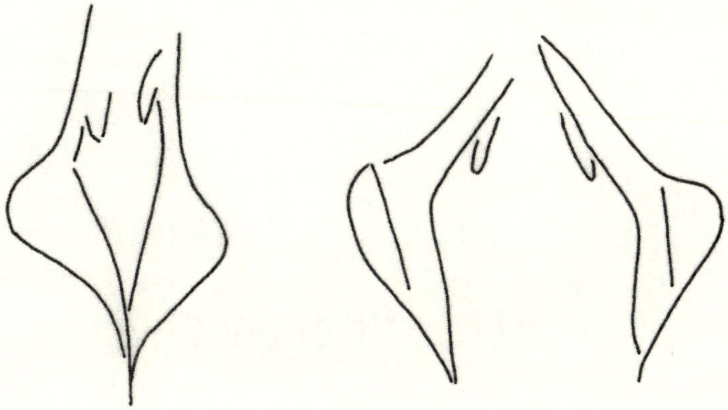

Engravings of stylised women of
Lalinde-Gönnersdorf type
(spirits of the mothers)

Left: couple from Gönnersdorf
(Neuwied; after Bosinski a.o., 2001).
Right: couple from Lalinde
(Dordogne; after Duhard, 1993).

Distance between Gönnersdorf and Lalinde is 1,000 km.

Catastrophic Climate Change

15,000 years ago, at the onset of the Late Ice Age, the climate in Europe abruptly got warmer and more humid. This happened as it were from one day to the next. Jordi Estévez mentions a temperature rise of seven degrees in only five years, at least in Greenland, but the team of Jörgen Peder Steffensen concluded that a temperature rise of ten degrees 'within a remarkable three years' was more likely; and all this without any noticeable human interaction (there are, for example, no signs of repeated, widespread bush or steppe fires)!

Initially, massive snowfall in winter produced a temporary extension of glaciers. Thick snow layers on the steppe will have killed a large part of the game that experienced serious problems in obtaining food. Deep snow dealt the deathblow to the already reduced groups of mammoth and rhinoceros in Europe, whereas the formerly large herds of horse, bison, saiga and reindeer were decimated. These Ice Age animals were adapted to cold, dry winters, but not to thick snow sheets, nor to wet winters.

We may compare this with a recent experience of Estévez, who had been working some time in Tierra del Fuego. He wrote that in a particularly harsh and wet winter, a single night of heavy snowfall killed two thirds of all the wild and domesticated horses and other hoofed animals. Jared Diamond for his part refers to Greenland, where in the winter of 1966-1967 twenty-two thousand sheep died due to cold and heavy snowfall.

Imagine the situation in Central and Northern Europe at the start of the Late Ice Age. Winter after winter game was exposed to heavy snowstorms so that only few animals survived. Only scavengers and carnivores, such as wolf, fox, wolverine, bear, raven, crow, gull, eagle and vulture took advantage of these circumstances. As soon as the snow melted in spring they could feast on the carcasses.
As a consequence, there remained insufficient game to be hunted in summer. People suffered food shortages and had practically no chance to respond the changing conditions. Of course, such disasters did not hit everybody at the same time, but this scenario explains why so many groups in Belgium, the Netherlands, Poland, Czechia and Switzerland disappeared virtually overnight, without leaving any trace. Only small families survived, presumably at the expense of weak, sick and elder family members. Everyone had to look out for their own self preservation. Compassion faded to the background as did the hospitability to strangers. The increasingly isolated groups drifted apart and traditions were forgotten. It would take many generations before new societies came into being.
Among these are the Hamburg* reindeer hunters on the North European Plain, or the Creswell* people in England, Wales and Scotland. Some groups may have tried their luck in Southwestern France, the former territory of their ancestors; returning to their roots. The author of the engravings in Lalinde, for example, was perhaps from Gönnersdorf, or did have relatives there. Who knows?

The consequences of this climate change will have been far more important than those of the Black Death in the Middle Ages that killed about one third of all Europeans.

It is true that in the fourteenth century tens of millions of people were killed, but, cynically speaking, many more survived so that the society could recover relatively quickly. At the onset of the Late Ice Age however the number of people in France was possibly limited to a few tens of thousands, and in Central Europe to a few thousands. The death of one third or half of them due to famine and associated illnesses ended in a real catastrophe. Notably in Central Europe did many groups become so small that they were no longer viable, and the same probably holds for their mutual contacts. Where and how could people find a partner, or get help in case of emergency?
Centuries would go by before this blow was overcome. The open steppe landscape became meanwhile encroached by forests of birch, poplar, willow, and pine, squeezing out the space for mammoth, rhinoceros, bison, saiga, reindeer, snow owl and ptarmigan. Their place was taken by red deer, roe deer, boar, black grouse and wood grouse.
The Magdalenian civilisation in Central Europe was replaced by the Federmesser culture, the assegai by bow and arrow. People clearly tried everything to adapt. Survival was the main driver. All else became trivial. There was no more time to fashion ornaments or to search snails, shells or fossils. They no longer went a short way round to get these; at least, that's the impression we have. People stopped engraving animals in bone and antlers, or carving figurines from ivory and stone; a most remarkable change! All this suggests that they abruptly renounced their religious beliefs, as if they suddenly concluded that the spirits could not help them in countering all those changes; that the spirits did not exist after all! That thought must have produced some sort of snowball effect. Within just a few centuries people stopped reproducing the images of animals and stylised women; a most fascinating change in their behaviour!
A piece of sandstone from Niederbieber seems to be the only exception. This site is situated at only a few kilometers from Gönnersdorf, where Magdalenian hunters engraved

hundreds of stylised women in shale. We have been talking repeatedly about these 'spirits of the mothers'. It is the subject of this book. We have interpreted them our way. That piece of sandstone from Niederbieber has been used by people of the Federmesser culture in smoothening arrow shafts; nothing special at first sight. Similar pieces are quite common across Europe. However, a number of deep incisions make this a unique stone. The outlines of extremely stylised women are unmistakable. The striking thing about it is the fact that these lines were carved only 13,000 years ago, two thousand years later than in Gönnersdorf! Had the faith in the spirits of the mothers held out that long, at least in this region? It seems indeed likely that the belief in the spirits continued to exist in the environs of Bonn, long after people had abandoned it elsewhere.

These changes passed more gradually in Spain and Southern France, where even in the coldest period of the Ice Age sheltered places existed for a wide range of trees and bushes, among which alder, ash, juniper, hazel, elm, lime and oak. These wooded places offered a refuge for so many deer that these became a catch as important as reindeer. Successful deer hunting in the woods required a new weapon: bow and arrow; the basis of the Azilian technique that became widespread in France and Spain. This seems to be the most logical supposition. The dramatic reduction of reindeer populations during the Late Ice Age was partly compensated by the rapid increase of roe deer and red deer in the rapidly expanding woods. Naturally, there were fish-rich rivers too and a long coast line with countless shells, snails, birds and seals. Thanks to this variegated food range the Magdalenian civilisation could persist in that area for quite a while, even after it had disappeared or absorbed in other, younger cultures in large parts of Central Europe.

Today, some people are extremely pessimistic about the rising global temperature. They fear that not only our welfare society but also mankind will not survive this. Naturally, we don't know if the temperature rise in the end will reach

extreme values. The IPCC has proposed with good reason various equally possible, less dramatic scenarios.
What we do know is that the temperature rose very quickly at the beginning of the Late Ice Age, 15,000 years ago. The human population was decimated in Central Europe and the Magdalenian civilisation collapsed, but the survivors did not dwell on fatalistic speculations. They developed new tools and new weapons. Many traditions and religious creed of the Old Stone Age vanished or changed by force of circumstances. People reorganised themselves into smaller groups and stopped traveling enormous distances. New regional cultures appeared and supplanted those of the Old Stone Age. Our prehistoric relatives adapted, no matter how. Adaptation was the keyword to survive this unprecedented catastrophe.

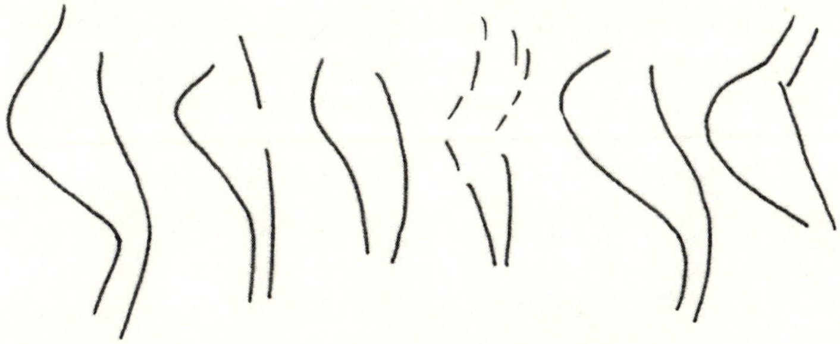

Engravings of stylised women of Lalinde-Gönnersdorf type
(spirits of the mothers)

From left to right
two specimens from Gönnersdorf
(Neuwied; after Bosinski a.o., 2001),
specimen from Felsställe
(Mühlen; after Bosinski, 1982),
specimen from Roc-aux-Sorciers
(Angles-sur-Anglin; after Pinçon, 2007),
specimen from Carriot
(Bouziès; after Duhard, 1993)
and specimen from La Vache
(Alliat: after Clottes & Delporte, 2003).

Distance between Gönnersdorf and Felsställe is 350 km, between Gönnersdorf and Roc-aux-Sorciers 800 km, between Roc-aux-Sorciers and Carriot 300 km, between Carriot and La Vache 250 km, and between Gönnersdorf and La Vache 1,200 km.

15,000 years ago

Uncertain Future

"Mama! Mama Leya!" Her daughter dashed into the tent like a little whirlwind. "Mama, help me!"

Tears were rolling down her cheek and she had blood on her face. She fell sobbing into the arms of her mother, who was carving new needles from a long bone.

"Tell me, my darling, what happened? Did you fall?"

"Oh, mama! The children called me all sorts of names, hitting me again and even pelting me with stones. Look! I am bleeding!"

Leya took her daughter in her arms, softly stroked her head and examined the wound. Then she soothed: "It is not that bad. Chin up! Try to be a big girl! Do I ever complain about anything?"

"But they called out that we are different, similar to the other ones! They want us to go away!" shouted he girl indignantly.

"Why do they compare us with the other ones? We live like they do, in huts and tents, near a cave to shelter. We hunt together with our neighbours, help them whenever they need. Don't you see that they come here to listen to my stories?"

"As soon as they believe that we can't hear them, they tell mean things about us," sobbed her daughter.
"Darling, you are wrong. It is not true!"
"Oh yes, mama! You are the only one, who doesn't want to hear this! Ask Krasser and Ursa! They know better!"
"What fault can they find with us?"
"Your clothes! Your strange way of talking! Your exaggerated faith in the spirits of the mothers! Why do you have to behave so differently? Oh mama, I feel so ashamed!"
The girl's torrent of words was unstoppable. Suppressed frustrations emerged abruptly. Leya heaved a deep sigh, not knowing how to react. Yet again the children were targeting her daughter.

The return of her friend provided a most welcome distraction. Ursa shook the water from her soaking hair and proudly showed the trout she had caught that morning. "Look! We will have a fine meal tonight."
Then she noticed the blood and the tears on the face of her niece. "Are we in trouble again? Does it hurt?"
"Fortunately, not," answered the girl, her face already brightening up.
"I can use a little bit of help," said Ursa. "All my gear is lying by the water side. Would you help your aunt? Would you clean it and bring it here?"
Her niece was beaming. Ursa needed her! She forgot the quarrel and ran outside to comply with her aunt's request.
Leya turned to Ursa: "I am glad you came. She was so sad. It is always the same story. What can we do?"
Her friend doubted. "Perhaps she should learn to cope with it. We have no choice. These are difficult times for us all. Who could imagine this when we left our winter camp? Do you know how many summers have passed since then?"
"Many, I would say. Look here, I have marked each summer on the shaft of my assegai. I remember that the families of the First Tribe received us with open arms and cheered: 'The narrator has returned; the narrator from the North and her friends!' They immediately requested you to

manufacture fish tools for everybody, whilst our neighbours asked Krasser to draw time and again the spirits of their favourite animals; last moon even a complete horse herd. Why do they get annoyed about our faith in the spirits of the mothers? We are not harming anyone; do we?"
"That's not the issue," was Ursa's reaction. "I think they are just frightened, afraid to suffer famine in the future. They transfer this fear in loathing for us, because we are Northerners, people who in their eyes not really belong here. The hunters have to cover larger distances these days and even then sometimes return empty-handed. They are now facing the same problems we have had in the North. Much game may die here next winter again because of heavy snowfall. Besides, how will we preserve our fish and meat supplies if it suddenly thaws, as in last winter? Where will we find enough game next spring and summer to feed everyone? Our neighbours believe that their children will be better off if we leave. That's the reason they want us to go away."
"Rumors are going that some people are urging the eldest to send away various families. Tradition has it that they did so before, in the Time of Great Change. Perhaps these times will come back! Everything is changing. Look at the Western Water that is no longer covered with ice in winter. Who remembers here the spirits of mammoth and rhinoceros? How many people still entrust themselves to the spirits of the mothers? Who knows what's awaiting us!"
Ursa interrupted the dark reflections. "There is no point in dwelling on it. No-one can look ahead. Perhaps it will not be so bad after all."
"Remember that winter, when we arrived at Big River after a journey that lasted eight summers. Remember how happy we initially felt and what came afterwards: the continuous snowfall, the increasing despair when we ran out of food and kindling, the arguments about nothing, the sudden thaw and Big River bursting its banks, and in the end the horrible choices we had to make. Even now, in the dark of the night, I keep wondering if our decisions were right. Will next winter be worse?"

Ursa stared blankly at her friend. "No," said she thoughtfully after a while, "It will never be so bad again. You must not think that I have forgotten what happened. I too have to face the question if we should have stayed there with your mother and the eldest, but in my dreams I see their spirits, assuring me that we would have died. No, staying there has never been an option."

"But we could have joined Prater's group. Did they survive? Should we have supported him? Have the spirits of the mothers protected him?"

"Leya; don't torment yourself with these questions! In this very moment they may be feeling as guilty as you because they did not come with us. That's a fair chance!"

"I know you are right, but I doubt that my little girl will be happy here. Possible food shortage is driving a wedge between us. People will only think of themselves. We are living here so long, Ursa, but to them we remain Northerners who should leave as soon as possible. Some of them don't hesitate at nothing, calling us other ones, although they know very well that our ancestors were born here. Who could imagine this before?

Krasser sometimes wonders if it would be better for our girl to part again. Who will later accept a Northerner as his wife? Do you recall the stories about that region behind the mountains, south of Western Water? Maybe we should give it a try."

"Leya, where did you get this idea? Do you really believe that life will be better there? If that would be true, everybody had moved already. No, that's only wishful thinking, and besides I don't want to begin another journey. And you, do you have the strength to travel so far?"

"Perhaps we should return to the North," suggested Leya. "Remember the Northerners living north of Northern River. They surely recall that we helped them with food and clothes. Like us, they idolise the spirits of the mothers. They will not treat us as other ones. Moreover, we have seen mammoths and rhinoceros in that region. Consider it, please."

"Well, we can propose it to the rest of our people. We should not make a rash decision. Talk it over with Krasser and his brother, while I will ask Durfal's opinion. Let us await their reactions and then decide."

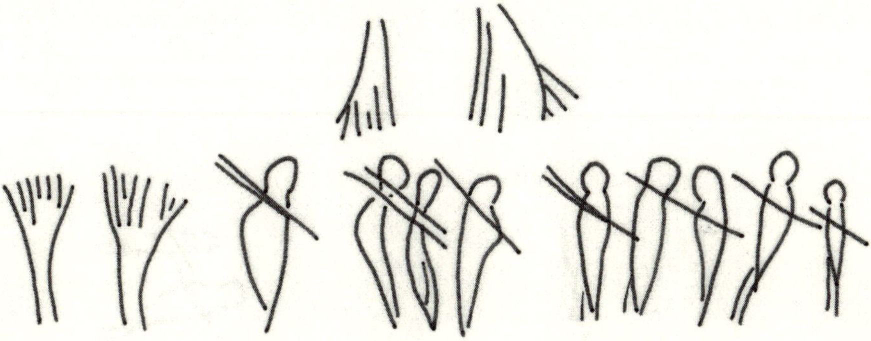

Late Magdalenian engraving

Château des Eyzies, Dordogne (after Cleyet-Merle, 2007) showing a hunting party, including men, women and children armed with spears or assegais. The branched signs to the left may represent two trees, whereas those on top may be interpreted as tents. This would be one of the very few exceptions of prehistoric people (or spirits) portrayed in a (primitive) landscape!

Epilogue

Should we send our friends on another journey? Leya's story has an open end. It is up to you to imagine how it continued. Maybe the food problems were resolved and our friends stayed on with the First Tribe, in the Dordogne basin. That's an option.

Anyhow, their children's children did travel westwards along the Seine from the environs of Paris. Engravings of stylised women in the caves of Gouy and Orival near Rouen prove that the worship of the spirits of the mothers also reached this remote corner. Were these images engraved in the white chalk by the last Magdalenian hunters or were they made by their successors of the Azilian culture? As pointed out by Yves Martin, only further research will answer that question. Together with the engravings of horse and aurochs at Gouy they represent the last convulsions of Paleolithic cave art.

The new environmental conditions were no good for reindeer. People had to adapt themselves by hunting horse, deer, aurochs and boar. The disappearance of mammoth and rhinoceros gave way to another giant, Megaloceros, also known as giant deer or Irish elk. This distinctive animal, its antlers up to twelve feet and with a conspicuous bump on its back, had been portrayed long before by artists of the Gravettian civilisation in France. Giant deer had practically disappeared since the start of the coldest period of the Ice Age, but the populations rapidly increased as soon as swamps and deciduous forests expanded again at the onset of the Late Ice Age. This explains why giant deer figured on the menu of the last Magdalenian hunters in Bonnières-sur-Seine; proof of the quick changes in climate, landscape, flora and fauna. The generation of Leya did however not live to see it.

Perhaps you are also interested to know what happened to the group of Stille and Prater who had decided to go from Gönnersdorf to the North European Plain. Since the beginning of the coldest period of the Ice Age, very few people had ventured into that region, but Prater's expectations came true. They discovered enough game to stay there and never returned to the old winter camp by the Rhine. Their children adapted to the changing conditions, just as the descendants of Leya and Ursa.
Improved techniques and weapons enabled small bands to become successful reindeer hunters on the open steppe. Moreover, there were plenty of foxes and hares, which they snared because of their fur, and they fished and fowled enough to get by. Their new tools made the offspring of Prater and Stille known as Hamburg hunters. Remnants of their campsites have been discovered from the Netherlands into Poland.

The group split up soon after. Several families (now known as Creswell people) went westward and crossed Doggerland, the name given by Bryony Coles to the North Sea area that became dry land in the Ice Age, due to the lowered sea levels and temporal uplift of the region. In the hills and valleys of Scotland, Wales and England they discovered a wide variety of game, including horse, reindeer, deer, boar, aurochs, hare; and even the last mammoths, as shown by a carving in the Cheddar Gorge.

However, living conditions will not always and everywhere have been ideal for these hunters. Hard evidence of cannibalism was recognised in Gough's Cave, where people will have faced starvation because of a life-threatening shortage of food. They may have been snowed up in winter and finally decided to consume their dead family members.
Don't fault our prehistoric relatives for this. In 1972, for example, the survivors of the 'Andes flight disaster' had to feed on their dead friends in order to stay alive.

The boundaries between these new cultures were not well-defined. Creswell camps occur in the region of the Hamburg culture and vice-versa. Creswell and Hamburg tools are sometimes found in Final Magdalenian bivouacs, for example at Bonnières-sur-Seine, indicating that the various groups have met with some regularity.
The sparse art products left behind by the offspring of Prater and Stille suggest that, equally to the descendants of Leya and Ursa, they did not spend much time to it. Their frequently clumsy engravings mark the end of Paleolithic cave art.

What did Leya really look like? Did she have dark hair, was she blond? Did she have brown or greenish eyes? By blurring the line between fact and fiction and stepping beyond, Leya and her friends became alive, people of flesh and blood.
They express our vision on the way of thinking and the daily doings and goings of our ancestors, humans like us, with the same qualities. Care for their kinsfolk and hospitality formed the base of a society that finally succumbed, due to growing self-interest and an increasing distrust of strangers.

DISINTEGRATION OF MAGDALENIAN CIVILISATION AFTER MAJOR CLIMATE CHANGE AT START OF THE LATE ICE AGE

I – Offspring of Leya and Ursa at Magdalenian-Azilian transition.
II – Offspring of Stille and Prater at Magdalenian-Hamburgian transition.
III – Offspring of Stille and Prater at Magdalenian-Creswellian transition.

1 – Lalinde (Dordogne, Late Magdalenian, engravings of stylised women of Lalinde-Gönnersdorf type).
2 – Bois-Ragot (Vienne, Late Magdalenian and Early Azilian).
3 – Bonnières-sur-Seine (Final Magdalenian with Hamburgian tools).
4 – Orival (Seine, Late Magdalenian or Early Azilian, engravings of stylised women of Lalinde-Gönnersdorf type).
5 – Gouy (Seine, Final Magdalenian or Early Azilian, engravings of stylised women of Lalinde-Gönnersdorf type).
6 – Andernach (Rhine, Late Magdalenian, engravings and figurines of stylised women of Lalinde-Gönnersdorf type).
7 – Gönnersdorf (Rhine, Late Magdalenian, engravings and figurines of stylised women of Lalinde-Gönnersdorf type).
8 – Elspeet (E-Netherlands, Hamburgian).
9 – Texel NW-Netherlands (Hamburgian).
10 – Poggenwisch (Elbe, Hamburgian).
11 – Zeijen (NE-Netherlands, Creswellian).
12 – Creswell Crags (Creswellian; engravings of aurochs[?] and deer[?] in Church Hole).
13 – Fairnington (Tweed Valley, Scotland, Creswellian).
14 – Kendrick's Cave (Great Orme, Wales, Creswellian).
15 – Gough's Cave (Cheddar Gorge, Somerset, Creswellian).
16 – Kent's Cavern (Devon, Creswellian).
17 – Presles (Hainaut, Belgium, Creswellian).

Bibliographic and Museological References

We frequently cross the limits between fantasy and reality in this book. We have already explained this. Perhaps you like to draw this limit yourself and consult some of our sources. Read a book on this topic, visit one of the many museums we have seen, or, even better, one of the caves or other archeological sites that are open to the public. It will give you a different perspective on the conditions of life and doings of our distant relatives, and on the climate changes they were exposed to.

For a start, we recommend a book by Sykes (*The Seven Daughters of Eve*, New York, Norton, 2002), explaining that the large majority of native Europeans descend through their maternal line from the hunters of the Old Stone Age or Paleolithic.

Of course, much information on the climate in past, present and future has been drawn from the Fourth Report of the IPCC (Solomon and others [eds], *Climate Change 2007 – The Physical Science Basis, Contribution of Working Group I to the Fourth Assessment Report of the Intergovernmental Panel on Climate Change*, Cambridge, University Press, 2007), a 'must' for policymakers in the entire world, but not easily understandable for laymen. Instead you better read Kroonenberg's book (*De menselijke maat – De aarde over tienduizend jaar*, Amsterdam, Atlas, 2007), with a wealth of information on the changing climate and sea levels since the last Ice Age. The extremely rapid temperature rise at the onset of the Late Ice Age (15,000 years ago) has been studied by Steffensen and others ("High-res-

olution Greenland ice core data show abrupt climate change happens in few years," *Science* 321, 2008, 680-684). Severinghaus and Brook ("Abrupt climate change at the end of the Last Glacial Period inferred from trapped air in Polar ice," *Science* 286, 1999, 930-934) explain that this change started exactly 14,672 years before the year 2000. The 'armada of icebergs' that sailed across the Atlantic 16,000 years ago has been described by Hemming ("Heinrich events: massive Late Pleistocene detritus layers of the North Atlantic and their global climate imprint," *Review of Geophysics 42,* 2004, RG1005, 1-43).
Examples of recent mass mortality among animals, due to exceptionally cold and wet winters, are found in books by Diamond (*Collapse: How Societies Choose to Fail or Succeed,* New York, Viking, 2005) and Estévez (*Catástrofes en la prehistoria, Barcelona,* Bellaterra, 2005). Most likely, Paleolithic hunters faced similar disasters heralding the collapse of the Magdalenian civilisation.
Guthrie (*Frozen Fauna of the Mammoth Steppe: the Story of Blue Babe,* Chicago, University Press, 1990) wrote a very special book on life and death on the mammoth steppe during the last Ice Age. His reconstruction of the way lions killed a bison in Alaska has been assimilated in one of Leya's stories.
You may be surprised that dogs already lived in the Ice Age, but their presence has been extensively documented by Germonpré and others ("Fossil Dogs and Wolves from Palaeolithic sites in Belgium, the Ukraine and Russia: osteometry, ancient DNA and stable isotopes," *Journal Archaeological Science 36,* 2009, 473-490).

The fate of the Middle Magdalenian Maszycka family, massacred in Southern Poland, has been described in detail by Kozlowski and Sachse-Kozlowska ("Magdalenian family from the Maszycka Cave," *Jahrbuch des Römisch-Germanischen Zentral Museums 40,* 1995, 115-205). In our book, the unfounded fear for *the other ones* is based on tales and myths that referred to this tragedy.

The Middle Magdalenian connections between Southwestern France and Switzerland have been analysed by Fritz and Tosello ("Le Tuc d'Audoubert et sa place dans la culture magdalénienne," in: Bégouën and others, *Le Sanctuaire secret des Bisons – il y a 14,000 ans, dans la caverne du Tuc d'Audoubert,* Somogy, Paris, 2009, 349-391).

Data on our ancestors' everyday life were derived from Baales ("Archäologie des Eiszeitalters – Frühe Menschen an Mittelrhein und Mosel," *Archäologie an Mittelrhein und Mosel 16,* 2005), De Beaune (Les hommes au temps de Lascaux – 40000-10000 avant J.-C., Paris, Hachette, 1995; and: *Chasseurs-cueilleurs: comment vivaient nos ancêtres du Paléolithique supérieur?,* Paris, CNRS, 2007), Nadel (Ohalo II: *A 23,000-Year-Old Fisher-Hunter-Gatherers' Camp on the Shore of the Sea of Galilee,* Haifa, Reuben and Edith Hecht Museum, Catalogue 20, 2002) and Otte (*Cro Magnon,* Paris, Perrin, 2008). Some aspects of the way of life of the Cro-Magnons may have resembled that of the Inuit studied by Gessain (*Les Esquimaux du Groenland à l'Alaska,* Paris, Bourrelier, 1953).

Desbrosse and Kozlowski (*Les habitats préhistoriques – Des Australopithèques aux premiers agriculteurs,* Paris, CTHS, 2001) describe numerous examples of prehistoric dwellings in a very readable booklet.

Claudine Cohen (*La femme des origins,* Paris, Belin – Herscher, 2003) has written an easily accessible book on the evolution of our concept of the role of women in prehistoric times. In *Man the Hunter* (New York, Aldine de Gruyter, 1968) by Richard Lee and Irven DeVore (editors) you will find amazing details on the life of present-day hunter-gatherers.

The earliest indications of human compassion have been summarised by Hublin ("The Prehistory of Compassion," *Proceedings National Academy of Sciences 106,* 2009, 6429-6430).

Information on the 'grave with the dog' of Bonn-Oberkassel has been published by Probst (*Deutschland in der Eiszeit,* München, Orbis, 1991), and on the baby skeleton of

Wylczyce by Irish ("A Late Magdalenian Perinatal Human Skeleton from Wylczyce, Poland," *Journal Human Evolution 55,* 2008, 736-740).

It is a real pleasure to mention the excellent illustrations by the brothers Adrie and Alfons Kennis (in: Arsuaga, *La Saga Humana – Una Larga Historia,* Madrid, EDAF, 2006) and Gilles Tosello (*Prehisto Art,* Le Touquet, Auréoline, 2005), which in a lively and scientifically accurate way portray our ancestors.

Bahn (*Cave Art – A Guide to the decorated Ice Age Caves of Europe,* London, Frances Lincoln, 2007) has published a useful catalogue of prehistoric caves with cave art, which are open to the public. The list does not include equally exciting places like La Vache, Mas d'Azil and Laugerie where the visitor gets a realistic impression of prehistoric dwellings and excavations.

Einwögerer and Käfer ("Die jungpaläolithische Flöte aus der Station Grubgraben bei Kammern, Niederösterreich, im experimentellen Nachbau," *Mitteilungen Gesellschaft Urgeschichte 7,* 1999) experimented with bone flutes from the Old Stone Age. This has resulted in a most remarkable CD (Österreichische Akademie der Wissenschaften, *Knochenklang – Klänge aus der Eiszeit,* OEAW MPK 36, Audio CD, Mitteilungen der Prähistorischen Kommission 36, 2000, ISBN 3-7001-2961-0).

Nobody knows how many or how few people were living in Europe during the Ice Age, but Rozoy ("Le Propulseur et l'Arc chez les chasseurs préhistoriques – Techniques et Démographies compares," Paléo 4, 1992, 175-193) and Zimmermann ("Zur Bevölkerungsdichte in der Urgeschichte Mitteleuropas," *Tübinger Monographien zur Urgeschichte 11,* 1996, 49-61) have tried to make a rough estimate.

The paper by San Miguel Llamosas ("El conjunto de Arte Rupestre Paleolítico de la Cueva del Linar [Alfoz de Lloredo, Cantabria]," *XX Congreso Nacional de Arqueología,* Universidad de Zaragoza, 1991, 95-103) inspired us to imagine that our ancestors really considered caves and caverns as the entry to the womb of the earth.

The journey of our fictitious narrator and her friends starts in Gönnersdorf, because of the wealth of available data. We especially refer to Bosinski (*Urgeschichte am Rhein*, Tübingen, Kerns, 2008), Floss ("Rohmaterialversorgung im Paläolithikum des Mittelrheingebietes," *Monographiën Römisch-Germanischen Zentralmuseums 21*, 1994) and Sensburg ("Die räumliche Organisation der Konzentration IIa von Gönnersdorf – Struktur und Dynamik eines Magdalénienzeitlichen Siedlungsbefundes am Mittelrhein," *Monographien Römisch-Germanischen Zentralmuseums 69*, 2007).
The depictions of seals and sea turtles in Gönnersdorf and Andernach have been interpreted by Bosinski ("Tierdarstellungen von Gönnersdorf – Nachträge zu Mammut und Pferd sowie die übrigen Tierdarstellungen," *Monographiën Römisch-Germanischen Zentralmuseums 72*, 2008) as an indication that the artists had observed these animals by the mouth of the Rhine (or Channel River) into the Atlantic.

Don't forget to visit the 'Museum für die Archäologie des Eiszeitalters,' Schloss Monrepos near Neuwied, with a permanent exhibit on the history of prehistoric man in Central Europe. The museum disposes of a fine collection of replicas of Paleolithic female figurines, including the highly stylised ones from the Late Magdalenian.

Our Magdalenian relatives bivouacked at many places in the Suabian Alb. Examples have been described in Hahn and others (*Eiszeithöhlen im Lonetal*, Stuttgart, Theiss, 1985) and Wagner (*Eiszeitjäger im Blaubeurener Tal*, Stuttgart, Theiss, 1979). Albrecht and Hahn (*Rentierjäger im Brudertal*, Stuttgart, Theiss, 1991) deal with the reindeer hunters of the Brudertal near Engen, in Southern Germany.
Information is also available in the 'Urgeschichtliches Museum Blaubeuren' (west of Ulm) and the 'Städtisches Museum Engen'. The latter one exhibits very instructive scale-models of the reindeer hunt in Brudertal. Our visit to

the Brudertal has proved to be very worthwhile in order to reconstruct that famous reindeer drive on site.

Middle and Late Magdalenian campsites occur in the environs of Schaffhausen. We refer to Bandi and others (*Die Kultur der Eiszeitjäger aus dem Kesslerloch,* Konstanz, Seekreis, 1984) and Höneisen and Peyer (*Schweizersbild – ein Jägerlager der Späteiszeit,* Schaffhauser Archäologie 2, 1994).
The 'Museum zu Allerheiligen' in Schaffhausen has dedicated a fine permanent exhibit to the subject, whilst you can visit the rock shelter of Schweizersbild on the outskirts of the town. Doubtlessly, the prehistoric hunters have frequently admired the Rhine fall, the largest in Europe.

The Swiss sites by Lake Neuchâtel and Lake Geneva were extensively studied by, respectively, Leesch and others ("Témoins d'implantations magdaléniennes et aziliennes sur la rive nord du lac de Neuchâtel," *Archéologie neuchâteloise 31,* 2004) and Stahl Gretsch ("Les occupations magdaléniennes de Veyrier – Histoire et Préhistoire des abris-sous-blocs," *Cahiers d'Archéologie romande 105,* 2006).
A visit to the 'Latenium' at Hauterive-Champréveyres is highly recommended. This museum by Lake Neuchâtel displays a wealth of data on the nearby sites of Champréveyres and Monruz.

The Rhône Valley has been frequently used for the transport of raw material (notably flint) by Magdalenian groups in the French Northern Alps as can be derived from the study by Pion & Mevel ("La fin du Paléolithique supérieur dans les Alpes Françaises et le Jura méridional," *Société préhistorique française Mémoire L,* 2009). The same publication also provides detailed information on Late Magdalenian vegetation and fauna in the Upper Rhône Basin.
A summary of the prehistoric caves along the Ardèche is presented by Roudil (*Préhistoire de l'Ardèche – le temps*

des chasseurs et leur art, Soubès, Conseil départemental de la culture de l'Ardèche, 1995). The likeness of Pont-d'Arc, the natural arc spanning the Ardèche, to a giant petrified mammoth has been noticed by André and Chabaud ("Le plus grand mammouth totémique de la préhistoire? Le Pont-d'Arc et son possible rapport avec l'ornementation de la grotte Chauvet [Vallon-Pont-d'Arc, Ardèche]," *Bulletin Préhistoire du Sud-Ouest 7,* 2000, 19-39). A really different story is the description of the stylised female figures in the Planchard Cave by Bosinski and Schiller ("Représentations féminines dans la grotte du Planchard [Vallon-Pont-d'Arc, Ardèche] et les figures féminines du type Gönnersdorf dans l'art parietal," *Bulletin Société préhistorique Ariège 53,* 1998, 99-140).
More information can be obtained in the 'Musée regional de Préhistoire' near Orgnac-l'Aven.

Excellent monographs exist on the caves of La Vache by Clottes and Delporte (*La grotte de La Vache [Ariège],* Paris, CTHS, 2003) and Niaux by Clottes (*Les cavernes de Niaux,* Paris, Seuil, 1995).
A visit to La Vache and Niaux, south of Foix in the Eastern Pyrenees, will open your eyes! We equally recommend the 'Parc de Préhistoire' near Tarascon-sur-Ariège with many superb replicas of the drawings in Niaux and art objects from La Vache.

The most important sites in Aveyron Valley are briefly dealt with by Ladier and Welté ("Territoires culturels au Magdalénien supérieur dans la vallée de l'Aveyron: éléments d'approche," in: Jaubert and Barbaza, *Territoires, déplacements, mobilité, échanges durant la Préhistoire – Terres et Hommes du Sud,* Paris, CTHS, 2005, 385-395). The description of Leya's visit to the cave of the ancestral mothers has been borrowed from Rouzaud and others ("Grotte de La Magdeleine-des-Albis à Penne [Tarn]," *Bulletin Société préhistorique Ariège-Pyrenées 44,* 1989, 21-70).

We can only guess at the exact locations of the (nowadays flooded) prehistoric sites at the Atlantic coast around the mouth of the Gironne. Thanks to the study by Serangeli ("La zone côtière et son role dans les comportements alimentaires des chasseurs-cueilleurs du Paléolithique supérieur," *BAR International Series 1105,* 2003, 67-82) we may presume that in those environs people have been hunting seals.

A complete library exists on the Magdalenian sites in the Vézère Valley. We limit ourselves to Delluc and others (*Discovering Périgord Prehistory,* Bordeaux, Sud-Ouest, 1992; and "La grotte ornée de Saint-Cirq [Dordogne] – Hommage à A. Leroy-Gourhan," *Bulletin Société préhistorique française 84,* 1987, 364-393).
The 'Musée du Périgord' in Périgueux disposes of a huge collection of original master pieces of Late Magdalenian art from the Dordogne area. Equally important is the 'Musée national de Préhistoire' in Les Eyzies. Visit both places as an introduction to the many unique caves in that region, among which Lascaux (a very good replica of the original is open to the public), Rouffignac, Combarelles, Font-de-Gaume, Cap-Blanc and Saint-Cirq. Booking in advance is recommended, especially in the high-season. A visit to Laugerie-Basse will help you understand the organization of a prehistoric dwelling and its posterior excavation.

Leya's trip from the Vézère Valley to the Auvergne has been based on a paper by Surmely ("Le peuplement magdalénien de l'Auvergne," *Société préhistorique française Mémoire 28,* 2000, 165-175).
Her stay in the environs of the then active volcanoes around the Puy-de-Dôme has been reconstructed thanks to the paper by Daugas and Raynal ("Territoire et occupation humaine au Magdalénien dans le basin moyen de l'Allier [Auvergne, Massif Central Française]: esquisse d'une géographie conceptuelle de l'espace humain regional. Arts et cultures de la préhistoire," *Documents préhistoriques 24,*

2007, 197-222). The flint road from Clermont-Ferrand and Roanne to the north has been described by Alix and others ("Determination et origine géologique de la matière première de l'industrie lithique du site magdalénien du Rocher de la Caille," *Société préhistorique française Mémoire 31,* 2003, 63-75).
The sculptures of Roc-aux-Sorciers have been portrayed in Airvaux (*L'Art préhistorique du Poitou-Charentes – sculptures et gravures des temps glaciaires,* Paris, Maison des Roches, 2001).
A detour from Poitiers or Tours to the 'Centre d'Interpretation de la Frise Magdalénienne du Roc-aux-Sorciers' in Angles-sur-Anglin is really worth the effort. With good reason the French journal 'Le Monde' described this relief as the 'Lascaux of prehistoric sculpture'.

Many publications have been dedicated to the Magdalenian sites in the Seine basin, east of Paris. We recommend Olive and others *(Il y a 13,000 ans à Étiolles, Paris – Argenton-sur-Creuse, L'Indre,* 1991) and Taborin ("Environnements et habitats magdaléniens dans le centre du Basin parisien," *Documents d'Archéologie française 43,* 1994). Pigeot ("Les derniers Magdaléniens d'Étiolles – perspectives culturelles et paléohistoriques," *Gallia Préhistoire Supplément 27,* 2004) refers to the stone with female curvatures that plays a role in one of Leya's stories.
The 'Musée regional de Préhistoire d'Ile-de-France' in Nemours is dedicated to the regional excavations around Paris; with very instructive reconstructions of the way of life of those prehistoric people.

Rozoy ("Séjours d'été en Ardenne des Magdaléniens du Bassin parisien," *Mémoires Société archéologique champenoise 13,* 1994, 139-156) argues that the Meuse Valley in the French and Belgian Ardennes formed part of the same territory of the people who hunted along the Seine and the Marne.

The last stop of Leya's journey was in Dutch South-Limburg. Rensink ("Regional-scale variation and the Magdalenian record of Northwestern Europe," *BAR International Series 896,* 2000, 133-146), and Deeben and Rensink ("Het Laat-Paleolithicum in Zuid-Nederland," *Archeologie 11/12,* 2005, 171-199) have placed this area in a regional context. The strategic location of Eyserheide suggests careful planning of their hunting parties. Utrilla and others ("A palaeolithic map from 13,660 calBP; engraved stone blocks from the Late Magdalenian in Abauntz [Navarra, Spain]", *Journal Human Evolution 57,* 2009, 99-11) recognised primitive maps, including rivers, mountains, lagoons and the location of game, in a cave in Northern Spain.

The last Magdalenians in the Seine valley have bivouacked at Bonnières-sur-Seine, west of Paris (Charier, "Il y a 13,000 ans à Bonnières-sur-Seine: une halte de chasse magdalénienne," *Catalogue de l'exposition 'La Prèhistoire en val de Seine,' Musée de l'Hôtel-Dieu, Mantes-la-Jolie,* 2008, 34-39), where they killed not only horse, deer and boar, but also giant deer. Data on the disappearance of mammoth and the return of giant deer in Europe at the onset of the Late Ice Age were taken from a publication by Stuart and others ("Pleistocene to Holocene extinction dynamics in giant deer and woolly mammoth," *Nature 431,* 2004, 684-689). Stapert ("Het Laat-Paleolithicum in Noord-Nederland," *Archeologie 11/12,* 2005, 143-169) suggests that flint points and sandstone arrow-shaft abraders with elongated grooves indicate that Hamburg and Creswell hunters already knew bow and arrow.

The genesis and destruction of Doggerland, the North Sea area that became dry land during the Ice Age has been described in detail by Coles ("Doggerland: a speculative survey," *Proceedings Prehistoric Society 64,* 1998, 45-61). Our ancestors traveled from the North European Plain across Doggerland to England. Pettitt and others (*Palaeolithic Cave*

Art at Creswell Crags in European context, Oxford, University Press, 2007) have edited a book on the spectacular discovery of Late Paleolithic cave art at Creswell Crags. Otte and others ("Maldegem et le Paléolithique recent du Nord-Ouest européen," *Helinium 24,* 1984, 105-126) deal with the influence of Creswell and Hamburg cultures in Belgium.

Terribly adverse conditions must have forced the Creswell hunters in Gough's Cave to feed on their dead relatives. Andrews and Fernández-Jalvo ("Cannibalism in Britain: Taphonomy of the Creswellian [Pleistocene] faunal and human remains from Gough's Cave [Somerset, England]", *Bulletin natural History Museum London 58 supplement,* 2003, 59-81) analysed the remains of two adults, two adolescents and a child, which had been subject of so-called 'nutritional cannibalism'. Read (*Alive: The Story of the Andes Survivors,* Philadelphia, Lippincott, 1974) gives a most compelling example of cannibalism in our days after a 1972 plane crash in the Andes. Mullan and others ("A Possible Engraving of a Mammoth in Gough's Cave, Cheddar, Somerset", *Proceedings University of Bristol Spelaeological Society 24,* 2007, 37-47) discovered evidence that the Creswell people have indeed observed mammoths in Southern England.

A very special place is Creswell Crags, the hiding place of the legendary bandit and hero Robin Hood. The valley, once shaped by advancing glaciers, was frequented by Neanderthals already 40,000 years ago and some ten thousand years later by our Gravettian ancestors. During the coldest period of the Ice Age no-one visited the region, but at the start of the Late Ice Age, when the climate improved, Creswell hunters arrived here some 14,000 to 15,000 years ago. Their heritage not only consists of stone and bone tools and preciously carved bone fragments, but also includes rock carvings in Church Hole, which represent the northernmost Paleolithic cave art in Europe. You may be one of the privileged visitors of this unique cave (prebooking required) and enter the discussion on the meaning of those

enigmatic signs, which are alternatively interpreted as birds or naked females.
We equally recommend you to visit Cheddar Gorge in Somerset, not only renowned for its cheese, but also for the prehistoric caves; Gough's Cave being the most famous one due to the 'Cheddar Man' who was buried there some 10,000 years ago. It is also the place, where Creswell hunters were snowed in 15,000 years ago, and eventually had to feed on their dead relatives. Last but not least, a mammoth has been carved in one of the walls of this cave, the only prehistoric picture of this animal in Britain!

Leroi-Gourhan (*Préhistoire de l'Art occidental, nouvelle edition revue et augmentée par Brigitte Gilles Delluc,* Paris, Citadelles & Mazenod, 1997) has made an effort to explain all prehistoric figures and signs in Europe in terms of male and female symbols. This hypothesis has become less popular, but yet it is conceivable that some of these signs refer to the spirits of men and women. Guthrie (*The Nature of Paleolithic Art,* University of Chicago Press, 2005) suggests that many drawings and engravings (especially the more 'erotic' ones) are comparable to modern graffiti and had been made by adolescents.

The illustrations of stylised women in this book (*spirits of the mothers*) were drawn after figures (photographs and drawings) in publications by Bosinski (*Die Kunst der Eiszeit in Deutschland und in der Schweiz,* Bonn, Habelt, 1982), Bosinski and Fischer (*Die Menschendarstellungen von Gönnersdorf der Ausgrabung von 1968,* Wiesbaden, Steiner, 1974), Bosinski and others (*Die gravierten Frauendarstellungen von Gönnersdorf,* Stuttgart, Steiner, 2001), Bullinger ("Le site magdalénien de Monruz, 1: Premiers éléments pour l'analyse d'un habitat de plein air," *Archéologie neuchâteloise 33,* 2006), Cleyet-Merle (*Musée national de Préhistoire, Les Eyzies-de-Tayac, Dordogne,* Paris, Réunion Musées Nationaux, 2007), Clottes and Delporte (*La grotte de La Vache [Ariège],* Paris, CTHS, 2003), Brigitte and Gilles Delluc (*La Vie des Hommes de la Préhistoire,* Brest, Ouest-France, 2003), Delporte (*L'Image de la femme dans l'art préhistorique,* Paris, Picard, 1993), Duhard ("Réalisme de l'image feminine paléolithique," *Cahiers du Quaternaire 19,* 1993), Fiedorczuk and others ("Late Magdalenian feminine flint plaquettes from Poland," *Antiquity 81,* 2007, 97-105), Hahn and others (*Eiszeithöhlen im Lonetal,* Stuttgart, Theiss, 1985), Ladier and others ("Rélations ou convergences entre Périgord et Quercy: le cas des figures féminines schématiques de type Lalinde-Gönnersdorf dans l'art mobilier," in: Jaubert and Barbaza, *Territoires, déplacements, mobilité, échanges durant la Préhistoire – Terres et Hommes du Sud,* Paris, CTHS, 2005, 397-410), Martin ("Authentification d'une composition graphique Paléolithique sur la voûte de la grotte d'Orival [Seine-Maritime]," *Compte Rendu Académie des Sciences Paris 332,* 2001, 209-216; and: "The engravings of Gouy: France's northernmost decorated cave," in: Pettitt and others, *Palaeolithic Cave Art at Creswell Crags in European Context,* Oxford, University Press, 2007, 140-193), Pinçon ("A la recherché du cheminement d'idées au cours du Magdalénien: Essai sur les representations féminines du Roc-aux-Sorciers [Angles-sur-Anglin, Vienne]," *Documents préhistoriques 24,* 2007, 55-63), Colette et Jean-George Rozoy ("Roc-la-Tour I, le Site des Esprits, le Magdalénien VI à Monthermé [Ardennes]: topographie, chronologie, art," *Bulletin Société préhistorique luxembourgoise 26,* 2004) and Sentis ("Les silhouettes féminines stylisées peuvent-elles caractériser des territories culturels?," in: Jaubert and Barbaza, *Territoires, déplacements, mobilité, échanges durant la Préhistoire – Terres et Hommes du Sud,* Paris, CTHS, 2005, 411-420).

Glossary

Assegais – throwing spears
Aurignacian – oldest Late Paleolithic culture in Europe, 30,000 – 40,000 years ago
Azilian – culture marking large part of the Late Ice Age in Spain and France, succeeding some 14,000 years ago the Magdalenian civilisation

Big River - Rhine
Blue Valley – Blaubeurener Tal, west of Ulm
Brother's Valley – Brudertal near Engen in Southern Germany
Bushmen or San – direct descendants of prehistoric hunters who lived more than 10,000 years ago in South Africa. Their circular huts are made from branches, grass and leaves. They resemble the wigwams or wickiups of North American Indians and serve as a model for the reconstruction of prehistoric dwellings

Channel River – prehistoric stream, running across the southern part of the actual North Sea, the present-day Channel and the Atlantic in between England and Normandy, which were dry land during the Ice Age, flowing into the Atlantic somewhere north of Cherbourg. The Rhine, Meuse, Thames, Scheldt, Somme and Seine for their part all discharged into the Channel River

Chuckchi – Eskimos in Northeastern Siberia

Coldest Period of Last Ice Age – between 25,000 and 20,000 years ago, but interrupted by several relative mild intervals. Period of maximum extension of ice sheets and lowest sea levels (one hundred and twenty meters below present one)

Creswell culture – name derived from the Creswell Crags in Derbyshire. Contemporary to Hamburg culture, latest Magdalenian and the first people of the Federmesser and Azilian cultures. More or less limited to Doggerland (the then dry North Sea area) and surroundings (Netherlands, Belgium, Northwestern France)

Cro-Magnon – prehistoric men, invading Europe some 50,000 years ago, named after the Cro-Magnon site near Les Eyzies in French Dordogne, where the skeletons of a child and four adults were discovered in 1868. In all aspects they were full members of Homo sapiens

Deep River – Rhône

Doggerland – North Sea area that became dry land during the last Ice Age due to lowered sea levels and temporary regional uplift

Federmesser culture – culture marking large part of the Late Ice Age in Germany, the Netherlands, Belgium, and Poland, succeeding some 14,000 years ago the Magdalenian civilisation

First Tribe – name given by Leya to people living in Vézère, Dordogne and Isle valleys, possibly the cradle of the Magdalenian civilisation

Goat – ibex or mountain goat

Gravettian – Late Paleolithic culture in Europe, 30,000 – 25,000 years ago

Great Auk or Garefowl – extinct bird (exterminated in

1844; Latin name: Alca impennis) with very short, penguin-like wings, incapable of flying. Several times depicted by Paleolithic artists in caves along Mediterranean and Atlantic coasts

Hamburg culture – name derived from Hamburg, where sites have been firstly described. Culture marks early part of Late Ice Age on North European Plain; contemporary to Creswell culture and latest Magdalenian
Holocene – geological period, in which we are living, that began some 11,000 years ago
Homo georgicus – early cousin of Modern Man, living 1.8 million years ago in the Caucasus
Homo heidelbergensis – early cousin of Modern Man, living 600,000 to 250,000 years ago in Europe; possibly the ancestor of the Neanderthals
Homo sapiens – Modern Man, originating some 250,000 years ago in Africa

Inuit – North American Eskimos

Jaranga – large, circular tent of Chucki in Northeastern Siberia, serving as a model for Bosinski's reconstruction of Magdalenian dwellings in Gönnersdorf
Jet – black or dark-brown fossil wood, usually with a clearly recognizable wood structure, that can be burned like lignite (used by prehistoric people for ornaments)

Large Lake – Lake Geneva
Late Paleolithic – last part of Old Stone Age in Europe, starting some 50,000 years ago with the arrival of modern humans in Europe
Long Lake – Lake Neuchâtel
Little Ice Age – relatively cold period in Western Europe, that lasted from 1430 to 1850, in which the mean temperature frequently was one or two degrees lower than that of the present reference period (between 1960 and 1990). Marked by a relatively large number of severe to very se-

vere winters and wet summers resulting in poor harvests and famine

Magdalenian – last civilisation of Paleolithic or Old Stone Age in Europe
Mezine-Meziritch culture – culture of Eastern Tribes in Ukraine, some 16,000 – 15,000 years ago, renowned for its cabins made from mammoth bones, skulls and tusks and for its highly stylised female figurines

Neanderthals – cousin of Modern Man, living some 250,000 to 24,000 years ago in Europe and Asia
Northerners – Magdalenian hunters living north of the Loire in the environs of present-day Paris and in the French and Belgian Ardennes. In Leya's story, the groups living in the Netherlands and Central Germany are also called Northerners
Northern Ice Lake – glacier lake that during last part of last Ice Age occupied the southern half of present-day Baltic Sea; bordered to the north by glaciers of Scandinavian ice cap
Northern River – Loire
North European Plain – lowlands of Belgium, the Netherlands, Denmark, Northern Germany and Poland

Paleolithic – Old Stone Age, starting some 2,500,000 years ago with the fashion of the first stone tools by Homo habilis, the first representative of the human line
Permafrost – permanently, throughout the year, frozen ground
Pont-d'Arc – natural arc spanning the Ardèche near Vallon-Pont-d'Arc

Salmon River - Meuse
Southerners – in Leya's story name of groups living south of Southern River (Ebro)
Southern River – Ebro
Southern Water – Mediterranean

Stylised female figures – also named 'stylised women of Lalinde-Gönnersdorf type'. Although some figures occur in younger cultures of the Ice Age, they are considered to be characteristic of the Late Magdalenian. Engravings only show a lateral silhouette of a woman without a head and with pronounced buttocks. The lower limbs usually end below the knees. Hands are practically never, arms rarely depicted. Breasts are frequently missing. Figurines were made from bone, stone and ivory. In this book they are interpreted as spirits of the mothers

The other ones – people who were not recognised as relatives and feared as potentially dangerous persons (in principle members of the Eastern Tribes)
Time of Great Change – mythical period of major migrations during Middle and Late Magdalenian due to famine
Time of Prosperity – mythical period in a vague past, when all human beings lived in harmony
Tool stones – stones, which fracture in an easily-controlled, predictable manner to fashion (prehistoric) stone tools. Especially 'chert,' 'flint' and 'quartzite' have been used in Europe. The chalky crust of the flint is commonly removed on the spot in order to reduce their weight
Treacherous River – Seine
Turbulent River – Ariège and Garonne
Twisting River – Marne

Uveran – storage space for food, cut out in the permafrost by the Chuckchi

Waterfall – Rhine Fall at Schaffhausen
Western Water – Atlantic
Wide River – Danube
Wigwam or Wickiup – circular to oval huts made by North American Indians from branches, grass and leaves
Winding River – Ardèche

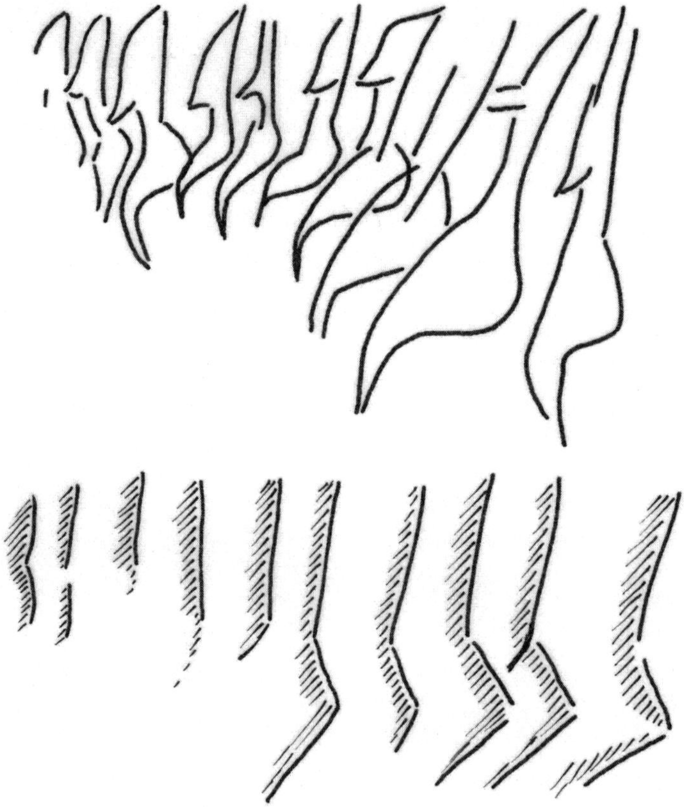

Engravings of stylised women of Lalinde-Gönnersdorf type

(Spirits of the Mothers)

Upper row: part of a larger group on shale, suggesting spirits of women in a choral dance from Gönnersdorf (Neuwied; after Bosinski and Fischer, 1974), Late Magdalenian, 15,000 years ago.

Lower row: group on sandstone, suggesting spirits of women in a choral dance from Niederbieber (Neuwied; after Bosinski, 1982), Federmesser culture, 13,000 years ago.

About the Authors

Initially, Cristi Fernández Narvaiza and Martin Bless devoted themselves to unlock geological science in the Meuse-Rhine Euregion (comprising the Region of Aachen in Germany, the German-speaking community and the provinces of Liège and Limburg in Belgium, and South-Limburg in the Netherlands) to the public.
This has resulted in a large number of lectures, papers, books and exhibits, not only elucidating the incredible journey of this region across the globe as a consequence of continental drift, but also the major changes in landscape, climate, vegetation, fauna and finally human occupation due to a wide range of geological processes.
The 'Time Tunnel' in the 'Centre Nature de Botrange' near Eupen has been built in 1997 after a draft by the authors, who monitored its paintings and also made the landscape models in this permanent exhibit.
The past decade they have focused their attention to the impact of these changes on prehistoric people in Europe. 'Spirits of the Mothers' is their first book on this subject.

9 789089 730282
09W17446/ T2/ 9789089730282